Missing Pieces

Audrey O'Riordan

ISBN 978-0-9562281-09

Cover Design by John O'Callaghan, Mallow

Printed & Bound by Carraig Print

Author

Audrey O'Riordan was born in 1960 in Little Island, Co. Cork. She moved to Ballincollig in 1983. She has been an avid reader all her life. Audrey has Diploma in Proofreading/Editing. After joining the Ballincollig Writers Class in 2003, she was inspired to write short stories, articles and her first novel. Today, she has her own business and she proofreads books in her spare time. She lives near Cork city with her partner. She has five grown up children and two stepdaughters.

Acknowledgements

Having grown up in Little Island, a rural area of Co. Cork, it was with growing sadness that I watched the agricultural Ireland of old metamorphose into a modern, heavily industrialised area. Magnificent Georgian houses were destroyed in the early '70s to make way for progress. In 'Missing Pieces' and its sequel 'Maria Rose', I attempt to recreate the Little Island of old. With much consulting of records and maps, and my own recollections, I hope I manage to portray a piece of Ireland as it was in the early 20th century. Similarly, Ballincollig received the same treatment.

Thanks to the Ballincollig Writers Class to which I have been going to for a number of years. A special thanks to Bernadette Leach, our tutor, who has been an inspiration to the entire class, past and present. Thanks to my daughter, Yvonne for writing the poem, 'The Rose'. Thanks to my other daughters, Kelley, Dannie and Samantha, stepdaughters, Yvonne and Amy and my son Gary for listening to me rambling about my book; half the time they didn't know what I was on about! And I have to mention my potentially biggest fans, Shane, Alexandria, Ryan, Dean, Kaylan, Tristan and my next as yet, unborn grandchild. Thanks to my brothers and sisters for listening to me saying for years, 'I've written a book!' Now they know it's true. I want to thank YouWriteOn.com and Legendpress.co.uk for giving me this chance to see my book in print. Last, but not least, thanks to Danny who always believed in me, encouraged me and fed me when I forgot to eat! Love you always.

For Lily and Gerard

North Infirmary
Cork
1972

Rose O'Shea rapped on the dingy taupe door and
waited. Her husband and daughter leaned against the brown
coloured wall, in the dim
corridor. Seconds later, the door opened and a nurse
appeared from the busy Accident & Emergency room. She
smiled at the family.
'Can I help you?'
'Hello nurse. My daughter here has injured her finger. I
think it's
broken,' the woman said. The nurse inspected the young
girls swollen middle finger. The girl winced in pain.
'It might be broken. It will have to be x-rayed. What's
the name?' the nurse asked taking out a small writing pad
and pen from the pocket of her starched white uniform.
'O'Shea. Adrienne O'Shea.
'Was she here before?' the nurse asked as she scribbled
in her note pad.
'Nurse, every one of my children has been here before.
We must be the most accident-prone family in Cork! We
have a path beaten to the North Infirmary.'
The nurse smiled.
'I think I remember the name. Were you here recently,
with a little boy, about two?'
'Yes. That was another finger! Not broken, just cut.
Four stitches!' the woman said, rolling her eyes. The nurse
laughed.
'We'll call you when it's your turn, but as you can see,
we're very busy. I'm afraid you'll be here a couple of hours
at least.'
Dark wooden benches on both sides of the corridor
were filled with waiting patients. A middle-aged man in a

1

black overcoat squeezed up on the bench and motioned to the woman to sit down. She smiled at him gratefully as she sat. The corridor was bustling with non-stop activity. Porters ferried patients in wheelchairs and on trolleys, up and down the corridor in the direction of the antiquated lift. Doctors in white coats darted past. Nurses in starched white uniforms passed in and out of 'Accident & Emergency'. Other patients joined the queue. The young girl sighed in boredom and she hunkered down against the wall carefully supporting her swollen digit. Her father, a middle aged balding man, folded his arms and settled down for the long wait. His wife was already in conversation with the other patients, initially inquiring about the various injuries and ending up with their life stories.

She puffed on a Woodbine and nodded sympathetically at the plump woman opposite her. Other patients joined the queue as it moved slowly along. Treated patients, in plaster casts, stitches or untreated bruising, left the hospital. Another trolley was brought in by two porters and left lying against the wall, while a nurse went off in search of a bed for the elderly female patient.

The old woman was in a half sitting position propped up on the trolley. A clear green plastic mask over her nose and mouth was helping her to breathe, which was laboured and shallow. She opened her eyes slowly and tried to focus on her surroundings. What were all these people looking at her for? They turned away, embarrassed. She tried in vain to twist away from their prying eyes but couldn't. She sighed, the pain in her chest hurting again. Her eyes rested on a dark haired woman chatting to a young man on the bench beside her. As the old lady watched, the woman turned to speak to a man and a young girl opposite her. The woman looked vaguely familiar.

'Why, that could be my daughter. Or rather, how I think my daughter would look now. How old would she be? She'd be forty-six. Imagine, I have a daughter of forty-six *who I haven't seen in over thirty years!' The woman thought.*

The old woman continued to stare at the younger woman until her tired eyes closed. She could overhear the hum of whispered conversations.

'We're from Little Island. We just got our first car, thank God. I was sick of dragging children up and down to the hospital on the train.'

The old woman's eyes shot open suddenly. She turned and looked at the woman.

'Maria!' called the old woman without thinking, staring intently at the younger woman.

The woman stopped in mid sentence and spun round. Puzzled she stared at the old woman, lying on the trolley. Her eyes widened in recognition. No, it couldn't be! Just then a porter returned with a nurse, who was telling him where to take the elderly patient. To the amazement of her husband and daughter, Rose got up and walked slowly towards the old woman. The women stared at each other as memories drifted back in both their minds.

'Nobody has called me Maria in donkey's years. Not since... my mother died nearly forty years ago. I was always called Rose,' whispered the younger woman.

'Rose? I remember now. You were called Maria, Maria Rose or just Rose. How beautiful. I think... I knew your mother. Was her name Noreen O'Mahony? Everyone used call her Nonie,' the old woman asked, not daring to hope.

'Yes, only I found out, a long time after she died, she wasn't my real mother,' the younger woman whispered softly, her eyes misting over. She paused.

'You're Elisabeth, aren't you? M-my mother? My real mother? You broke it.'

'What?' asked the old woman, crying, her now alert eyes shining with tears.

'The vow? In the letter? You wrote me a letter and you vowed....'

3

'Excuse me, we have to take Sister Elisabeth up to the ward,' the nurse interrupted.

'Adrienne O'Shea!' the casualty nurse called suddenly, from the Accident & Emergency door.

The younger woman looked at the older woman. After all this time, were they to be parted again? Rose grasped the withered hand of the older woman.

'I've got to go now. It's our turn. I'll find you later. Nurse, what ward is she going to?'

'Are you a relative?' asked the nurse.

'No.'

'Yes,' the old woman interrupted, 'this is my daughter, Maria.'

'Well, your mother is going to St Bridget's ward, on the first floor,' the nurse said as she began to wheel the trolley with the porter.

'I'll be up in a little while,' the younger woman called, as the trolley was pushed away.

The old woman smiled weakly and nodded. Rose stood in the centre of the noisy corridor staring after the trolley, her thoughts in confusion.

'Mrs O'Shea, are you coming in with your daughter?' asked the casualty nurse, impatiently.

'Yes.'

An hour later, Adrienne and her mother emerged from the Accident & Emergency, the injured finger confirmed to be broken. Adrienne sported a heavily bandaged finger attached to a wooden splint. She glanced at her mother, who was acting weird ever since talking to that old lady on the trolley.

'Tim, will you take Adrienne home. I-I want to go see that old lady, you know, that was here earlier. Remember? She was my... mother's best friend and I haven't seen her for nearly forty years. I-I really need to talk to her; you know why, don't you? I have my coat and my bag and some money. I'll get the train home afterwards. I won't be long.'

4

Surprised, Tim O'Shea looked at his wife and smiled.
He had seen the way his wife had been looking at the old
lady. He remembered things, things that his wife had told
him before they married twenty-five years earlier. The
mystery surrounding Rose's real mother. He shrugged his
shoulders and smiled. If Rose wanted to see her, he wouldn't
stand in her way.
'All right. I'll see you later. I'll clean the kitchen before
you get home. Come on Adrienne.'
Rose watched as father and daughter ambled towards
the tall hospital door. She turned and looked up the first
flight of stairs that branched off in both directions under the
tall stained glass window on the first level. Slowly, she
climbed the stairs, wondering if she was doing the right
thing. On the first floor, she followed the arrow pointing in
the direction of St Bridget's. She stopped in the doorway of
the high ceilinged ward. Six beds, three on each side, lined
both sides of the dreary magnolia ward. She looked from bed
to bed at all the elderly patients, hardly remembering what
the old woman looked like. She spotted her, last bed on the
right, near the tall window. She tiptoed towards the sleeping
woman. The old woman slowly opened her eyes as Rose
approached. She smiled weakly and whispered,
'Hello, Maria, I've waited my whole life for this
moment.'
Rose sat down on a hard plastic chair beside the bed,
and looked at the frail old woman. So many questions.
Afraid of the answers. Rose didn't know where to begin.
'Maria, I don't know where to begin. How much of your
background do you know?'
Rose sighed. What did she really know?
'Well, I didn't know anything until I was eighteen. I
always believed Nonie and Patsy were my real parents. I
was very upset the day I found out. It was a complete shock.'
'Who told you, my child?'
'Molly. She was...' Rose began. Liz nodded.

'She was Nonie's niece. I met her once or twice and of course I saw her at both Nonie's and Patsy's funerals. How is she?'

'Molly's dead. Died last year.'

'Oh! I didn't know. I'm sorry.'

'It was after Molly died; I discovered all your letters to Nonie. They told me a lot. You see, Molly found out about...you being my real mother and she used it as a weapon against me.'

'How did you feel when you heard I was your real mother?'

Rose paused as a lifetime of memories flitted through her mind. She shook her head as she struggled to contain her emotions.

'To be honest, I hated you. Then, when I discovered you were my real mother and you were alive, I loved you and wanted to see you. Then, I hated you again. I had a terrible ... life, and I couldn't understand why. Why my own mother would give her baby to her friend to rear. Why? Why did you give me away? How could you give your newborn baby away? I've gone through nearly thirty years torturing myself because my mother never wanted me! I was two days old when I got christened. I had problems getting married because I didn't even have a birth certificate. All I had was my baptismal cert. All I ever wanted to know was why?'

Rose sobbed, her eyes brimming with tears.

Liz looked at her only daughter, her own eyes glistening with tears. She reached for Rose's hand and covered it with her own bony hand.

'You were right earlier. I broke my vow. I never came for you, did I? Little Maria, I am about to tell you everything. Judge me then. But remember one thing; I have always, always loved you, thought about you and prayed for you.

I got married to my husband Jack McCarthy in nineteen twenty one. It was an arranged marriage. I was a young girl

6

of twenty, my husband was fifty-three. Marrying for love was out of the question in those days. I worked here in the city, in a dressmakers shop in Oliver Plunkett Street with Nonie. We were best friends ....'

Prologue
January 1921
Ballincollig, Co. Cork.

The young bride gazed at her reflection in the long bevelled mirror on the wooden stand in the corner of her parents' bedroom. Staring back was the reflection of twenty-year-old Elisabeth Moran. Tall and slender, her jet-black hair cascaded around her shoulders. Wearing a white linen wedding dress trimmed with Youghal lace, she stood silent and unsmiling as her mother fussed with her veil. The white ankle length, long sleeved gown had taken weeks for her mother and herself to make. On her feet she wore a pair of low-heeled white-laced boots. Her make-up consisted of ruby red lipstick on her full lips and a hint of rouge on her high cheekbones. Her deep blue eyes showed no interest in her forthcoming marriage. Finally her mother finished arranging Elisabeth's veil and stepped back to admire her only daughter in her wedding attire.

The short plump woman was wearing her Sunday best, a long grey gathered skirt, crisp white blouse and hand knitted cobalt blue cardigan. Her grey hair was scraped back into a bun. On her feet she wore her good pair of black ankle boots.

'It's nearly time Liz. My, you look like an angel sent down from Heaven!' Her mother whispered, a look of pride on her lined face.

Chapter One

The village matchmaker rapped loudly on the kitchen door of the Moran house. He rubbed his hands together and stamped his feet to keep warm on the cold winters night. The top half of the door opened a crack, and Michael Og Moran peered out. Outside, shivering in the gale force wind, Pat Murphy stood on the doorstep. Michael Og opened both halves of the heavy bog oak door.

'Hello Pat, come in, come in,' Michael Moran called from the kitchen table. Slamming the door behind him, Pat came into the small kitchen and nodded at the family members seated around the warm peat fire. The pigs' pot, hanging on the swinging crane was simmering on the hearth. Above the fire, tucked into the recess, cloth bags full of apples and onions could be seen. From the riddy pole hung the fire irons and pot hangers.

Michael's wife, Peggy, the fire bellows in her hands, sat in the stone hob of the fire. Elisabeth and Michael Og's wife Maire sat on the settle.

Elisabeth's face was deathly pale. She knew why the matchmaker was sent for. Michael Og returned to the three-legged stool he had been sitting on. Seated on the two sugan chairs were Michael's two middle sons, Padraig twenty-six, and Sean, twenty-five. Padraigs wife Aine had already retired to the bedroom. On the kitchen table stood a solitary tilly lamp. Under the narrow stairs was the large pine kitchen dresser. Gleaming willow patterned plates were displayed on the shelves above the closed cupboard. The large plates adorned the two top shelves while the smaller plates rested on the lower two shelves. Willow patterned cups hung from hooks screwed under the shelf. A tilly lamp stood on the dresser alongside two wood framed photographs.

The tiny windows rattled as the wind blew more ferociously. The low ceilinged darkened kitchen disguised the whitewashed wattle and daub kitchen walls. Pat Murphy, a short stocky bachelor in his mid forties had been the village matchmaker for the last ten years since his father the previous matchmaker died. He lived in the village of Ballincollig, a mile away. His matchmaking skills were also called for in the neighbouring villages of Inniscarra, Ovens, Cloghroe and Waterfall. He rubbed his hands together to warm them. Sitting at the small kitchen table, Michael eyed him in anticipation as he puffed on his clay pipe. His tobacco supply had already dwindled, so he mixed the remaining dregs with coltsfoot and dried rose petals to keep him going till his next outing to Cork city. Slowly he removed the pipe from his mouth, extinguished it carefully and placed it in the pipe bowl on the table. He pushed it to one side and leaning towards Pat, he said in low voice,

'Did you do like I asked?'

'Ya, Michael, I found one possible match. As you know there isn't many single men left, what with the Great War an' all. Makes my job more difficult, trying to come up with any match at all, let alone a suitable one,' Pat whispered his voice barely audible.

Elisabeth strained to hear their conversation.

'Well, spit it out; who have you in mind for our Liz?' asked Michael.

'Jack McCarthy, from Inniscarra, ' Pat replied shielding his mouth behind his hand, not wanting Elisabeth to hear.

'NO!' cried Elisabeth suddenly. Everybody jumped.

'Be quiet girl, you'll do as I say. You're twenty and no sign of a marriage. I can't keep you any longer. The bloody house is overflowing. As Pat here says, many men fell in the Great War and now we're in the middle of an all out bloody civil war. You can't afford to be too choosy,' Michael bellowed harshly at his only daughter.

'But Father, Jack McCarthy is an old man. Older than you. I cannot marry him. I WON'T!' Liz said her voice rising in anger.

She stood up and began to walk towards the stairs.

Michael stood up suddenly and slapped Liz across the face as she passed. She stumbled against the kitchen dresser. Her cheek stung from where her father had struck her, a red handprint clearly imprinted. She didn't utter a sound. She wouldn't give him the satisfaction of seeing her cry. Besides, she had worse beatings from him, they all had. She stood there looking at her feet, trembling.

'Jack McCarthy is the same age as myself, it's true. But he has a fair bit of land in Inniscarra, enough to keep you from ever going hungry. He will keep you well. Besides, it's already agreed, and if you know what's good for ya, you'll keep your mouth shut and just get on with it. Do ya hear?' Michael shouted into her face, towering over her as she cowered. The rest of the family sat in silence, knowing it was futile to interfere. With a sob, Liz ran up the narrow wooden stairs as quickly as she could. When she reached the landing, she stopped suddenly as great sobs shook her entire body. She placed her arm wearily against the wall outside her bedroom and rested her forehead on it. Her face felt like it was on fire. She stood there crying as she listened to her father finalising the details with Pat Murphy.

Shortly, he would hand over the fee to the matchmaker, ten shillings, that's what her life was worth. That's the going rate to sell your daughter into marriage.

'Is that you Liz?' Aine, her sister- in-law called from the bedroom.

Aine was expecting her and Padraig's first child in little over a month.

'What's all the commotion downstairs?'

Liz tried to stifle her sobbing. Wiping her tear-streaked face with the backs of her hands, she opened the bedroom door and slowly walked in. The night candle cast a soft glow in the sparsely furnished bedroom.

Sitting up in the high double bed, Aine looked even younger than her twenty years. Her long flaxen hair reached nearly to her waist in a thick braid. Her swollen tummy looked like it was going to burst at any moment. Everybody loved Aine. She had the gentlest nature, and was kind to everybody. She had a concerned look now on her pretty face. Liz sat down on the edge of the bed. Instinctively, Aine held out her arms to Liz, who fell into them gratefully. The two young women held each other tightly for a few minutes. At last, Aine gently pushed her sister-in-law away from her.

'What's wrong, love? It can't be all that bad,' Aine said gently.

'Oh Aine, Father got the matchmaker in and he's only gone and matched me with Jack McCarthy, you know, from Inniscarra? He's too old! It will be awful! I wanted to pick my own husband. I wanted to fall in love with somebody my own age, and now, everything is ruined. What am I going to do? Father hit me again when I told him I wouldn't marry Jack. He says he can't keep me any more. Keep me! He has a cheek! I work long hours in my job in the city. And when I am here, I do most of the work in the house with Mother, as well as look after the poultry and pigs. And, …. I hand up most of my wages to him.

Every Friday evening he is waiting when I walk in the door, his paw out for the money. I earn eight shillings a week and he takes seven. Then he goes and drinks it in the porter house!' Liz said, all in one breath.

'Oh, you poor cratoir. You know, you might be better off to marry so, because then you can give up work. Only tend to the poultry for Jack. You'll be a lady of leisure!' Aine said, tilting Liz's face to her as she examined the bruise now visible on her cheek.

'But I don't want to give up work. I like being a tailor. I have friends there since I started work seven years ago. Nonie is my best friend in the world. We tell each other everything. I went to her wedding last year remember? When she wed Patsy. Now's there's a couple who really love each other! She pretends to get cross with him all the time, and he's so easy going, he lets her! He works with

Great Southern Railways in Cork. They both get the early train from Little Island in the mornings. Then he walks her to Crowley's. I want someone to love me like that, who I can love back. I can't marry Jack. I refuse to marry him! I don't care what Father says. I'll leave home! Yes, that's what I'll do,' Liz said defiantly, sitting up straight on the bed.

'But Lizzie, where will you go? Young women have to stay at home 'til they get wed. No respectable place would take in a single lass. Maybe you could go into service in one of the big houses in the city? Yes, that's what you should do!' Aine said, patting Liz on the arm like the problem was already solved.

'No, I don't want to leave my job. Nonie and Patsy said they would have me to stay any time. I could go there. Just 'til Father sees that I have no intention of marrying Jack McCarthy,' Liz said, a glimmer of hope appearing in her eyes. She gingerly touched her cheek. She could feel the swelling. Suddenly she felt very tired. It had been a long day and the news of her impending marriage was a terrible shock.

'I'll go to bed now, Aine. I might wake up in the morning and realise it was all a bad dream. Goodnight,' she yawned, rising from Aine's bed.

'Goodnight, Liz. Things will work out in the end, you'll see,' Aine said as she waited for Liz to walk the two paces to her own narrow bed in the opposite corner. When Liz lit the candle on her little bedside table, Aine blew out the candle on hers. She then turned over and settled down under the colourful patchwork quilt.

Padraig always waited till Aine and Liz were in bed before he went up. Liz looked around the small bedroom. Apart from the double bed and the single bed, the only other items were the two bedside tables, the clothes chest, the washstand and basin, and the po, discreetly pushed under the double bed. Her feet were cold on the darkened floorboards. The timber shutters rattled on the small window as the wind increased outside.

Liz quickly removed her black woollen socks. She untied her long grey linen skirt and let it fall to the floor. Next, she pulled her black knitted geansai over her head and reached for her nightgown under the pillow. She pulled it over her head and gathered her clothing to hang on the end of her bed. Walking to the washstand, she filled the basin with cold water from the jug. She picked up her facecloth and washed her face and hands thoroughly before drying herself with a worn grey towel. Releasing her hair from its braid, she shook her mane of sleek dark brown hair. She sat for a while staring at her reflection in the cracked mirror suspended over the washstand.

*   *   *   *

Liz was formally introduced to her future husband the very next day. Her father forbade her to go work and insisted that they visit Jack McCarthy as quickly as possible. Michael Moran climbed into the trap and glowered at Liz. Reluctant, she made her way towards the trap and pulled herself up beside him. A strong wind swirled around them as the horse and trap trundled out of the yard. Grey clouds hung low in the sky as they turned left, over the humpbacked Maglin Bridge and turned left again along the narrow borreen. Half a mile up, Michael flicked the reins to steer the Clydesdale to the right, in the direction of Inniscarra. Taking the road to the right again, the horse continued at a steady trot until it neared Inniscarra bridge. Liz searched the hillside until she spotted the whitewashed farmhouse on the windswept hill on the other side of the river. After crossing the narrow stone bridge, Michael steered the horse right, then a sharp left up a steep narrow borreen until they entered the dilapidated farmyard. Liz looked around despite herself. She noticed the dingy peeling whitewash on the large farmhouse and the thatch with great tufts missing. A tilly lamp glowed invitingly in the small window. There was a stone well in the centre of the yard complete with chain and bucket. A tall tree stood between the house and the sheds and outhouses. In the far corner she saw a pond. Next to the pond was what she guessed to be a chicken coop, although no sounds came from it. Beyond the pond she could see a timber gate leading upwards to the fields, and cows grazing peacefully. Michael pulled the horse and trap up near the shabby door.

'It mightn't be so bad,' Liz thought, miserably as she stood on the doorstep of Jack McCarthy's farmhouse in the twilight. Michael Moran rapped loudly on the door. The top half of the door opened a crack and Jack peered out. Hurriedly, he pulled back both halves of the door, holding it open for them to enter.

'Come in, come in, Michael, I'm glad ye came at last, ' Jack McCarthy said as they entered the draughty kitchen. Michael and Jack shook hands while Liz looked around. It looked much like their kitchen, only bigger, shabbier, dirty and smelly. The fire hadn't been lit at all that day. She finally looked at Jack and tried to suppress the shudder of revulsion she experienced.

Over fifty years of age, he stood six foot four and nearly as broad as he was long. He had a large round head, bald on top, with straggly grey hair reaching his shoulders. His eyes bulged from their sockets. A large bulbous nose seemed to take up most of his ruddy wrinkled face. He hadn't shaved in a while and grey bristles grew thickly on the lower half of his face from which a pair of thick rubbery lips protruded. He wore a shabby grey tweed jacket over a striped shirt and black work pants, tied with string at the ankles. On his large feet, he wore a pair of thick black woollen socks.

Looking around, Liz spotted a pair of black Wellington boots just inside the kitchen door, from which a distinctive manure smell emanated. She wrinkled her nose in disgust. Turning back to Jack, she shivered involuntarily. He was leering at her in a most unsavoury manner.

'Jack, it's a pleasure. This is Elisabeth, we call her Liz. She's twenty. A good girl, always has been. Not a bit of trouble. She's a tailor in Miss Crowley's dressmakers in George Street. She'll make a fine wife for you, you mark my words,' Michael said nudging Liz forward.

Jack's eyes hadn't left Liz's face. He was still leering at her.

'Well, hello there young Liz. You're a picture so you are. You won't need to work in that shop anymore after we wed. Best hand in your notice to your boss. You'll have plenty to do here. I have a few hens but I'm getting more and a few ducks an' all. You'll have the cows to milk too and the pigs to feed. This house needs a woman's touch again. No woman has been 'ere since me poor ma died twelve year ago. Me sister, me only family that's left, lives down the road on the next farm with her husband and eight childer. She'd given up hope of me ever marrying. Come to think of it, I'd given up meself! I never thought I'd get a little beauty like Liz 'ere,' Jack said, still leering at Liz, his eyes roaming over her slender body.

She shrank back against her father.

'Well girl, say something to your husband to be,' Michael said, smiling jovially. Liz stood silent, staring at the mound of ashes in the hearth. This was worse than she imagined. Michael and Jack stared at her expectantly. She swallowed hard.

'I -I can't get married. I'm sorry, but, I can't get married,' she said, looking from one to the other. Silence. The sound of a sharp slap broke the silence, as Michael struck Liz's face. She put her hand to her left cheek; it was always her left cheek. Last night's bruise was still visible. She looked at her feet. Although her cheek stung, she wouldn't give in and cry. Michael grabbed her roughly by the arm and shook her. Her eyes widened in fear.

'I warned you last night. You are getting married

whether you like it or not. Any more trouble out of you and I will give you the hiding of your life. D'ya hear me? Answer me!' Michael said in a low menacing voice.

'I hear you,' she whispered hoarsely.

'Jack, Liz has 'Grand' notions about herself. You'll have to knock it out of her, and fast,' Michael said, turning to Jack.

'I'll go to Father Murphy first thing in the morning and have the banns read at mass,' Jack replied, seemingly unmoved at the sight of his future wife being hit by her father.

In the days that followed Michael hardly left Liz out of his sight. A few nights later, Jack called to the Moran household amid torrential rain. Liz saw him as he pulled up outside the kitchen door on his donkey and cart. She turned back to washing the delph in the basin of water. Her mother, standing beside her, looked at her.

'Liz,' she whispered pleadingly, 'why don't you settle down and just get on with it. Your wedding is arranged. That's the way things are done. Don't fight it anymore, because he'll take it out on all of us, you know that.'

Liz nodded. Aine stood on the other side of her, tea cloth in her hand. She saw the look of dread in Liz's eyes. Michael opened the door and Jack entered, brushing the rain from his straggly hair.

'I just came from Father Murphy and the weddin' is on Tuesday the ninth of January. The banns will be read at mass the Sunday before,' Jack said excitedly. He glanced at Liz's back expectantly, hoping she'd turn around. Liz was standing as still as a statue.

'That's great news, Jack. Isn't it Peggy? We're going to have the Free State any day now, after this bloody Civil War. De Valera is going to do great things for Ireland. We'll get rid of them Black and Tans out of the country once and for all. They have the country destroyed the bastards. Starting the New Year with a wedding, eh! It's like a new beginning; it is a new beginning! Ye'd better start the preparations now, you know, the dress an' all that,' Michael said, grinning from ear to ear.

'Michael, we-we didn't agree anythin' yet. You know? For Liz? By way of a bit of a-a dowry?' Jack asked, his face reddening with embarrassment. He glanced at Liz again, disappointed she hadn't turned around.

'Oh, right. I was going to give two cows, two pigs and the sum of twenty pounds. How does that sound? After all, you're getting a grand girl. She'll make a great wife.'

Liz hadn't moved. Seeing the look of dismay on her face, Aine reached out and placed a comforting hand on Liz's shoulder.

'Well, I think that's very fair. Aye, she'll make a grand wife, and who knows? Maybe by the end of next year, you might have another grandchild, if I have anything to do with it,' Jack replied with a laugh, turning to look at Liz again. She could feel his eyes on her and froze. Aine squeezed Liz's shoulder reassuringly.

* * * *

News of the burning of Cork city reached the Moran household on Sunday morning 12th of December. Michael Moran and his wife returned from seven o clock mass in St Mary and St Johns church. Peggy was dabbing her eyes with her handkerchief while Michael's face was grim. Liz and her brothers looked at their parents. Liz rested her hand on her mothers arm as her mother's body heaved with the effort of her sobs.

'Mother, what's happened?' she asked fearfully.

'Those bloody Black an' Tans!' Michael muttered under his breath as he leant on the windowsill, his back hunched. Without warning he thumped the nearby table. Liz jumped.

'Them bastards. Them evil English bastards,' he shouted, 'they've gone and burnt Cork to the ground.

Bombed it. They went crazy last night.'

'But dad, they've been burning houses and buildings for the last few weeks....' Padraig Og began.

'The city has been razed! It's destroyed! Roches is gone, the Munster Arcade, Cashs, Sunners, the English Market,.... they're still burning.'

Michael and his sons were secret members of the Irish Volunteers as were some of the local men. They didn't perform active duty; only helped to hide people and weapons.

Liz's heart felt a flutter of hope. There wasn't anywhere to buy the fabric for her wedding dress! Maybe the wedding could be postponed or better still, cancelled. Who would be in the mood for a wedding with Cork City burnt to the ground?

Michael Moran and his sons went with some of their neighbours in to see the ruined city five miles away. When they returned, Liz was shocked to see her father openly crying. It was to be the only time in her life she saw him cry.

Liz got on the Muskerry tram as usual the next morning, wondering would any work be done at all that day. Alighting from the tram at the Western Road terminus, she couldn't believe her eyes; a cloud of smoke trailed into the grey sky and the once vibrant city seemed strangely quiet. The first thing that Liz and her fellow passengers noticed was the foul burning smell. The crowd made their way along the silent street. No horses and carts, or trams trundled by. Only people on foot. On Washington Street, the first signs of fire damage were to be seen. But nothing prepared Liz when she turned the corner onto the Grand Parade. Crowds filled the once bustling street now strewn with rubble and broken glass and awash with water, mud and charred remains. Glancing across to Crowley's dressmakers on the corner of Georges Street she was relieved to see it standing and intact although still closed. Looking around she could see hundreds of people standing on Patrick Street and this is where she

21

headed, swept along with the throngs of people headed in the same direction.

Turning the corner a collective shocked gasp rang out from the crowds. Patrick Street was no more. All that remained were a few broken walls, a street filled with mounds of debris and smouldering ruins. Horse drawn fire brigades with exhausted firemen who had been on call since the previous night, were still trying to douse smaller fires. The people of Cork including Liz wept openly at the destruction of their fine city. Despite everything children played happily among the ruins. Hundreds of people suddenly were out of work two weeks before Christmas. It was when she picked her way down what was once Corks main shopping street that the full scale of the tragedy unfolded. Most of Patrick Street and Georges Street as well the City Hall and the Library were obliterated.

*   *   *   *

Liz's brothers, Michael Og, Padraig and Sean, and her father, waited patiently in the warmth of the kitchen. They were dressed in their Sunday best. Black suits, starched white shirts and black ties. Maire, Michael Og's wife, wore a long crimson skirt, high necked white blouse and her best black shawl. On her head, she wore a white caipin lasa. Aine wore a navy linen skirt, white blouse, black shawl and a caipin lasa. In her arms she cradled baby Cormac, born three weeks earlier. He was dressed in a white linen gown, white knitted cardigan, matching bootees and a white hooded crochet shawl. All eyes were on Liz as she emerged from her parents' bedroom, her mother following behind. Despite Liz's hopes of the wedding being cancelled, Miss Crowley came to her 'rescue' and kindly donated a few yards of Youghal lace for the making of her wedding dress.

'The pony and trap is outside. Better hurry. It's quarter to ten and the snow is getting worse. By the way, you look

… lovely, Liz, really lovely. I'm real proud of you, you know. I really am,' Michael said in a soft voice, as he looked at his only daughter.

She nodded slowly as tears came into her eyes. Carefully, she pulled on her heavy bainin cloak over her wedding attire while her father struggled into his heavy black overcoat. The family, except Liz and her father, left for the church along with some of the neighbours. The wedding breakfast would take place at Jack's house in Inniscarra, two miles away.

Snow was swirling heavily as Liz and her father arrived in the pony and trap to St Mary's and St John's church in Ballincollig. Padraig was waiting patiently for them in the falling snow. He helped Liz from the trap and led the pony to the side of the church where the other ponies were tethered. Michael, Liz and Padraig hurried to the heavy outer church door and stepped inside. Padraig walked in ahead of them. Liz removed her cloak while Michael took off his overcoat and they hung them on the wooden coat stand. Michael peered through the open inner door waiting for the signal from Padraig to proceed. Holding on to Michael's arm, Liz stared straight ahead, her eyes glistening with tears.

'Good luck, cailin. It's for the best. Remember that,' Michael whispered, patting her hand gently, just as Padraig nodded at them.

Everybody in the church turned and watched, as, side by side, Liz and her father made their way slowly up the aisle. Father Murphy was standing in front of the altar waiting. As they drew near, Liz saw Jack standing at the altar, looking remarkably clean and neat in his Donegal tweed suit, starched white shirt and black tie. His hair was neatly combed over and oiled. He was looking at her with his now familiar leer. Finally they reached the altar and Michael gently released Liz's cold hand from his arm as she stood beside Jack. Shivering in the cold, the ceremony went ahead but to Liz, everything was a blur. Finally, she was Mrs Jack

McCarthy.

The snow fell gently on the ponies and traps as they made their way from the church along the winding road, and over the Inniscarra Bridge. Turning right, the little convoy continued up the narrow lane to Jack's whitewashed farmhouse, now almost invisible under a veil of snow. Jack and Liz sitting side by side in Jack's pony and trap headed the procession. As they neared the farmhouse, Liz could see smoke billowing out of both chimneys. The light in the kitchen window cast a warm glow as they pulled up outside the kitchen door. Jack jumped down, walked around and helped Liz from the trap. He pushed the kitchen door open for her before leading the pony to the barn. Liz stood on the threshold of her new home and looked in. In the last few weeks Jack had recruited the services of his only sister Cait in cleaning up the house for the wedding.

A peat fire crackled in the hearth. A solitary candle on the windowsill cast a warm glow on the wedding table, laid with the good 'delph' crockery and recently polished silver cutlery. Within seconds Jack was back, a light covering of snow on his shoulders. Just then, the other ponies' hooves could be heard approaching the house.

'What are you waiting for, girl? You'll let all the heat out,' Jack said as he gently guided her into the warm kitchen. Jack's sister Cait came in and busied herself preparing the food at the hearth. The other guests filed in, chatting as they shook the snow from their caps and cloaks. Liz walked to the window and stared at the flickering candle flame, seemingly unaware of her wedding guests. Nonie walked over to her.

'It was a lovely wedding Liz,' she said gently. Liz didn't move.

'Liz, what's the matter?' Nonie whispered.

Liz turned and looked at her friend, her eyes welling up with tears.

Behind them the guests chattered loudly.

'I can't do it Nonie. I feel like I've been sentenced to gaol and I'm never going to be free again. I wish I were dead. He's already on at me to give up work, but I'm not going to,' she said defiantly. Liz wiped her runny nose with the back of her hand. Nonie put her arm around Liz's shoulders and gave her a quick squeeze.

'Liz, you've got to snap out of it. You've got to get through the day. You've no choice. You're married now. You've got to make the best of it. Come, people are looking at us now. Big smile!' Nonie said squeezing her friend's shoulders again. Choking back tears, Liz wiped her eyes with the back of her hand. Taking a deep breath she looked at Nonie with a watery smile.

'Thanks Nonie, for being here for me. Promise me you'll always be my friend?' Liz asked squeezing Nonie's hand.

'But of course we'll always be friends. I'll always be here for you. I promise. Now come on, try and cheer up.'

Together they joined the other guests at the table. The wedding party feasted on large helpings of bacon, eggs, brown and white soda bread and pots of tea. Afterwards, Cait and Peggy gathered up the dirty ware and carried it to the earthenware sink under the kitchen window. Jack stood up at the table and cleared his throat.

'Order, order, everybody! I'd like to say a few words. Today, me and Liz here, got married and shure, I'm the proudest man in Ireland. I'd like to invite ye all into the parlour for a few drops of the hard stuff, by way of celebration,' Jack said, as he started to walk out of the kitchen, across the gloomy hall and into the parlour, closely followed by the guests.

The fire had been lit that morning in the little used room that was only used for special occasions, indeed, the last time was for the wake when his dear mother had died, years ago. The parlour was a large room with a polished wooden floor. The smell of lavender wax polish filled the warm room. Along the far wall was the brightly polished sideboard. Amongst the few family photographs and delph figurines were a few dozen bottles of Murphys stout, two bottles of Jameson whiskey and an ominous looking earthenware tankard of what could only be poitin. The sugan armchairs and couch, complete with delicate lace antimacassars, were pushed back against the walls.

The Dutch oak grandfather clock, standing at least seven and a half feet, stood in the far corner of the room. Faded family portraits in wooden frames adorned the walls. A mahogany framed picture of the Sacred Heart hung centre stage on the wall above the sideboard. A serene looking Our Lord gazed out, his stigmataed hands outstretched, a glowing red heart pulsating in his chest. A soft glow emanated from two highly polished brass oil lamps. The heavily lined curtains were drawn to keep out the draught.

Jack stood near the sideboard, opening and passing around drinks. His new-father-in-law, Michael, Michael Og, Padraig, Sean, Father Murphy, Patsy, Pat his brother-in-law and his two neighbours from the neighbouring farms, Ned Hogan and Sean McDonagh, surrounded him. Liz, along with Nonie, Aine and baby Cormac, Peggy, Maire, Cait, Mary Hogan and Mary McDonagh huddled near the warm peat fire in the hearth. Liz tried her hardest to appear cheerful. Nonie sat beside her occasionally squeezing her hand reassuringly.

Suddenly, the group of men went quiet and the beautiful tenor voice of Michael Moran could be heard singing 'When Irish eyes are smiling' by John McCormack. As the dulcet tones filled the parlour, Ned Hogan lifted his fiddle and from its worn leather case.

Michael Og lifted his accordion onto his lap and pulled the straps over his arms. Padraig pulled the tin whistle from his inner coat pocket. The musicians quietly consulted amongst each other while Michael finished the song at which they simultaneously launched into a rendition of The

Haymakers Jig. Jack looked across at Liz, a big smile on his ruddy face. In a moment, he crossed the floor and held out his hand to Liz. Hesitating for just a second, she took his outstretched hand and followed him to the middle of the floor. Holding hands aloft they made a gallant attempt at dancing a two-hand reel. Patsy and Nonie joined them, as did Michael and Peggy. Shortly afterwards the group of dancers were joined by Sean and Mary McDonagh, Pat and Cait, and Aine and Maire. Mary Hogan sat talking to Father Murphy; the sleeping baby nestled in her arms.

The remainder of the non-dancing guests clapped their hands in time to the music. The walls reverberated with the sounds of the ceili music. Liz looked at her family and friends enjoying themselves and for the first time in weeks she smiled.

'Tonight, I'm going to enjoy my wedding. I'll worry about the rest of my life, tomorrow,' she thought, as Jack swung her around again. She threw her head back and laughed heartily.

*   *   *   *

Liz woke early next morning, her first in her new home. She turned and looked at her new husband sleeping beside her. Mouth open, eyes closed, the occasional snore. Liz still felt repulsed at the sight of him.

Sitting up in bed, she sighed wistfully. He was never going to be her Prince Charming but he was her husband now. She had to make the best of it. Thankfully, Jack had not sought his conjugal rights last night; probably due to the copious amounts of alcohol he'd consumed!

She pulled back the bedclothes and tiptoed across the polished floorboards to the bedroom window. The windowpane was frosted over. The snow had gotten heavier during the night and the farmyard was carpeted in white. Shivering, she pulled on her dressing gown and tiptoed downstairs to the kitchen.

The women had cleared the mess in the kitchen and parlour the previous night. The guests had all departed before six o'clock, trying to get home before the snow got worse. Jack and herself had waved off the convoy of ponies and traps. A glowing oil lamp on either side lit each trap. All the travellers were wrapped in their overcoats and cloaks and covered with their travelling blankets.

Walking to the log box, Liz lifted the lid, took out a handful of cipini and the matches. She raked over the ashes in the grate, which fell down into the ash hole. She arranged the cipini in the grate and lit them.

Hurriedly, she placed small pieces of peat on top, watching as the fire crackled into life. The grandfather clock in the parlour struck the time on the quarter hour. Quarter to seven. Time to call Jack. She ran up the stairs and found Jack sitting on the edge of the bed yawning and stretching. He smiled at her.

'Come 'ere wife,' he said softly, patting the bed beside him, 'I know you got a week off work for your honeymoon, but there's no need for you to work any more. And now that those bloody Black an' Tans burned Cork to the ground, I don't think its safe to work in the city. There's a lot of unrest still. God knows what'll happen next. The city is in an awful state and it'll take six months at least to put it right. I told you already. You'll have enough to do around the farm. Why don't you pack in the job?'

Liz looked away for a moment. She turned back to face him.

'Jack, I really want to keep my job. Miss Crowley has agreed to let me work just three days a week. And the fires only happened on Patrick Street and the City hall. I know things are uneasy around the city, but I for one, won't give in to them Black an' Tans. Please don't make me give up my job and my friends. I promise I'll do everything that's expected of me, but please, let me keep my job? Please?' she pleaded. Jack looked at his beautiful young bride. His heart melted. Wasn't he already a lucky man to have such a beauty? And if she wanted to work, why not?

'All right Liz, you can keep your job, if that's what you want, just remember, you can give it up anytime you want. And you must be careful. Right?'

'Thank you Jack, thank you. I won't let you down,' she said gratefully.

With that, he leaned towards her, large lips puckered for a kiss, but she jumped up quickly.

'Jack, it's nearly seven! I'll help you milk the cows. They're probably wondering what's keeping you. Now, come on!'

Chapter Two
Little Island

Liz settled into a routine in no time at all. She continued to work at Crowley's on Tuesdays, Wednesdays and Thursdays. Jack and herself would rise at cockcrow each morning at six thirty. Jack would milk the cows while Liz fed the pigs, hens and ducks before leaving for the city. Jack would take her in the pony and trap a mile up the road to the railway hut at Leemount Cross. From there, Liz would catch the Muskerry tram to the city sighing with impatience at the slowness of it, as it all but crawled up the Carrigrohane straight road. After disembarking at the terminus on the Western Road, it was only a short walk to the corner of Grand Parade and Oliver Plunkett Street to Crowleys Ladies Dressmakers. Over the coming months, Liz and Nonie watched with interest as Cork City was slowly rebuilt. Patrick Street, which took the brunt of the bombing by the Crown Forces, was a hive of reconstruction. On her return from work she usually walked from the railway hut, back to the farmhouse.

On her days off, she'd clean the farmhouse from top to bottom, bake bread, mend clothes, and tend the vegetable patch and garden. Jack, for his part, was very happy with his new wife. He made no demands on her. Occasionally, he expressed his wish for a baby to which Liz would respond by telling him she wasn't ready for a baby yet.

One Sunday a month, weather permitting, Liz, sometimes accompanied by Jack, would visit Nonie and Patsy in Little Island. The following month, Nonie and Patsy would visit Liz and Jack in Inniscarra. Liz loved Little Island and its picturesque splendour. She'd set off after mass, at eleven o'clock in the pony and trap, heading for Cork city, six miles away. Penny the pony, her sleek black coat glistening in the morning sun, loved these excursions. After leaving the bustling city behind, Liz would take the busy

Youghal road, through Mayfield and downhill into the little village of Glanmire. Then she'd turn right and follow the Glashaboy River until she came to a low bridge. Just past the bridge on the right was North Esk, which was just inside the boundary of Little Island on the eastern side of the Island. From here, Liz would turn to look at the white turreted house North Esk House as it flashed by.

Just beyond North Esk, almost hidden among the tall sycamore trees was Bury's House. The Cork to Cobh track ran alongside North Esk and Bury's House. A small stone bridge above the train line was the only entrance to North Esk. Liz would continue on up the steep hill, turning to look at the tall Martello tower perched on top of the hill, like a sentry, guarding the entrance to Cork Harbour. Another mile up the road and she would arrive at Caherlag Cross. Turning right, it was downhill for nearly a mile until she'd reach Sacred Heart Church in Glounthaune.

Turning right again, she knew she was on the home stretch towards the entrance to Little Island. A stone humpback bridge linked Little Island to the mainland.

Penny would trot carefully over the train tracks that traversed the road, until she neared the Island Cross. They'd pass the little shop near the cross before turning left. On the corner stood the little thatched post office. Further up on the left, was Little Island National School. Liz would continue on until she came to the fork in the road at Ballytrasna. Straight ahead was Courtstown. The road to her right, led up the small incline onto Clash Road, which is the one she followed.

Whitewashed thatched cottages dotted both sides of the road. A mile up on the left was Nonie and Patsy's cottage. Liz loved their charming whitewashed thatched cottage, which was always a kaleidoscope of colour in summer. Old black pots filled with colourful geraniums stood either side of the bog oak half door. The narrow garden in front of the house was awash with colour with geraniums, anemones, dahlias, wallflowers and rose bushes. The top of the whitewashed boundary wall contained a rainbow of pansies, freesia's and gladioli.

Little wonder then that the stone plaque on the pillar read 'Rose Cottage', the letters written in bitumen. A tall green cast iron water pump stood outside the wall. The wide cast iron gate was always left open when visitors were expected. A high-whitewashed wall on the left of the cottage surrounded the driveway. At the end of the driveway near the back of the cottage, was a low sycamore tree, its gnarled trunk leaning towards the cottage. Beyond the tree were the sheds and the outside toilet. Hens, ducks and geese wandered freely. Near the bigger shed was a tiny pond in which the ducks splashed happily.

Liz loved spending time with Nonie and Patsy in their 'bit of paradise' as they called it. Nonie was shorter than Liz and more curvaceous. She wore her long sandy hair in a tight bun at the nape of her neck. She was easy going and had a wonderful sense of humour, and as Liz's father said 'she'd talk the hind legs of a donkey.' Patsy, on the other hand, was a man of few words. He was quite content to let Nonie do all the talking. Few people knew it, but he had a stutter, so he refrained from speaking as much as possible. When he did speak, everyone listened, for he was a highly intelligent man who chose his words and the subject matter wisely. He was a tall slim man who liked to smoke his clay pipe in the evenings. He was devoted to his talkative wife and save for work, the couple was seldom apart.

Sometimes, Liz and Nonie would walk down to the end of Clash Road where the road turned sharp left onto the Well Road. On the right was Lough Mahon, part of Cork Harbour. On the other side of Lough Mahon was Passage West and Monkstown. Up the narrow passage on the right, running along the shoreline, was a narrow pathway leading into Cork Golf Club. Founded in eighteen eighty-eight, it was one of the first golf courses in Ireland. Part of it was built in the depths of the old limestone quarry. On the outer corner of the junction of Clash Road and Well Road were two wrought iron gates. Outside the gates, there was a square shaped thatched lodge right on the bank of the river. Beyond the gates, a long winding lane wound along the waters edge on one side, and on the other side was a great stretch of green rolling fields, leading to the picturesque Carrigrennan House.

Where the lane turned left away from the shoreline, an ancient Norman tower stood like a sentry on the edge of the shore on the right. Liz and Nonie loved to sit and talk on the grass verge near the lodge. As they basked in the sunshine they'd breathe in the salty sea air, listen to the waves gently lapping the edge of the rocky shore and the screech of the seagulls as they soared overhead.

Other days, they'd walk down the tree lined Well Road to the very end and sit on the edge of the shore, looking across the narrow channel of water at Cuskinny, on the road to Queenstown.

One day Nonie and Liz walked fifty yards from the cottage up the road on the right, and into the top of the old limestone quarry. Liz marvelled at the breathtaking view of the quarry overlooking the sixth hole of Cork Golf Club, the smooth rolling fairways, the tall rugged cliffs surrounding the elegantly trimmed green, in the centre of which was the hole bearing the flagpole.

For over a hundred years limestone had been hewn out of the quarry by local men and used in many buildings around Ireland as well as being transported abroad. The sixth tee, overlooking Lough Mahon was clearly visible, the afternoon sun twinkling and rippling on the gentle waves. Clumps of gorse bushes dotted the rough terrain on either side of the fairways. Nonie pointed towards a thicket of trees in the distance and told Liz of the mysterious Green Water. The Green Water was a sinister stretch of water in the middle of the quarry, feared by generations of local people.

Over the years, this relatively small body of water claimed many lives by those unfortunate enough to fall into its slimy green depths. Legend has it that it was bottomless and anybody who fell in was never recovered.

*　　*　　*　　*

1925

'Jack, I'm just off now. I should be back about seven. Your dinner is simmering on the hearth,' Liz called as she climbed into the trap. Jack was leading the two horses out of the barn.

'All right. Tell Nonie and Patsy I was askin' for them and I'll see them next week, please God,' Jack called as he placed the harnesses on the horses.

Liz turned Penny towards the lane and the pony set off at a trot. The sun shone as bright as a summers day even though it was only mid April. An hour later, as she neared 'Rose Cottage', Liz noticed the open half door. She pulled into the driveway just as Nonie and Patsy came out. Patsy helped Liz down and took the reins from her. He led Penny to the back of the cottage as Nonie linked arms with her friend.

'How are you? How was your journey? How's Jack?' Nonie asked all in one breath.

'I'm fine. The journey was good; the city wasn't busy at all. Jack is fine but he is very busy, and, he sends his best wishes,' Liz replied smiling.

A murmur of voices came from the kitchen. Liz looked at Nonie inquiringly.

'We have visitors staying for a few weeks. Patsy's sister Nellie is down from Kildare with her husband John. Come on in and I'll introduce you,' Nonie said as she whisked Liz into the dim kitchen. Two people were sitting at the kitchen table. The woman turned and smiled at Nonie and Liz. In her late twenties, she was small and slightly plump. Her ginger hair was coiled loosely near the crown of her head. The man, his back to them, got up and turned round. Liz stopped in her tracks, a smile frozen on her face. He was tall, well built with a head of wavy jet-black hair. Liz, her heart beating faster than normal, couldn't take her eyes off him. She felt her cheeks redden. The man appeared to be similarly mesmerised, his deep blue eyes boring into hers. After what seemed an eternity, he stepped towards Liz.

'Good afternoon. I'm John Flynn, and this is my good wife, Nellie, pleased to meet you,' he said politely, extending his hand to her.

Liz took his outstretched hand. A current surged between them. John held her hand longer than was necessary and seemed reluctant to let go.

'I- I'm Liz. Liz McCarthy. I work with Nonie in the city. We've been best friends for years,' Liz stuttered looking into his eyes, her face reddening.

'I know. We've been hearing all about you. A pleasure to meet you.'

Liz walked to the table and held out her hand to Nellie, who shook it, a smile spreading across her pretty face.

'Hello Nellie. How do you do? Patsy talks a lot about you. He says you moved to Kildare eight years ago. Do you like it there?'

'It's no different to Cork to be honest. I was very homesick when we moved up first after getting married but I'm used to it now. John and meself came down because John lost his job and he's hoping to get work around here, if only for a while. You're married yourself, aren't you Liz?' asked Nellie.

Liz sat down at the table as Patsy entered the kitchen and stood near the hearth talking to John. Standing behind her, Liz could feel John's eyes boring into her.

'That's right. Married three and a half years. I live in Inniscarra, a little village about sixteen miles away. My husband Jack has a farm.'

'I'll make a pot of tea and I've some freshly baked brown bread and cakes,' Nonie announced as she busied herself at the hearth. She placed a large plate of brown bread and Madeira cake, a butter dish, a jug of fresh creamy milk, crockery and cutlery on the table.

'Patsy, when the kettle is boiled, make the tea and bring it over here,' Nonie instructed, as she sat at the table between Liz and Nellie. Patsy nodded in reply. Liz, Nonie and Nellie chatted together.

After a while, the discussion turned to children.

'Nonie, any luck yet, you know, in getting in the family way?' Liz whispered to Nonie.

'No,' she replied sadly, ''tis not from the want of trying. I even went to the doctor. He was no help. He just said its Gods will if we're not blessed with children. What about you?'

'I told Jack I don't want a baby yet. He's a good man, but oh, I don't want to be stuck with a baby yet. Not until I absolutely have to. What about you Nellie? Any sound of the patter of tiny feet?' Liz asked, smiling.

Nellie stopped smiling. There was an awkward silence.

'Actually, I've lost four babies. Two were born dead and I miscarried another two. I'd give anything to have a baby to hold in my arms,' Nellie said sadly, her bottom lip quivering.

'Oh, Nellie, I am so sorry. I had no idea. I didn't mean … I'm sorry I mentioned it now,' Liz said, placing a hand on Nellie's arm, 'please forgive me and my big mouth.'

Nellie smiled again. A sad smile.

'It's all right Liz; I know you didn't mean any harm. We would love to have a baby. We're still trying. Maybe someday, please God. Only thing is, we're nearly thirty now.'

Patsy brought the large china teapot over and placed it in the centre of the table. John followed him and squeezed in between Liz and Nellie. An animated conversation followed and a very enjoyable afternoon passed all too quickly.

'Well, I must be going, or Jack will be wondering where I've got to,' Liz announced, rising from the table. Patsy and Nonie started to clear the crockery away, helped by Nellie.

'I'll harness up the pony for you, Liz,' John offered.

Liz's heart began to beat faster. He followed her out into the setting sun. They walked to the old tree where Penny was tied up.

'How long will it take you to get home Liz?' John asked as he harnessed the trap to Penny.

'Just over an hour,' she replied, 'it's Nonie and Patsy's turn to visit us next week. You'd be more than welcome to come with them. And Nellie too, of course.'

Standing beside her, he suddenly straightened up. He towered over her. He was so close she could feel his breath on her face. She didn't look up at him. Instead she diverted her gaze towards the corner of the house waiting for the others to appear.

'Thank you Liz, I'd like that. Very much…so would Nellie. Have a safe journey home,' he said in a soft voice. He held out his hand to help her into the trap. His warm fingers intertwined with hers and their eyes met. She felt like she never wanted to let go of his hand. They heard the voices of the others coming around the corner. Liz hurriedly stepped into the trap and let go of John's hand.

'Goodbye Liz, see you next week,' Nonie called to her.

'Liz very kindly invited Nellie and myself to her home next week too,' John said, his eyes still on Liz as she sat in the trap, holding the reins.

'Oh, that's very nice of you Liz. Thank you. We look forward to seeing you next week,' Nellie said smiling happily, 'goodbye.'

''Bye Liz, have a safe journey,' Patsy called as the pony and trap moved off from the drive.

'Goodbye everyone, I had a lovely time. See ye next week,' with that, she flicked the reins and Penny set off at a trot. Glancing back, she saw that John Flynn was the only one still standing at the gate.

*   *   *   *

Jack stopped outside the kitchen door, his hand on the door handle, when he heard the sound of the pony's hooves approaching. The pony and trap pulled up in front of him. He helped Liz down and led Penny to the barn. While she waited for him, Liz noticed how tired he looked.

'How are Nonie and Patsy?' he asked.

'They're fine. Were you working 'til now?' she asked.

'Yes, yes I was. I could do with someone to help around the farm. There's loads to be done now come harvest time, I'll be even more rushed. I'm seriously thinkin' of gettin' a farm hand. I'll ask around the village and in Ballincollig too,' he said wearily, wiping the sweat from his brow with the back of his rough hand.

Liz thought for a moment.

'Jack, Patsy's sister and her husband are down from Kildare and they're staying with Nonie and Patsy for a while. Nellie, that's Patsy's sister, said her husband lost his job and they're here to look for work. Why don't you ask him? His name is John and I invited them both here next week with Nonie and Patsy,' Liz said, all in one breath.

Jack scratched his jaw thoughtfully.

'Now there's an idea! Leave it with me for a while. Sure, I can talk to him next week if I think it's all right, now let's get some supper, I'm starvin'!'

*   *   *   *

Liz entered Miss Crowley's shop at five to eight the following Tuesday. She made her way behind the counter to the workroom behind. This was where Nonie and Liz worked alongside two other machinists. The business was mostly ladies clothing; dresses, blouses, skirts and coats for everyday wear. Occasionally, they made dresses for eveningwear. The other two machinists, Sheila and Mary, were already at their Singer sewing machines. Taking off her shawl, Liz swung around as Nonie entered the shop, walked across the floor and in behind the counter.

'Morning Liz, how are you?' Nonie called as she removed her cardigan and hung it on the hook.

'I'm fine. How're the visitors settling in?' Liz asked, as she stood at the large rectangular wooden table, measuring a paper pattern. Liz was the pattern cutter. Her job was to cut all the fabrics. The paper patterns were standard and had to be adjusted for each new garment before being cut. Noreen was a machinist. Miss Kathleen Crowley worked in the shop, taking care of the customers and taking their measurements.

Nonie adjusted the caipin lasa on her head. All married women wore white caipin lasa whenever they were away from home. Unmarried women like Sheila and Mary didn't.

'They are getting on all right. John went out today to look for work. They might settle here if he finds steady work. T'would be nice if they did. I'm very fond of Nellie, and so is Patsy, of course.'

'Nonie, Jack is looking for a farmhand. He has been expanding the farm a bit and the work is getting a bit much for him. I mentioned it to him about John. Do you think John would be interested in farm work?'

'He might. I'll say it to him tonight,' Nonie said, sitting at her sewing machine.

'Actually, don't say anything yet. Ye're coming out on Sunday. We'll wait and see what happens then. All right?' Liz said, she picking up the large scissors.

'Ya sure.'

*   *   *   *

40

The cock crowed at its usual time, six thirty, from his usual perch, the pigsty gatepost, as Sunday dawned. Liz lay awake in bed. Soon, Jack would rise and the daily chores would begin. He snored loudly. Like clockwork he woke, rubbed his eyes and sat up yawning and stretching.

'I'll have the breakfast on the table for quarter past,' Liz said as he got out of bed.

'I'll be back by then,' he replied as he dressed in his working clothes. Liz heard him go downstairs and put on his Wellington boots. The kitchen door closed behind him. Liz got out of bed and washed her face and hands in the washstand basin. She pulled on her black skirt and white cotton blouse. She stared at her reflection in the long mirror on the stand, twisting first one side then the other. She peeled off the blouse and took her new pink, short-sleeved blouse from the clothes chest. She had made it herself.

'I'm sick and tired of boring black and white clothes,' she thought as she brushed her hair carefully. She fixed it in a more elegant style, pinning it into place with hairpins, long tendrils curling down her back.

Preening in front of the mirror, she couldn't help but notice her eyes shining and the rosy glow in her cheeks. She smiled. Nonie, Patsy, Nellie and John would be arriving about twelve thirty. She had loads to do before going to eight o'clock mass in Ballincollig.

*   *   *   *

The sound of the pony's hooves alerted Liz and Jack to the arrival of their visitors. They walked out into the farmyard as the pony and trap came to a halt in front of them. Patsy and John helped their wives from the trap.

'Jack, how are ya? This is my sister Nellie and her husband John,' Patsy said. Jack held out his hand to John first, who shook it firmly, then Nellie.

'Pleased to meet ya, John, Nellie. Welcome to

41

Inniscarra. I'll just put the pony in the shed,' Jack said taking hold of the pony's reins and leading him to the shed. John's eyes lingered on Liz. She blushed before turning away. Liz invited her guests into the kitchen, where the aroma of boiled bacon and turnip wafted in the air.

'Dinner's nearly ready. We're having bacon and turnip and spuds of course. Sit at the table and I'll serve ye,' Liz said.

Nonie and Nellie helped Liz. The men were already sitting at the table. John sat on the far side from where he watched Liz as she set about serving dinner. All week long he thought of little else but this tall beautiful woman. He also felt a bit guilty. After all he was married to Nellie. She was a good wife; the best. Once, Liz caught him looking at her and she quickly turned away.

'My, something smells good,' Patsy said as he sniffed the air appreciatively.

'It sure does. Our Liz is a great cook,' Jack said, beaming with pride.

Soon the three men were deep in conversation. The women served the dinner and sat down at the table. They all enjoyed the dinner and the fresh apple tart and cream afterwards. Later when the kitchen had been cleaned, the six of them walked out into the dazzling afternoon sunshine. The women strolled around to the front of the house. Pots of geraniums stood either side of the little used front door. A hedge at least seven feet high surrounded the neat garden with its gently rolling lawns. An enormous oak tree stood in the corner. The women sat on the wooden seat beneath the parlour window, in the cool shade. In the yard, Patsy and John sat on an empty hay cart while Jack leaned against the oak tree, each of them holding a bottle of Murphy's stout.

'Liz tells me that you're looking for work, John. I don't know if she told you, but I'm looking for a farmhand. This place is too much work for one person,' Jack said wiping the sweat from his brow with the back of his hand.

'I'd be very interested in working for you Jack, but I have a wife and I'd need somewhere local to live,' John replied taking a swig of Murphy's.

'No problem there, I've a cottage just down the road. It's a bit of a mess. T'would need a bit of fixing up, but ye could have it rent free, if you take the job.'

'In that case, I'll definitely take it. I just have to mention it to Nellie first, but I'm sure she'll agree,' John said excitedly.

'That's settled then. When can you start?'

'I'll say it to Nellie in a minute, but all in all, I'd say we could be moved in by the end of the week, if that's all right by you?'

'Shure, that's great. By the way, any children on the horizon?'

'Poor Nellie has lost four babies in the last five years. Doctor reckons she'll never have one now. Her age is against her. We would have liked a few, but it doesn't look like that's ever going to happen,' John said sadly, watching the women, Liz in particular, as they came around the side of the house.

'That's rough. I'm always asking Liz when is she going to present me with a child but she says she wants to wait another while. As you can see, I'm getting on in years so she'd want to start soon. What about you Patsy?' asked Jack, wiping his brow again.

'We've been married six years and we thought we'd have at least two children by now. Can't understand it. The doctor can't either,' Patsy said sadly.

'Well, here's to us producing at least one son and heir in the next twelve months!' Jack said raising his bottle of Murphy's in the air. John and Patsy clinked bottles with him.

John was clearing out the cottage, not far from the entrance to the lane, when Liz stopped on the road outside on her way home from work on Thursday evening. He came down the path towards her.

'Hello, how are ye settling in?' Liz asked.

'Great. We've tidied it up a fair bit. Nellie is having a lie down. How was work?'

'Oh, same as usual. No change.'

Liz carefully stepped down from the trap and holding the reins, she led Penny up the narrow lane towards the farm with John falling into step beside her. Her heart was beating wildly in her chest.

'Do ya take the pony and trap into the city all the time?' John asked, stroking Penny on the side of her head. She leaned her head towards him.

'No, not when I go to work. Jack was too busy to drive me to the cross this morning. That's where I get the Muskerry tram to the city. So I take Penny here, and she waits ever so patiently for me to come back. Isn't that right Penny?' Liz said smiling and nuzzling against Penny's neck.

'She's a lovely pony, is Penny,' John said watching Liz.

'When are you starting work, John?'

'First thing in the morning. Have to be up at the farm before seven. I want to thank you, Liz, for fixing me up with the job. I know it was you that mentioned me to Jack.'

John dug his hands deep into his pockets trying to resist the urge to hold Liz's hand.

'Don't mention it. Jack was looking for someone anyway. I hope ye like it here,' Liz said, her face blushing bright red.

'I know I'm going to love it here! I mean, we....we're going to love it. Well, here we are. I'd better get back to Nellie. See you...Liz,' John turned abruptly and walked quickly down the lane.

Liz stared after him for a few seconds before continuing on into the farmyard. Later that night, Liz rose from the kitchen table.

'I'm off to bed now. See you in the morning,' she called as she headed for the narrow stairs.

'G'night,' Jack called without looking up. He sat at the

table smoking his pipe. From time to time he had to relight it when it went out. The pungent aroma of tobacco wafted around the kitchen. Liz walked into the bedroom and lit the candle on her night table. The bedroom glowed cosily. In bare feet she padded across the wooden floor to the window, which overlooked the cottage at the end of the lane. The upstairs bedroom in the cottage was illuminated by candlelight. Liz stood staring at the cottage.

In the cottage, Nellie slept soundly while John stood looking out of the window in the direction of the farmhouse. He suddenly saw candlelight appear in the upstairs bedroom. After staring out the window in the darkening sky for a minute or two, he walked back to the night table and blew out the candle.

Chapter Three
Inniscarra

John proved to be worth his weight in gold. He was a
good worker, always on time and willing to do anything that
was asked of him. The summer of 1925 was a scorcher.
Most evenings Nellie would call to Liz and they would sit in
the garden at the front of the farmhouse. The women became
firm friends. They'd sit for an hour or two on the wooden
bench under the parlour window.

Liz loved watching the River Lee as it meandered below
the hillside farm on its way from Gougane Barra through
Cork City onwards to the mouth of Cork Harbour and finally
merging with the Atlantic Ocean. Its rippling surface always
had a calming effect on her. Almost directly below the farm
was the 'Weir' where the fast flowing river cascaded like a
miniature waterfall as it sped on its way towards the city.

The sun shone on the front of the house in the evenings
and the women loved to sit in its cooling rays. The sounds of
the flowing river, birds chirping, butterflies fluttering and
bees humming lifted their spirits as they talked and laughed.
Nellie, on hearing John's voice, would jump up excitedly,
say goodbye to Liz and hurry around the side of the
farmhouse to greet her husband with a peck on the cheek.
Linking her arm in his, they would walk down the lane. Liz
resolutely avoided John.

One day in July while Liz was washing the laundry in
the large tin bath in the yard, she spotted a figure walking up
the laneway. She stopped scrubbing and shielding her eyes
from the sun, she waited and watched till the thinly built
man came nearer. The man hastily took off his dirty cap and
smiled a toothless smile. His clothes were shabby and filthy,
his grey hair greasy and unkempt.

'Good day, Missus, how are ya? Me name is Dan Lucey
and I'm your new neighbour. Me uncle Charlie from the
farm next door, God rest his soul, left me the farm. Well,

I'm his only family so his solicitor contacted me and told me I am now the proud owner of a farm. Shure, I know 'tis small but I have big plans for it.'

Warily Liz looked at the stranger.

'How do you do, Dan? I'm Liz McCarthy. My husband Jack is working in the fields. I was sorry to hearing of the passing of your uncle. I didn't know him that well, but Jack knew him well enough. You're not from around here are you?' she asked.

'Naw. I'm just back from sea. I was away for six months. 'Twas a bit of a surprise all right to be greeted by a solicitor. I met your husband once or twice before. Well, tell him I was askin' for him and I'll probably see him in the local pub sometime. I bid you good day mam,' with that Dan Lucey put back on his cap and with another smile walked down the lane. What a funny man, Liz thought.

Later when Jack returned from the fields, Liz recalled her encounter with Dan Lucey. Jack rolled his eyes to heaven as he wolfed down his dinner.

'That scoundrel! You'd want to watch him. He'd rob the eye out of your head and come back for t'other one! Charlie Lucey couldn't stand the sight of him. He must be turning in his grave that his farm went to his nephew. Poor Charlie had nothin'. Just a few stony acres. No livestock or nuthin'. He only grew spuds, which he'd sell in Ballincollig and Inniscarra. As for Dan Lucey being at sea, he only says that when he's in jail. I'm warning ya, you gotta watch him like a hawk.'

'Is he really that dangerous?' Liz asked worried.

'Naw, he's harmless, just very light fingered.'

Late summer turned to autumn and there was no let up in the brilliant weather. Jack and John were busy with the harvesting. The other farmers in the area took turns at helping each other with the backbreaking work. Most of it was complete by the middle of September. Jack and John had three fields left to harvest. Sometimes they were so busy that one or other of the women would take a lunch up to the two men in the fields.

One Saturday, Liz and Nellie set off for the 'top' field with wicker baskets containing food for their husbands. They walked uphill through tilled fields scorched by the relentless sun before finally entering the largest field on the farm. In the middle of it the hay cart was piled high with freshly cut barley. The large Clydesdale horse stood patiently beside the water trough in the cool shade of a sycamore tree. Jack and John were busy cutting the barley. Jack wore a striped work shirt, sleeves rolled up, over trousers tied at the ankles with twine. A homemade straw hat was perched sideways on his head. John, on the other hand, wore trousers tied at the ankles, but was bare-chested and bareheaded. His dark skin was burnt a deep shade of brown by the sun. As the women drew near, they could clearly see the perspiration dripping from the men's faces.

'Jack! Lunchtime. Come on,' Liz called while Nellie spread the tablecloth on the stubbly remains of the cut barley. The men stuck their pitchforks into the mound of barley on the hay cart and walked towards their wives. Liz took out the food from the basket along with a pitcher of water, while Nellie lifted out home made soda bread, thick slices of bacon, home made cheese and a freshly baked apple tart. The men hunkered down at the make shift table and drank water thirstily. Wiping their mouths they helped themselves to the bacon and cheese sandwiches, which they devoured noisily. Their wives, heads covered in cool muslin bonnets, good-naturedly scolded their husbands about their lack of table manners.

'If ye were as hungry as us, ya wouldn't remember your manners either,' Jack said as he received a sharp smack from Liz. She smiled back. John was watching her and she quickly looked away. Turning to Jack again she asked, 'How long more before it's finished?'

'If the weather holds, two more days. What d'ya think

John?'

'I'd say you're right, Jack. Will I go down later to milk the cows?'

'There's no need,' Liz butted in, 'all my chores are done and I'm still on holidays, so I'll do the milking again. Ye carry on here.'

'Ya, best let Liz do it John; the quicker we get the harvesting done the better. Never know when the weather will break. Better get back to it, come on John. Thanks for the lunch, see ye later,' Jack called as he and John walked back towards the hay cart. Liz gathered up the remnants of the lunch into the wicker baskets, while Nellie scattered the crumbs towards the circling crows. They headed back down the hill. John paused, pitchfork in mid air, and watched as the two women walked away, chatting and laughing with each other.

A couple of hours later, after rounding up the cows, Liz started the milking. When Liz worked in Crowley's, Jack usually did the milking twice a day. On her days off, Jack and herself either did the milking together or they took turns. The coolness of the byre was a welcome relief from the searing heat of the sun. Liz sat on the three-legged stool and milked the first cow. Five minutes later, she emptied the pail into the large churn. She pulled the stool over to the next cow. More than half the herd were milked when she heard a noise at the open door behind her. Turning, she saw John standing in the doorway.

'Oh John, it's you. You gave me a fright. I thought ye were still in the top field,' Liz said breathlessly, standing up and tucking loose tendrils of hair behind her ears. Hastily, she smoothed down her grubby white apron.

'Jack sent me down to give you a hand. The top field is just about done for today. After that there's only one more field. That'll take another few days if the weather holds,' John said as he leant against the door casually. Now dressed in a plaid shirt open to the waist, Liz glimpsed his rippling chest muscles gleaming with sweat. The whites of his eyes looked whiter in his bronzed face. Flustered, Liz looked away.

'There's no need. Really. I'll have this lot done in half an hour. I'm well used to it.'

'You work too hard, Liz. You're a great worker and you have your job in the city as well. Jack's a very lucky man to have such a good wife. And, and... a beautiful one at that,' Jack said, his eyes boring into her back as she turned and sat on the stool. Liz froze. She quickly regained her composure and continued milking the cow. She blushed under her light golden tan. She heard John pulling up the other stool to the next cow.

'Liz, I hope you don't think I'm being brazen or forward,' she heard him say from the other side of the cow.

'No...no...of course not. You...you're a good worker yourself, John. Jack would be lost without you.'

'And you Liz?'

'And me, what?'

'Would you be lost without me as well?' John said softly peering at her from under the cow's belly. She blushed furiously.

There was a pause.

'I'm sure I don't know what you mean, John.'

Liz rose from the stool and tipped the pail of creamy milk into the churn. John stood up and pail in hand, stepped nearer to Liz.

'Liz, I think very highly of you. I think you're the most beautiful, intelligent....'

Liz whirled around suddenly, her eyes blazing.

'Stop it! What are you trying to do, John? If you have something to say, for heavens sake spit it out and stop all this beating about the bush.'

'I love you, Liz.'

The empty pail clattered loudly as it hit the stone floor. The sound echoed around the byre. Liz stooped to pick it up at the same time John bent to retrieve it. Their eyes met.

'Liz, I had to tell you. I've loved you from the first moment I saw you. I couldn't tell anybody. I know nothing can happen between us, ever, but please, please tell me you feel the same way,' he looked deep into her eyes; into her very soul it seemed. She rose slowly. John stood nearby towering over her. Liz didn't know what to say, or where to look.

'John...., I don't think you should have said ...what you just said. I don't know what you expect me to say. I'm married to Jack. You're married to Nellie,' she said, perplexed.

'Tell me you feel the same way.'

Placing his hands on her shoulders he massaged her gently. She relaxed slightly as she stared at her feet, her emotions threatening to unleash themselves. She couldn't allow that to happen. Breaking free of his grasp, she turned.

'John Flynn, I don't feel anything for you. How could you think that? You're the husband of a dear friend of mine and may I remind you, my husband employs you. Now I am very busy. The cows have to be milked and then I have to make my husband's dinner. So stop this tomfoolery. I'll forget we ever had this conversation and I strongly suggest you do the same.'

With that she strode to the next cow, sat on the stool and furiously pulled the cows teats. The sound of the milk hitting the sides of the empty pail, echoed around the byre as Liz milked the animal. John stood for a few moments, watching her back, then quietly walked out of the byre. Hearing his footsteps fading, Liz leaned over and rested her head in her hands.

*   *   *   *

Late September and there was no let up in the sunshine. A perfect 'Indian' summer. One morning Liz opened the kitchen door and went out, bucket in hand, to feed the ducks and geese. It was oddly quiet. She walked to the pond and stopped in astonishment. There wasn't a duck or a goose to be seen! Where on earth could twenty ducks and twenty-eight geese have gone? She looked around the yard, checked in the byre, even in the pigsty. She dropped the bucket and ran up the fields. In the distance, she saw Jack and John cutting barley in the field.

'Jack, Jack,' she called breathlessly. Jack and John looked at Liz running towards them. Jack walked towards her.

'What's wrong?' he asked worried.

'It's the ducks and the geese!' she gasped, sweat rolling down her face.

'What do ya mean, it's the ducks and geese?'

'They're gone! All of them! I came out to feed them and there's not one left.'

Jack and John looked at each other.

'They were there when we left at quarter to seven,' John said.

'You're right. Are you sure you haven't been at the whiskey, Liz?' Jack asked smiling.

She looked at him indignantly.

'Of course not! I'm telling you, they're all gone!'

Jack stopped smiling suddenly.

'It's Lucey! Dan flamin' Lucey! I bet he took them. Right! I'm going around there now.'

He turned abruptly and marched back towards the yard. Liz and John glanced at each other before running after him. Jack was fuming when he saw the empty pond.

'I'm coming too,' Liz announced.

Jack, John and Liz climbed into the pony and trap and drove the short distance to Dan Lucey's newly acquired farm. It was much smaller than Jack's and extremely shabby. As they alighted from the trap, they heard an unusual sound. Ducks quacking! Old Charlie Lucey never had ducks or geese. Looking around, Jack spotted a newly dug pond at the side of a rundown shed. Just at that moment, the kitchen door of the run down little cottage was flung open and Dan Lucey emerged, a rifle in his hand. He stared at the three of them.

'Get off my land,' he spat. Jack glowered at him.

'You took our ducks! And our geese! And we're taking them back.'

'They're me own ducks and geese. They're bought and paid for. Now get off my land before I shoot you off,' Dan Lucey shouldered the rifle. John stepped protectively in front of Liz.

'I want my ducks and geese now because if I don't get them, I'll go to the police and you will be back in Cork gaol before you know it.'

'Can you identify them?' Dan Lucey asked.

'What?'

'Can you identify them ducks an' geese? How can you tell if they're yours?' Dan Lucey said with a smirk.

John and Liz looked at each other incredulously. A smile broke out on John's face, which he tried to hide behind his hand. Liz glared at him.

'They're ducks and geese! How can anybody identify them? I just know they're ours, now I want them back,' Jack shouted, his face red.

'Well, you go to the constabulary and get a search warrant, and, a description of each duck and goose, and we'll let the police handle it then,' Dan Lucey smirked again.

John's shoulders heaved up and down with suppressed laughter. Even Liz smiled.

'Are you mad? A description of a duck? Shure, they all look alike,' Jack spluttered angrily.

'Exactly! How do you know them ducks are yours? Now get out, I'm busy.'

Jack was shaking in anger. John put his hand on his arm.

'Jack, come on, he's right. We can't prove they're your ducks and geese. Let's go back to the farm and plan our next move,' John said quietly.

With one last look at Dan Lucey, Jack turned and catching Liz's arm turned towards the trap.

'Jack, you go, let me try talking to him,' Liz said in a low voice.

Before he could reply, Liz had turned and walked towards Dan Lucey. He eyed her suspiciously. John and Jack watched.

'Mr Lucey..,' Liz began, ' I can ..identify the ducks. And the geese. I've fed them for the last few years, so I know they're our ducks. If you let us take them back, I'll give you a few goslings and ducklings when they're born.'

Dan lowered his rifle and swallowed. Whatever about threatening men with his empty rifle, it didn't seem right to aim it at a lady. He scratched his jaw thoughtfully. Handing back the ducks and geese would be like admitting he stole them in the first place.

'As I said missus, them's me own ducks an' geese. We'll let it up to the police to decide,' he said then turned abruptly went inside and slammed the front door.

'Let's go, there's no point in talking to that eejit,' Jack said catching Liz's arm again. The three of them climbed into the trap. John was still struggling to control his laughter. Jack eyed him angrily. John raised his hand.

'I'm sorry for laughing but you have to admit, its funny. Can you identify them?' John mimicked Dan Lucey, his eye screwed up in a squint just like Dan.

Liz burst out laughing then stopped when she saw Jacks sour expression. John patted Jack on the back as he flicked the reins.

'Don't worry, we'll get them back!'

Exactly one week later, John came running up the lane at six-thirty just as it was getting dark. He opened the kitchen door before striding in. Liz was sitting in the sugan chair by the glowing turf fire, reading Great Expectations. She looked up in surprise when John burst in without knocking. He was grinning from ear to ear. He nodded at Jack excitedly. Jack jumped up immediately and pulled on his jacket.

'Where are ye goin'?' asked Liz suspiciously.

'Nowhere!' they chorused innocently.

'We won't be long,' Jack said as he and John hurried out.

Much later, after Liz had gone to bed, she heard the pony and trap returning. Half an hour later, Jack came up the narrow stairs. Liz sat up in bed.

'Where were ye?' she demanded. Jack was beaming as he sat on the bed to take off his shoes.

'Dan Lucey went to the pub tonight in Inniscarra. John was watching out all week. So we went and stole our ducks and geese back. Not only that, we filled in his new pond with rocks!' chortled Jack as he climbed into bed.

Liz shook her head not knowing whether to laugh or be cross.

'What if he steals them again?' she asked.

'Well, we'll steal them back again,' laughed Jack as he blew out the candle.

At the beginning of October, the sun cooled only slightly. The leaves began to fall, the roadsides strewn with leaves of different hues of yellow, amber and brown. Liz did everything in her power to avoid John and in doing so, didn't see much of Nellie either. Lately Jack spoke of little else but having a baby. Up until now, they hadn't made love very often. She had grown fond of Jack, he was a kind man, but she didn't love him. There was no affection, no intimacy between them. The occasional time when they did make love it was for Jack's sake. Liz was only doing her 'duty'.

Until recently Liz had continued to visit Nonie and Patsy one Sunday every month, sometimes accompanied by Nellie. One warm day in the middle of October, Liz and

Nonie walked along the road along Clash Road.

'We haven't seen much of Nellie and John in a while. How are they?' Nonie asked.

'I don't see much of them myself. Jack and John have been busy lately and I have loads to do in the house,' Liz replied, breathing in the fresh sea air. They sat down on a patch of grass near the strand and looked out across the water. The water reflected the sun twinkling like little stars on the crests of waves as they raced towards the shore.

'Is everything all right? With you and Jack, I mean. It's just that you haven't seemed yourself lately,' Nonie asked. Liz smiled.

'Oh, everything is fine, just fine. Don't worry about me.'

Liz watched idly at a small boat being rowed from Little Island to Passage West.

Liz arrived back at the farm at six o'clock, as the sun was setting. She led Penny into the shed and unhooked the trap. She crossed the yard and went into the kitchen. It was strangely quiet. The fire had gone out in the hearth. She relit it within minutes. Where was Jack? It was dark now so he wouldn't be working. Probably gone to the public house in Inniscarra. She tidied the kitchen and settled by the fire with her book. She was an avid reader and was half way through Jane Eyre by Charlotte Bronte. A loud rap at the kitchen door woke Liz. Sleepily she looked around.

'Who's there?' she called out rising to her feet.

'It's me John. Can you open the door quickly because I've got a present for ya,' John said laughing.

Liz couldn't believe the sight before her eyes, when she opened the door. Standing on the doorstep was John and Jack. Unfortunately, John was propping up Jack who was asleep and snoring on his shoulder.

'What's wrong with him? Is he hurt?' Liz asked anxiously.

'Naw, just drunk!' John grinned as he dragged Jack into

the kitchen, 'where will I put him?'

'Drunk? The eejit! What's he doing, being this drunk on a Sunday? Take him upstairs and drop him on the bed. I'll deal with him later.'

John half dragged, half carried Jack upstairs. Shaking her head in disgust, Liz poked the flames in the hearth. She knew that Jack liked his few drinks from time to time, but he must have drunk a fair amount to get into that condition. She could hear the sound of somebody being dropped onto the bed. That settles it, she thought, I'll sleep in the guest room tonight.

John came downstairs, still smiling.

'He's sleeping like a baby. He'll have some headache in the mornin'.'

'He'll have more than a headache when I lay into him. In the name of God, how did he get in that condition?' Liz hung the kettle on the swinging crane while John took a seat at the table.

'He called to me not long after you left, about one o clock, and asked me to accompany him to the pub in Inniscarra. I said no. I called to the pub tonight for a pint and he was in that condition, along with a few of his neighbours. Dan Lucey was with him. It seems they patched up their differences and Dan had brought along a jug of homemade poitín.'

'Jesus, Mary and Joseph, Dan Lucey! Poitín! I've told him loads of time not to touch that stuff. I don't mind the few pints of Guinness, but I remember my own father when he used to come home after drinking poitín. He'd be like a lunatic. There was always a fight at home. My poor mother usually bore the brunt of it. Anyone trying to help her would get a few slaps as well. 'Twas often I'd get a beating too, just because I'd try to help me mother. 'Tis lucky that him upstairs is asleep. I don't think I could handle it if he was like me Da,' Liz said as she spooned the tealeaves into the freshly scalded teapot. She poured the boiling water into the pot and placed it on the table along with cups and saucers and milk.

'Thank you for bringing him home John, although I don't know if I should be thanking you at all, the state he's in! Still, I suppose it's better than him being found in a ditch.'

'No thanks needed. Glad to be of some help. How are you Liz? I haven't seen you in a while,' John said softly staring intently at her.

'Oh, I'm fine, same as usual. I went down to Nonie and Patsy today. They were asking about ye. Said ye don't call much. They send their love anyway,' Liz sipped her tea. John put down his cup.

'Liz, we have to talk.'

'Talk about what?'

'About me an' you. You can deny it all you like, but I know you have feelings for me. The same feelings that I have for you. That's what we have to talk about.'

'John, please, my husband is upstairs. Your wife is just down the road. Even if I did have 'feelings' for you, where would it get us? I'll tell you. Nowhere! There's nothing at all we can do. We're married. To other people!' Liz said angrily.

Silence.

'Thank you, Liz. You have finally admitted that you feel the same way about me as I do about you,' John lifted the cup to his mouth and sipped his tea while watching Liz.

'I most certainly do not, I.. I mean…' she stuttered and her face reddened.

Putting down his cup, John reached across the table and took her hand in his. Tenderly, he stroked it with his other hand. She sat there basking in the warmth as he lovingly stroked her. Her whole body tingled in a way it had never done before. All the same she couldn't bring herself to look into his eyes.

'Liz, look at me.'

Slowly she raised her head and looked into his eyes.

'I love you so much and I don't want anybody to get hurt. I care deeply for Nellie but it doesn't come any way near what I feel for you. Jack loves you very much. He always talks about you. Of course he doesn't realise how much it hurts to hear your name. He told me tonight how much he'd love to have a baby and that you keep putting him off. He's a decent man. These last few weeks of not seeing you were hell. Please Liz, don't avoid me again. I can put up with anything, so long as I know you are near. I need to see you every day. I need to know you love me the way I love you. I know nothing can come of it, but I need you.'

John looked at their clasped hands and slowly Liz put her other hand on top. He looked up and saw tears in her eyes. His grip tightened.

'John…I shouldn't be saying this. I do…love you. The reason I don't want to have a baby with Jack is that I can't bear him to touch me. I do my 'duty' every few months. Yet, I'm fond of him. He's good and kind. I'd love to have a baby, but I …can't stand him touching me. And you, you have a wife. She's a very dear friend. She worships the ground you walk on. I could never hurt her and you shouldn't either. So it's best all round if we admit we have feelings for each other but, carry on as before. You'd better finish your tea and go home. Nellie will be wondering where you are.'

Together, they sat, hands entwined for what seemed like a long time.

'Nellie thinks I'm in the pub. She won't be expecting me for another couple of hours,' John said as he got up and still holding her hands, walked around the table where Liz was sitting. Gently, he pulled her up to a standing position beside him. Without a word they embraced, Liz laid her head against his muscular chest. John stroked her silky black hair with his cheek. Eventually, Liz raised her head and looked into his eyes. John returned her gaze. Slowly, he lowered his head until their lips met. The kiss was like nothing she had ever experienced. She felt sensations she had never experienced coursing through her body. For the first time she knew what it felt like to be truly loved.

'Oh, Liz, I want you. I don't care how. I just need you so much. I want you so bad right now,' John whispered softly into her hair. She pulled away from him abruptly. Catching hold of his hand, she gently led him to the bedroom door under the stairs. Tiptoeing across the darkened room, she lit the candle on the night table, while John remained standing by the door. She turned around and looked at him shyly. He walked towards her and wrapping his arms around her, he caressed her in the flickering light of the candle. Eventually John led her to the bed where still entwined, they lay down on top of the patchwork quilt. He leaned over and blew out the candle.

Liz woke with a start when the cock crowed from his usual perch, the pigsty gate. Six thirty. It was dark outside. Remembering the night before she turned over. John was already gone. She pulled the blankets around her naked body. Her clothes, hastily discarded the night before were strewn on the wooden floor. She ran her fingers distractedly through her waist length hair.

'Oh God, what have I done?' she said out loud. Shivering, she got out of bed and hurriedly dressed.

I'd better wake Jack or I'll have to do the milking myself, she thought. She hastily plaited her hair, and walked into the kitchen. She lit the kitchen fire without raking it out. As she stood up she caught sight of the teapot and cups still on the table. She picked them up and took them to the washbasin. She rinsed and dried the cups and saucers and hung them on the cup hooks on the kitchen dresser. Then she ran up the stairs to the bedroom. Jack lay on the bed, still fully dressed, his boots on his feet. His mouth hung open as he snored noisily. A trail of spittle rolled out of the corner of his mouth. From the doorway, Liz could get the putrid smell of stale alcohol from his breath. His straggly grey matted hair had fallen over his eyes.

'Get up Jack, you have to milk the cows,' she shouted, shaking him roughly.

Jack slowly opened his eyes. It took a few moments for the room to come into focus. With bleary bloodshot eyes he looked at Liz standing over him. Yawning, he struggled to sit up. He closed his eyes for a few seconds, blinked, and then shook his head hard. He groaned as he held his head in his hands.

'Jaysus, it feels like there's a little man in my head with a huge hammer and he's banging on me skull.'

'Don't look for sympathy from me, Jack McCarthy. I can't believe you drank poitin. How much of it did you drink for heavens sake?' Liz asked, disgusted.

'I had four pints of Guinness then Dan Lucey came in with two large tankards of poitin. Between the four of us, I reckon we had at least a pint of poitin each. Oh God, please stop the bangin' in me head!' He exclaimed loudly, clutching his head again.

'Ya eejit. Well, a hangover is easily cured. There's a shed full of cows waiting patiently to be milked. Now, get up!' She shouted angrily as she turned and began to walk away.

'By the way, how did I get home? Last thing I remember was laying me head on the table in the pub to rest my eyes.'

Liz stopped dead in her tracks. She didn't turn around.

''Twas John. He brought you home. Just as well. God only knows what might have happened to you.'

Her cheeks scarlet, she continued on down the stairs.

Chapter Four
Crowley's

Thursday morning, Liz arrived at Crowley's. She
entered the shop and slammed the door to shut out the gale
force wind. The weather had changed abruptly in the last
few days. Nonie was already in the back of the shop taking
off her cloak and bonnet as she chatted to Sheila and Mary.
Liz shivered. Thank God Miss Crowley lights the fire at half
past seven on the cold mornings, Liz thought.

'Hello, Liz, great news. My niece Molly is coming to
stay with Patsy and me for a while. Remember I told you
about her? She is the eldest of my sister Nora's children.
She's twenty. Nora's at the end of her tether since her
husband died last year. She's struggling to feed all nine of
them but it's very hard. She's asked the five eldest to leave
home. Luckily, they're working. They're gone to stay with
neighbours and friends. Patsy and me give her two shillings
a week every week but it's not enough. Lucky for her the
workhouse was abolished or she definitely would be in there
by now, along with her children. Anyway, Molly is coming
to live with us. She works in the railway. Patsy and me will
enjoy the company,' Nonie said excitedly.

'Well, that's great news. You'll have to introduce us
soon,' Liz said taking the scissors and measuring tape from
the drawer.

'You look a lot happier lately. Happier than you've been
in a long while. What's put the colour back in your cheeks?'
Nonie was smiling as she sat behind her sewing machine.
Liz blushed.

'I don't know what you mean. Shh! Here's Miss
Crowley,' she whispered as the door slammed.

Seconds later, Miss Kathleen Crowley appeared in the
doorway.

'Morning, Ladies. Ye know we have a lot of orders to
finish in the next two weeks. Liz, any chance you could

work a five day week? Just for the two weeks. Otherwise, we'll be into the Christmas rush,' she asked.

'I don't mind at all, Miss Crowley.'

All the girls enjoyed working for Miss Kathleen Crowley. She had high standards in her tailoring business and her employees worked extremely well as a team. Miss Crowley worked in the shop, taking orders, measuring customers and advising them. She was in the tailoring trade for the last twenty years. In her early forties, she was slim and petite and always neatly dressed. She wore her auburn hair elegantly coiled on top of her head. Her sister Majella occasionally took charge of the shop if Kathy had other business to attend to. Unfortunately, Majella Crowley was the opposite of her sister. The girls were always on edge when she was in the shop. Whereas, kindly Miss Kathy had no objections to the women chatting while they worked, Miss Majella kept their noses to the grindstone and, absolutely no talking. She looked for the slightest little thing so as to wield her authority over the workers. The women sometimes pulled funny faces at her behind her back; so far they hadn't been caught!

Liz threw herself into her work. It helped take her mind off 'that' night. She hadn't seen John since. Jack couldn't apologise enough for getting drunk on poitin last Sunday night, which made Liz feel even guiltier. Although she had declared her love for John, she resigned herself to nothing coming of it. She relived their night of love over and over in her mind. She never imagined in her wildest dreams that such exquisite pleasure existed. She did wonder what explanation he had given Nellie for coming home in the early hours of Monday morning.

Liz woke to the sound of the rain pelting against the bedroom window next morning. Jack opened his eyes when he felt Liz move.

'I'll make breakfast,' Liz said yawning and stretching as she got out of bed. She shivered as she went downstairs.

The mornings were getting colder as November approached. She raked out the ashes in the hearth. After lighting the fire, she filled the kettle and placed it on the swinging crane above the hearth. As she rose to go back upstairs, she suddenly felt light headed. As she reached the landing, she felt slightly nauseous. I hope I'm not coming down with a cold, she thought.

'I'll be back in an hour,' Jack said as he descended the stairs. Liz dressed quickly. She pulled on her newly knitted cardigan. Returning to the kitchen, she got out eggs, bacon and dripping to cook breakfast for herself and Jack. As she cooked the food on the griddle, she suddenly felt a queasiness in her stomach. She cooked only enough for Jack. Jack returned from the byre, took off his oilskin jacket, and sat at the table. Liz served his breakfast to him and sitting opposite him, poured two cups of tea and handed one to Jack.

'You not eating anything?' Jack asked, eating his bacon hungrily.

'No, I'm not hungry,' Liz answered, 'I think I'm coming down with a cold.'

'Hope it's only a cold, and not T.B. Maybe you shouldn't have taken on that extra work,' Jack said.

'I'll be all right. It's only a cold. I don't mind doing the extra work. It's only for another week,' Liz said, sipping her tea.

'You must have a fair old nest egg by now. I've never seen so much as a farthing of your wages,' Jack said, smiling.

'Jack, you know where I keep my wages. If you want it, you're more than welcome to it,' Liz replied.

'I'm only kiddin'. That's your money. It'll come in handy whenever we have a baby. I'd really love to have a baby in the next year, Liz. Nothing would make me happier. How about it?' Jack asked, as he picked up his cup of tea.

He watched her over the rim of his willow pattern cup.

She blushed crimson as she remembered her one night of love with John.

'Mm. Yes. Maybe. Yes, I suppose... I suppose it's time we did. Yes, I'd like a little baby too,' she said, looking at Jack. His eyes lit up in surprise.

'I've got to go now Jack, or I'll be late for work. We'll talk about it tonight. I promise. 'Bye.'

With that she put on her black winter cloak and walked towards the door. Jack remained at the table, still staring at her. A wide grin slowly spread across his face. At last! They were going to have a baby. As Liz pulled open the kitchen door, John was standing on the doorstep, hand poised, ready to knock on the door. Their eyes met briefly.

'Mo- morning John, I'm in a rush. I'll be late for work. 'Bye,' she said quickly, as she hurried past him, head down. John stared after her then turned and walked into the warm kitchen. Jack was still grinning as he drank his tea.

'John, I have great news! Liz said she wants to have a baby. I hope we'll be starting one tonight,' he said excitedly.

John was stunned. He felt like a sharp knife was plunged into his heart and was being twisted over and over. The last thing he wanted to hear was the woman he loved having a baby with Jack. He wished she'd have a baby with him instead. He still longed to have a baby of his own, but he knew he and Nellie would never have one.

'That's - that's very good news Jack, I wish ye all the best,' he said with a forced smile.

*   *   *   *

Liz was on her feet all day, cutting out pattern after pattern. Most of them were for ladies winter coats and cloaks. Others were for ladies gowns. The nauseous feeling got worse as the day wore on. She felt weak and light-headed. Her face was a shade whiter than normal. Nonie watched her closely. She noticed that Liz ate nothing for her lunch. Liz cradled her cup of tea, occasionally sipping it.

'You look sick, Liz. Why don't you ask Miss Crowley can you go home,' Nonie said, concerned.

'I'll be fine. I think I'm coming down with a cold. There's only another two hours to go anyway,' replied Liz as she smiled weakly.

Later, after returning home she entered the kitchen and took off her cloak. She shivered. Quickly, she stoked up the dying embers of the fire and added more turf and a few blocks. She felt weak and had to sit down to peel the potatoes, carrots and onions for Irish stew. Jack came into the kitchen as she was putting the vegetables and mutton into the pot. He sat at the table.

'You still sick?' He enquired.

'I don't feel too bad now, just tired,' she answered wearily.

Later, she washed and dried the dishes. She had eaten very little. Liz announced she was going to bed early.

'I'll come with you,' Jack said, as he began to get up from the table.

'Jack, I don't feel well. I have a sick stomach and my head is pounding like the hammers of hell. I really need a good nights sleep,' Liz pleaded.

Jack looked crestfallen. He looked at Liz. She did indeed look very pale, dark rings under her eyes.

'Of course. You go on up so. I'll stay down here a while for a smoke of me pipe. Hope you feel better soon. Goodnight,' he said as he fetched his pipe bowl.

Liz continued on up the stairs. She undressed slowly. After washing herself, she pulled on her warm nightgown and slid into the cold bed. She fell into an exhausted sleep within minutes.

Liz woke early next morning. She was dismayed when she realised she didn't feel any better. The morning after that, she still felt sick and nauseous and ate very little. The rush at work was over and she was back on her normal three day week.

'I'm going to Dr White this morning. This cold is dragging on a bit,' she told Jack after another two days of feeling sick.

'Ah, good. Good. The doctor might give you a tonic as well. Build up your strength. You'll need it if we're to make a baby,' Jack said winking. He had been disappointed that they hadn't made love lately.

*   *   *   *

Dr White sat writing notes at the solid oak desk in the surgery. Liz emerged from behind the flimsy linen screen. Moments earlier, Dr White had prodded and pressed her tummy as he asked her questions. She sat opposite the doctor and waited. He continued writing.

'Do you know what's wrong with me, Doctor? What can I take for it?' Liz asked anxiously.

Dr. White looked over his spectacles at Liz. He smiled suddenly.

'Mrs McCarthy, there's nothing wrong with you. You're in the family way. Congratulations! I estimate your due date is the first week in July.'

Liz sat in stunned silence. Her mouth went dry.

'Are you sure doctor? I mean …., could you be mistaken?'

'I'm a doctor, Mrs McCarthy; I can tell when a woman is expecting a baby. You and your husband must be delighted,' the doctor said smiling.

'Ya. Delighted. Goodbye Doctor.'

Liz walked out of the surgery in a daze. The afternoon sky was overcast and dark. Grey clouds scurried overhead as the wind increased. Liz pulled her cloak around her and shivered. She stared blankly ahead. What am I going to do? It can't be Jack's baby; sure, we haven't made love in months. Oh my God! It has to be John's! Oh no!

She climbed into the trap and flicked the reins. Penny headed towards Inniscarra. What am I going to do? Nothing for it but to let Jack make love to me tonight. Damn! I wish I didn't feel so sick, she thought. The wind howled around her as the pony and trap pulled into the farmyard. The grey sky looked as if it would burst at any moment and spew its contents in a heavy downpour. Jack was in the byre. He came out when he heard the clip clopping of the pony's hooves on the ground.

'What did the doctor say?' Jack asked as he helped Liz from the trap. John entered the yard at that moment. He stopped momentarily and glanced at Liz. She looked at him briefly then turned to look at Jack. She forced a smile.

'Dr White thinks it's an upset stomach. He says I'll be as right as rain in a day or two. Nothing to worry about. I'd better start the housework,' she said brightly as she headed towards the kitchen.

'Did he give you something for it?' Jack asked as he led Penny towards the barn.

'What?' Liz asked, turning around as she reached the door.

'Your upset belly. Did he give you anything for it? The Doctor?' He repeated.

'No. No, he said it'd pass in a day or two.'

She opened the door quickly, stumbled inside and shut the door. She stood for a long time with her back against the door. She raised her hands to her face, and then clasped them over her mouth as she tried to think straight. How did I get myself into this mess, she thought. If Jack ever found out, it would kill him. Or he would kill her. She shuddered. He must never find out.

Later, Jack got out his pipe box and sat at the table. Liz was standing by the crackling fire. Outside the wind continued to howl around the farmhouse. Clearing her throat Liz sidled towards Jack.

'Jack,' she whispered.

'Ya?' He replied absentmindedly, as he cut slivers of tobacco from the square of tobacco with a sharp knife.

'If…if you're in the mood, I… we… I mean, I think we could start, you know, making a baby. Now. Tonight,' she said, her face reddening from embarrassment. She gently placed her hand on his shoulder and stroked it. Jack stopped cutting. He looked at Liz.

'Are you sure? I mean, do you mean now? Right now?' Jack asked incredulously.

'If you'd rather have your pipe first, that's all right. I'll wait,' Liz replied softly.

Jack jumped to his feet, lifted Liz clean off her feet, and swung her around as he hugged her tightly. She squealed in surprise as she clung to his thickset neck.

'Oh Liz, come on now! Me pipe can wait. I want to get started with making my son and heir!' he said, as he released her. Gently, he held her hand and led her towards the stairs, a big smile on his face. Behind him, Liz's smile was strained. I feel like a lamb being led to the slaughter, she thought.

Hours later, Liz lay in bed twisting and turning, unable to sleep. She felt dirty, disgusting and ashamed after being manhandled by her husband. Why do I feel like this? I hate making love with my own husband. I spent one night with John Flynn and he made me feel loved and wanted. He made feel …alive. I love him and I know he loves me. And now, I'm going to have his baby; a baby he should be having with his wife. Nellie! I feel so guilty about what I have done. And to Jack too. I have to pretend to everybody that this is Jack's baby. I ll never tell another living soul that it's John's baby. That's what I'll do. I'll just have to keep my mouth shut. Jack will be a good father. I'll have to keep John out of my thoughts from now on.

Chapter Five

Two weeks to Christmas and Crowley's was well into its Christmas rush. Everybody wanted new coats, cloaks, skirts, blouses and dresses in time for Christmas. Liz's morning sickness was almost gone. So far she hadn't told anybody that she was expecting a baby. Lunchtime came at last. Nonie and Liz brought their cups of tea to the fireplace in the shop, as well as a plate of buttered brown bread and cheese. Huddling by the flickering flames of the log fire, Nonie and Liz shivered as they cradled their cups.

'How is Molly getting on?' asked Liz.

'Very well. She's working in the railway in the little fruit and sweet shop. She's going out with a soldier from Collins' Barracks no less! She met him six weeks ago. She gives her mother money every week towards feeding the little ones. Nora, my sister works a few hours in the mornings in a little bakery. She's up at five and is home in time to get the young ones to school. Patsy and me haven't seen Nellie or John in a while. I know the weather is terrible an' all. How are they?'

Liz caught her breath.

'I don't see much of them myself,' Liz replied after a pause, 'Nonie, I have something to tell you, which I haven't told anybody else yet. I don't know if I should tell you or should I tell Jack first...'

'Stop babbling an' spit it out.'

'I'm going to have a baby!'

Nonie stopped drinking her tea. She looked at Liz. She saw the strained look about her eyes and although Liz was smiling, her smile didn't quite reach her eyes.

'Are you happy about it? Was that morning sickness you had a few weeks ago? You know, I guessed you were expecting,' Nonie said quietly.

'Oh no, no. I'm only a few weeks gone and yes, I'm happy. I'm going to tell Jack tonight, so please, don't tell anybody yet.'

Nonie smiled suddenly. She put down her mug and stretched out her arms towards Liz.

'Come here till I give you a hug. Congratulations. I wish you and Jack all the best. Ye'll make good parents,' she said.

Liz fell into her embrace and they hugged tightly. A single tear rolled down Liz's face.

'Thank you Nonie.'

'I wish, well, I wish I was having a baby of my own so, I'm a little bit jealous of ya,' Nonie said wistfully as she looked at Liz, 'don't mind me. I'm so happy for you and Jack.'

Liz patted Nonie on the shoulder and she smiled sadly.

'I know how much you and Patsy want a baby. I'll share my baby with you!'

'I'll hold you to that! Well, what about work? You'll be giving it up of course?' Nonie asked.

'Not yet. I'll wait till nearer my time. It's due at the end of July. Come on, we better get back to work or we'll have to stay on!'

Grey clouds scurried across the sky as Liz neared the farm in the pony and trap. She glanced at the cottage at the end of the lane as she passed. A lighted candle in the window shone like a beacon. In the kitchen Liz could make out Nellie hunched over the hearth, no doubt cooking dinner for her husband. Liz felt a pang of guilt as she watched her friend singing to herself. As she headed up the lane to the farm the rain started. Hurriedly she led Penny into the barn and unharnessed her. Coming out of the barn, she could see Jack and John returning from the fields. Both of them wore oilskins and Wellingtons. She scurried towards the kitchen door and wrenched it opened.

Stepping inside, she removed her cloak. She poked the dying embers of the fire and added more turf and logs. Within minutes the flames were licking around the logs. She heard Jack's heavy footsteps as they neared the kitchen door.

The door opened and he came in, rubbing his hands together to warm them. After removing his oilskins and Wellingtons, he sat at the table while his wife prepared dinner. After peeling and slicing potatoes and turnip, she placed them on top of the mutton pieces in the pot. She added water, and covered the pot with a plate. She swung the crane over the blazing fire. Drying her hands on her apron she walked to the table. Her mouth went dry. Jack looked at her.

'What's wrong?' he asked gruffly.

'Nothing. I just wanted to tell you that we're going to have a baby,' she said.

Jack stared at her incredulously. Suddenly he leapt from the chair, delight dancing in his eyes.

'Oh God Almighty! A baby! Our baby! Oh that's the best news! I bet it's a boy! Wait till I tell everybody. When will it be born?'

'It's due at the end of July,' she replied quietly.

'A summer baby! Well there now! Come on, we'll go straightaway and tell your Ma and Da,' he said reaching for his overcoat and cap.

'Jack, it's raining. It's late. It's dark. I'm tired and the dinner is on!' Liz said.

Jack stopped in his tracks.

'Oh, right. I'll go see them tomorrow while you're at work. Talking about work, you're giving it up aren't ya?'

'Later on, at the start of the summer. I'll have to tell Miss Crowley soon.'

'Of course. She's a decent woman. Now don't go putting any strain on yourself. If it gets too much in that shop, will you promise to give it up?' Jack asked as he draped his arm around her shoulders. He gently stroked her abdomen with his other hand. She squirmed out of his reach and walked to the pot, which was bubbling above the hearth.

Winter gave way to spring. Liz had given up her job in January. She continued doing her chores around the farm.

Now at the beginning of March, she was rooting around in the outhouse beside the byre. John and Jack returning from the fields stopped in their tracks as they heard noises coming from the little used shed. Jack motioned to John to follow him as they inched their way towards the open door. Peering around the door Jack was surprised to see his wife inside searching for something. He stepped into the dim shed.

'What the devil are you doing?' he said.

Liz jumped in fright and dropped the old wicker basket she held in her hands.

'Oh! You frightened me,' she gasped, clutching her chest. She stared at John standing in the doorway.

'I was looking for the wicker basket,' she said the colour rising to her cheeks as she hastily tore her eyes away from John. John was staring at her. He thought she never looked as beautiful as she did now, halfway through her pregnancy. Her hair never looked as glossy, her pale skin glowed with health. Her stomach was more rounded. She brushed her hair back from her now flushed face.

'I'm going to give Dan Lucey a couple of ducklings,' she said a smile lighting up her face.

'Why?' Asked Jack and John together.

'I kind of promised him that time, that we'd give him a few ducks,' she said bending to pick up the basket. Instinctively Jack stepped forward picked it up and handed it to Liz.

'But he stole our ducks. And geese!' Jack said.

'I know, but he's not that bad really. He wandered in this morning while I was doing the washing near the well. Would you believe he washed all the clothes and hung them on the line? And told me stories that almost made my hair curl!' she said with a smile. She walked past Jack and John and towards the pond. She dropped the basket and clutching her lower back, knelt beside the pond. Jack shook his head, a smile on his face. He loved his beautiful kind wife more than ever and could not say no to her. He threw his hands up in mock despair as he walked towards the kitchen.

John knelt beside Liz. Together they tried to catch the fluffy yellow ducklings that kept slipping from their hands. They both laughed as another one made his escape.

'There! Got one,' John announced proudly as he carefully placed the duckling in the basket.

'Quick,' Liz shrieked as she captured another frightened duckling. John pushed the basket towards her and helped her lower the squirming duckling into it. Laughing, she turned to John, her eyes glowing. He looked into her eyes.

'I haven't seen you in a while. You seem to be avoiding me,' John said softly taking the wicker basket from Liz and holding out his hand to help her up.

'I see Nellie nearly every day, she's almost as excited about the baby as me and Jack,' Liz said, standing.

'I meant I haven't seen you. I miss you…'

'Stop this right now John, I have things to do. I want to take these over to Dan now before I cook the dinner.'

'Well I hope you'll allow me to walk you down the lane, seeing as how I'm going that way anyway,' John said taking the basket from Liz. Hesitating a second, she fell into step beside him. Together they crossed the yard and passed the open kitchen door, watched by Jack. A strange feeling crept over him.

Walking down the lane, John and Liz chatted easily about the ducklings, the weather, anything but the passion that existed between them. Liz spotted Nellie sweeping around the front door of the cottage.

'Hi Nellie, hard at it I see,' Liz called.

Nellie smiled as she leant on the broom handle.

'What have ye got there?' she asked. She was delighted that Liz was expecting her first baby although she couldn't help feel a bit envious. She knew she would never be a mother herself.

'Ducklings for Dan Lucey!' Liz announced, 'would you like to come with me to present them to him?'

'Why not? Half an hour won't kill my husband,' Nellie said, leaning the broom against the whitewashed wall. She patted her hair into place and walked down the short path to the little wooden gate. Opening it she smiled at her husband as she took the basket with the squealing ducks in it from it.

'Come Liz, you can tell me about the baby kicking,' she said as she linked arms with Liz and together they strolled down the lane.

May dawned bright and sunny. Liz was blooming. Her long dark hair was glossy, and her skin was radiant. She loved getting up on these glorious sunny mornings. Occasionally she glanced into the baby's room as she passed. It was next to their bedroom. The handcrafted wooden crib stood silently in the corner waiting for the new arrival. Neatly folded in it was the white crocheted quilt that Liz had made. Crisp new cotton sheets and new blankets, that Liz had cut to fit, topped the pile. The drawers of the clothes chest contained an assortment of matinee jackets, bootee's, leggings and bonnet's knitted by Liz. Nonie had given Liz a gift of hand made linen baby vests and gowns. Soon now she had to buy cotton sheets to cut into squares for baby napkins! Eight weeks to go, although she told everybody it was twelve. She planned on telling people the baby arrived early. Jack had a constant smile on his face these days!

*   *   *   *

Wednesday May 5th dawned, another picture perfect summers day. Liz hummed to herself as she cooked breakfast for Jack. She turned the sizzling strips of bacon on the griddle with the long fork. She flipped over the eggs as Jack opened the half door, back from milking the cows. He smiled as he listened to Liz humming. He sat at the table and Liz served him his breakfast. Just then John appeared at the half door and opened it. He walked into the kitchen and stared at Liz, then at her burgeoning abdomen. She lowered her gaze. Jack who hadn't looked around, noticed Liz looking downwards.

'I'll be with ya soon, John. There's tae wet if you'd like a cup,' Jack said, still watching Liz.

'Ya, I'd love a cup,' he replied sitting at the table.

Liz got up quickly and got a cup from a cup hook on the kitchen dresser. Putting it on a saucer, she leaned across John and placed it on the table in front of him. She didn't look at him once. John, on the other hand, followed her every movement discreetly. Or so he thought. Jack noticed the way he followed Liz with his eyes. Jack was puzzled. He raised his cup to his mouth and gulped his tea.

'Thanks Liz,' John said gratefully.

'We'll plough that field, you know, the nearest one. That's the last one. We're ready for sowin' then. We can start planting the barley tomorrow. We'll harness the plough onto the horse soon as we're ready,' Jack announced as he drank his tea.

'All right Jack,' John replied as he hurriedly drank his tea.

Moments later, both men put on their caps, and still discussing the days work, they left the kitchen and walked across the yard. Liz tidied the kitchen. Then she made her way to the byre to begin making butter. Walking in, she assembled all the utensils she would need. A large milking can of milk stood nearby. She poured the three day old milk into the earthenware vessel. She skimmed the cream from the milk with the milk separator. Liz poured the cream into the timber churn and plunger, and agitated the cream until it was 'grained'. After removing the thick substance from the churn, she washed it several times with cold water from the earthenware sink in the corner. She pressed the creamy butter into the butter moulds. After levelling it, she pressed the rubber butter stamp firmly on top. She smiled as she admired the shamrock emblem on her freshly made butter. She poured the watery remains, the buttermilk, into a milk jug. She wiped tendrils of hair from her face and sighed with pleasure. Almost two hours later, the butter making process was complete and the clearing up nearly done. As she turned around, Liz saw him, watching her. How long had he been there? With her hand supporting her back, she straightened up.

'Hello John,' she said hesitantly, 'I...I thought ye were still in the field?'

'Part of the plough broke and I came back to get some bits of wood and a hammer and nails, to try to mend it,' he replied, leaning against the doorframe of the open door.

'Oh!' she said, 'I've just finished the butter. I have to put it into the larder along with the buttermilk.'

'Liz, you've been avoiding me for months. You won't talk to me. Nellie says you don't talk much to her any more either. You look away when I try to catch your eye.'

Neither of them noticed Jack entering by the open door at the other end of the byre. He saw them talking and quietly stepped back behind the door to listen.

'We have nothing to talk about, John. You work for my husband. You're a farmhand. I've no reason to talk to you,' Liz replied, turning her back to him as she placed the utensils on the wooden shelf.

'How can you say that? You know what you mean to me. You love me! You told me! And I love you more than anything on this earth. The baby you're carrying; I believe it's mine. You say it's due at the end of July. I'd bet a week's wages that baby will be born at the start of July. Nine months after we shared a night together,' he said, watching her closely.

Her face reddened and her heart beat wildly in her chest. She turned suddenly and looked him in the eye.

'Don't be silly, John. Of course it's not your baby. It's mine. And Jack's. It's OUR baby.'

'You don't fool me, Liz. Look, I know you're excited about the baby. And so is Jack. He talks about nothing else. Please, Liz. Come away with me. We'll leave here. Right now! I know people, Jack and Nellie, they'll be hurt. But I've been hurting for months now. Why can't I have what I want? What we both want? Why am I expected to think of everybody else's feeling's all the time? I want you and I want our baby.'

'It's not your baby! It's mine and Jacks!'

'Do you still love me?'

'What?'

'I need to know. I need to know the truth. Do you still love me? Are you carrying our baby?'

On the other side of the open door, Jack could scarcely believe his ears. As he leaned his head against the door, his chin trembled and silent tears ran down his face. His heart beat wildly in his chest. This is not happening, he thought, Liz will tell him to go to hell any second now. Sure, of course it's my baby! The man is mad! He clenched and unclenched his fists.

'John, Please! Don't do this. Can't you leave me alone? I just want to do the right thing. I'm giving birth in a few weeks. Jack and me are going to raise the baby together. Our baby! Why can't you leave us be? Please!' She pleaded.

He walked the few paces that separated them and stood before her. He saw the tears in her eyes.

'I know you don't love Jack. How could you? He's a decent man, sure enough. But he's old. Didn't you tell me yourself, how you hated him touching you? By God! You were clever enough to let him touch you when you found out you were carrying a baby. My baby! And he fell for it! And he thinks it's his baby! You'd let Jack raise MY baby! What am I supposed to do? Pretend it's not mine?' John said angrily.

Liz put her hands up to her cheeks to try to stem the flow of tears streaming freely down her cheeks. Great sobs shook her entire body.

'John, Please! I beg you! Stop this now! Leave Jack and me alone! Please!' She implored as she placed her hand on his arm. He took her hand between his two hands and stroked it lovingly against his cheek. She could see tears running down his face.

'Liz, please tell me. Is it my baby? Do you love me? I need to know,' he asked gently.

'Yes,' she whispered, after a pause, 'It's your baby. It's due in less than eight weeks. And yes I love you, but....'.

Before she could go on, an ear splitting roar came from the direction of the far door. Startled, John and Liz sprang apart as Jack advanced towards them. His face was contorted with rage.

'You bloody bitch! You bitch! You whore, you! You – you whore!' He screamed at Liz, who shrank back in fear.

John instinctively stepped in front of her protectively.

'Jack, Jack, now calm down. It's not how it looks, just calm down,' John said fearfully.

'I heard every bloody word. My wife, the whore, is carrying YOUR bastard! And she was going to pass it off as mine. And you tell me to calm down!' He shouted at both of them looking from one to the other, his eyes wild.

Liz trembled in fear. She had never seen Jack like this before. He was truly frightening. He stood almost nose-to-nose with John for a few moments. Without warning, Jack lashed out with his fist and struck John full in the face. John was knocked backwards to the ground, blood spurting from his face. Liz, rooted to the spot, screamed. Jack picked up a shovel and swung it above his head.

'No!' Screamed Liz as she jumped in front of Jack to try and grab the shovel. They wrestled with it as John stumbled to his feet unsteadily. Suddenly, Jack swung the shovel catching John on the shoulder. He fell to the ground again, dazed. Pushing Liz to the ground and throwing the shovel aside, Jack advanced towards John. John tried in vain to get up. Jack kicked him viciously, once, twice, three times. John lay there curled up in agony, and groaned. In shock, Liz was still lying on the cold hard stone floor, unable to move.

'John Flynn, get up and go to your poor wife, who probably doesn't know about any of this. You have one hour to get off my property. Otherwise, I will kill you,' Jack gasped, turning to Liz, 'and you, ya whore, get into the kitchen NOW!'

John clutching his aching ribs looked across the cold floor at Liz who was struggling to get up. A trickle of blood edged from the corner of her mouth.

'Liz, don't go in the house. Don't go in there! You've got to leave now! He'll kill you!' whispered John as Liz stumbled to her feet unsteadily. They looked at each for a long moment. Liz shook her head, tears spilling down her face.

'Go. Just go John. There's nothing you can do now, nothing anyone can do,' she replied in a toneless voice. John struggled to his feet. He looked at Liz then looked at Jack. Slowly, he staggered out into the glorious sunshine, blood and perspiration mingled on his face and squinted. Jack watched as John staggered down the lane. Liz pushed past Jack without a word, out of the byre, across the yard, opened the half door and went into the kitchen. She was weak, exhausted and drained. She knew nothing was ever going to be the same again. She wiped the back of her hand across her sore mouth and looked in horror at the thin stream of blood. The whole course of her life had changed in an instant. The future filled her with dread. She feared for her unborn baby.

Wearily, she sat at the table, staring at her feet. Seconds later, Jack entered and kicked the door shut. For several minutes, he paced the kitchen, his fury mounting. Suddenly, he thumped the table. Liz jumped.

'How could you? How could you, Liz? I would have given you anything. Done anything for you. I heard him, you know. He said, you hated me touching you! Is that true? Do you hate me that much? I'm your husband! I have a god given right to touch you! And you and John... Oh my God! John Flynn. All he is, is a Spailpin! A farmhand. A penniless farmhand. With a wife! Oh, he knew what he was doing all right. He wanted a baby. His poor wife couldn't have one so he decided he'd have one with you! Where did ye do it?' he shouted, thumping the table again. Liz winced in fear; she couldn't speak.

'Answer me! Where did ye do it?' he shouted again, spittle spewing from his mouth.

'In the downstairs room,' she mumbled.

'Where?' he demanded.

She nodded in the direction of the bedroom door under the stairs. He followed her gaze. He sat down heavily opposite her, put his head in his hands and sobbed. Liz sat rigid on the hard kitchen chair. She felt her baby move inside her and laid a hand protectively on her swollen stomach. Eventually, he looked across at her, his eyes blazing.

'I can't believe you did it under my roof!'

He jumped to his feet again, knocking the chair backwards. He resumed pacing the floor again. Liz didn't dare look at him. With an anguished roar he reached out his arm and swept it across the pine dresser. Crockery and ornaments clattered noisily to the floor.

Suddenly he lashed out with the back of his hand. The blow sent her flying sideways from the chair and she crashed to the floor heavily. She lay in a crumpled heap on the cold flagstone floor.

Without warning, she was dragged to her feet. He shoved her hard against the kitchen dresser. She staggered and fell amongst the broken crockery. She felt the bone in her wrist snapping and screamed in pain. A clammy sweat broke out on her forehead and she felt faint. Her eyes went blurry, her head unfocussed.

'No, Jack, no, stop, please, stop. The baby…', she said weakly. He stood over her.

'The bastard, you mean. I hope it dies!' he said as he yanked her up by the broken wrist. She screamed in pain again. He slammed her face first hard against the stairs. She passed out. He knelt beside her. She barely felt the punch to her face, followed by another one and another one. He tried to drag her to her feet but she was as limp as a rag doll. From her pain filled semi-conscious state, Liz heard another voice. Somebody was trying to drag Jack off her. Nellie, barely reaching Jack's shoulders was desperately pulling on his arm. He swung around.

'Jack, stop! You'll kill her. She's having a baby!' Nellie screamed in terror. She had never witnessed anybody in a temper like Jack. He stood up, panting.

'Did he tell you? Did he?' Jack shouted, panting, his angry face red.

'Jack, what's got into you? What have you done to John? He's in terrible pain. He sent me up to check on Liz. He said you'd gone mad.'

'He didn't tell you so?'

'Tell me what?'

'Well, you have to know sometime. Your husband is going to be a father soon. Yes it's true, because my wife is carrying his baby!'

Nellie looked like she had been struck. She let go of Jack's arm and looked at Liz, lying on the floor among the broken shards of crockery, semi conscious, then she looked at Jack disbelieving. She shook her head slowly.

'No, it's your baby Jack.'

He looked at her pityingly.

'Believe it or believe it not. I heard them with my own ears.'

Tears welled up in Nellie's eyes. She turned again and looked at Liz on the floor. Walking over to her, she knelt beside Liz. With tear filled eyes Nellie pushed back Liz's hair from her damp forehead.

'It's not true shure it's not Liz? About you and....' Nellie choked back a sob. She put her hand over her mouth, trying to stop herself from screaming.

'Nellie, dearest Nellie,' sobbed Liz, trying to focus on her friend, 'I'm sorry, I'm so sorry. Please, forgive me.'

Nellie, crying uncontrollably now gently hugged her.

'I'll do whatever I can to help you, Liz, because of your... condition, but I doubt I can forgive you. My husband! John! And you. I never thought...' her voice trembled as she stifled a sob, 'can you stand up? Maybe sit on a chair?' putting her arm under Liz's arms, she tried to lift her up from the floor.

'Jack, help me. She's in a bad way. Jack! Help me NOW!'

Dazed, Jack was standing staring blankly into the hearth, his anger suddenly gone. It was replaced by a disbelieving numbness. At Nellie's command, he lurched forward and helped Nellie carry Liz to the armchair. While Nellie examined Liz, she noticed that the back of her skirt was drenched in blood. Her hair had been pulled from its braid and hung around her face and shoulders. Her left eye and cheek and nose were swollen and turning a dark blue in her blood spattered face. Nellie could clearly see the bone jutting out of Liz's right wrist at an awkward angle.

'Jack, we have to get her to the hospital fast. Now! Look at the blood! Go and get the pony and trap, quickly.'

Jack's temper had diffused by now, and suddenly he was afraid. Afraid at what the outcome of the recent revelations would be. He ran out the door to get the pony harnessed to the trap. Nellie fetched a clean tea cloth and a bowl of cold water. Gently, she washed Liz's tear-stained, swollen bloodied face and gently pinned her hair back from her face. Liz watched her, her eyes full of tears.

'Nellie, I'm so sorry. I never meant to hurt you. You're a dear kind friend,' she sobbed her words slurred, her body shaking uncontrollably.

Nellie looked into her eyes. Her own eyes were brimming with tears. She stroked Liz's good hand. She nodded as she stifled her own sobs.

'I know Liz. But it's all changed now. There's no going back. What's done is done. We have to get you to the District Hospital immediately. You're seriously hurt. Look, Jack's outside now. We'll put you in the trap. And then, I have to leave you. Jack will take you in. I'll fetch a blanket.'

Nellie ran towards the stairs, stopping abruptly when she saw the pool of blood at the foot of the stairs. The metallic stench of blood made her feel nauseous. Stepping over it, she ran upstairs and pulled the patchwork quilt from the bed. She reached the bottom of the stairs just as Jack came in. Together, they gently wrapped Liz in the quilt and between them carried her outside. Jack laid her on her side in the seat. Nellie looked at Liz for what was to be the last time. Both women were crying.

'Goodbye, Liz. And God bless you.'

Liz lay there, eyes glazed, her mouth opening and closing, unable to speak. Jack climbed into the trap and knelt on the floor. He flicked the reins, and Penny set off at a fast trot down the lane. Nellie pulled out the kitchen door. She walked slowly to the centre of the farmyard. She crossed her arms and hugged her shoulders. The sun shone brightly. The birds chirped sweetly, bees buzzed as they flitted from flower to flower. In the distance she could hear sheep baaing. Her pent up grief finally released itself and she let out an anguished cry. She stood there, sobbing loudly, her body shaking uncontrollably, her heart broken.

Minutes later, John ran up the lane. Bruises and grazes covered his face, which had been washed clean of blood. He stopped suddenly when he spotted his wife, her back to him. Her head was slumped forward and her body was shaking violently. From where he stood, he clearly heard the loud sobs convulsing her body. When he reached her, she turned her tear streaked grief-stricken face and looked at him. He stopped dead. Tears sprang to his eyes when he saw the measure of her pain. She knew!

'I'm so sorry Nellie,' he whispered, his eyes closing in shame. He had caused untold hurt to the people he cared most about. His wife: Liz: Jack; and his unborn baby.

May God forgive me for everything I've done, he prayed silently.

Gently, he put his arms around her shoulders and held her tightly. She clung to him and sobbed into his chest. They stood there clinging to each other, crying, almost drowning out the sounds of summer.

Chapter Six

Jack drove Penny as fast as he possibly could, flicking
the whip at the pony. Behind him, in the trap, Liz lay curled
up, moaning. People walking on Ballincollig's main street
stopped and stared in astonishment at the speeding pony and
trap on a hot sunny afternoon. Every few minutes, Liz cried
in pain. She squinted against the glare of the sun as the pony
galloped on. The trap rocked violently from side to side,
every jolt sending another bolt of pain surging through her
broken body. Sweat bathed her face. Jack, his anger gone,
realized what he had done. He was numb. He glanced back
at her pain-racked face.

Oh God; It wasn't meant to be like this at all, he
thought.

Finally, he drove through the tall gates of the City
District Hospital on the Douglas Road. He looked around. A
nurse, dressed in a long blue shift, with a white starched
apron and a nurse's hat on her head, was coming towards
him.

'Excuse me, Sister, would you be so kind as to point me
in the direction of the place where women give birth?' he
asked.

She pointed at a building directly in front of him. He
hurried towards it. He pulled up outside two tall wooden
doors, one of which was open. Jumping down, he ran into
the building. Two nurses were talking.

'Please help me! My wife. She's outside. She's...she
needs a doctor,' he said, urgently.

Together, they followed Jack outside. They looked at
Liz, barely unconscious, then looked at each other, and
looked sharply at Jack.

'Go get the orderlies to bring the stretcher, Sister,' the
ward sister instructed her colleague.

Within minutes, two orderlies, dressed in black
uniforms appeared with a stretcher. Gently, they lifted Liz,

still wrapped in the quilt, from the trap. The nurses and the orderlies noticed the bloodstains on the quilt.

'Take her to Maternity, quickly,' the Ward Sister instructed the orderlies, 'and Sister, tell Dr O'Connor to come immediately. It's an emergency!'

Jack followed the group into the hospital. The orderlies walked quickly along the long corridor, followed by the Ward Sister and Jack. As they reached the double doors at the end of the corridor, the Sister turned to Jack.

'You can't come in Sir. What is your wife's name?' she asked.

'Liz. Elisabeth McCarthy. From Inniscarra.'

'And what is her due date?'

'Not for a few more weeks. Four, I think. No. Eight. Oh, I'm not really sure,' he replied.

'I see. Wait here, Mr McCarthy. We'll call you.'

With that the sister followed the orderlies, nurses and Liz in through the double doors. Jack sank heavily onto a nearby wooden bench and leaned back against the wall. The smell of carbolic soap and polish irritated his nostrils. A continuous flow of people, patients, orderlies, nurses and doctors streamed past him in both directions as he sat on the uncomfortable bench, unaware of anything else but the heaviness in his heart.

Two hours later, the nurse appeared from beyond the double doors. Jack stood up quickly. In her arms she carried the neatly folded bloodstained quilt.

'Mr McCarthy, your wife is in labour. Unfortunately, she's very poorly. Her baby is not due for another few weeks. Your wife and baby are in a bad way. Could you tell me what happened to your wife?' The nurse asked, 'she has a broken wrist, a broken cheekbone, broken nose, black eyes and she is very bruised and swollen. She's lost a lot of blood and is in a state of shock.'

Jack opened his mouth to speak, but no words came. He stared at the bulky bloodstained quilt in his hands. He tightened his grip as he recalled the nights Liz sat opposite him by the fire as she sewed the coloured patches together. They'd chat contentedly about their day. Those days will never happen again. He choked back a sob. The nurse looked at him.

'Mr McCarthy, are you all right?' she asked in a concerned voice.

'It-it was an accident,' he blurted, 'wh-when will the ...baby be born?'

'It's hard to tell, Sir. Are you going to wait?'

Jack stared at the floor, deep in thought.

'Sir, are you going to wait?' The nurse asked again. He shook his head vigorously.

'No. I'll go home. Tell her...tell her, I'll be in tomorrow,' with that he turned and quickly walked back along the corridor.

'Mr McCarthy. Mr McCarthy! Your wife is seriously ill. She could die!' The nurse called after him.

He kept walking.

*   *   *   *

Searing pain. Disjointed voices. Distorted figures coming in and out of view. Hot burning pain. Pain rising up inside, reaching a peak. She screamed and cried at the same time.

'John help me! Stop the pain, please, please stop the pain! Help me, God help me!'

The pain ebbed after a few minutes. Blurred faces hovered over her. She lapsed into unconsciousness. As the pain washed over her again, she jerked awake screaming. Again, she passed out. As each pain gripped her, the spasms intensified. Suddenly, she was hurtling along a white tunnel away from the intense pain. In the distance, she saw a bright light. Looking back she saw the pain looming like a giant black mass. She turned and ran as fast as she could towards the beckoning light. The dazzling light grew bigger and brighter as she got nearer.

'Elisabeth, go back now! You have to go back!' she heard a voice say.

She stopped. Looking back she saw the great dark mass of pain as it encircled her. Everything went black.

Through her euphoric haze, Liz saw a shadowy figure lean over her. The figure placed what looked like a white bundle into Liz's arms. Indistinct words floated in the air.

'...a baby....You....proud....husband....so pleased....daughter.'

'No, no, what's happening to me? Where am I? What's this? Take it away? I want ... to sleep now. I'm tired.' She slipped into unconsciousness again.

*   *   *   *

The sound of people whispering woke Liz. Slowly, she opened her eyes. She tried to turn over, towards the voices. Pain shot up her arm and she moaned softly. The two people in the room looked at her. Fragmented pieces of conversation invaded her thoughts.

'She's coming round, Doctor.'

Slowly, her misty vision cleared and she saw a nurse and a doctor at her bedside. The doctor, wearing a white coat, stethoscope around his neck, held her left hand.

'Mrs McCarthy, I'm so glad you woke up. My name is Dr O Connor. You've been unconscious since you gave birth to your baby, a baby girl, yesterday. It was touch and go I must tell you. Your baby was born a month or more early. Your condition was extremely serious. Apart from the birth, you seemed to have suffered some serious injuries. Could you tell us how they came about? Even more worrying is the fact your husband didn't even come to visit you. A couple that say they are your friends came in yesterday. Unfortunately, we had to tell them to go home, as you were seriously ill. I believe they said they'll call again today,' the doctor said in his cultured accent.

The nurse stood at his side and looked at her in a kindly way.

'I.. I.. have a baby?' Liz asked in a faltering voice.

'Yes, my dear, a beautiful baby girl. She's the spit of you. Thick mop of black hair. She weighed four pounds,' the nurse said, smiling down at Liz.

'Oh!' Liz said, unable to take it in.

Suddenly, it came flooding back to her. John, Jack, the confrontation, the beatings. She started to cry softly. Tears flowing down her black and blue swollen cheeks.

'What happened to you my dear?' The doctor asked gently, stroking her hand.

'It was…. was, my husband. That's all. I'll get over it,' she sobbed. The doctor stared intently at her sad battered face, her two eyes, black and puffy.

'All the same, Mrs McCarthy, you will be very weak for a long while. Your husband shouldn't…. be violent with you. It will be hard enough as it is to cope with a new baby. You'd best be careful not to upset your husband again, judging by the severity of your injuries. Now, do you want to see your beautiful baby?'

Liz tried to clear her confused mind. She felt broken. Everything had happened so quickly since yesterday and now she had a baby to think of. Pain stabbed its claws into every part of her including her mind. She knew her face was cut and swollen. Her broken right wrist was bandaged onto a wooden splint. Her ribs and abdomen were swollen and sore. She felt very weak.

'Can I see my baby please?' she asked.

'Of course. I'll get her now,' the kindly nurse said, patting Liz's arm.

She turned and left the room. Liz looked around. She was in a little room. All it contained was the single bed on which she lay, a chair and a bedside table. It was spotlessly clean and she could detect the smell of carbolic soap. Sunlight streamed in the tall window. The doctor hovered over her.

'Mrs McCarthy, I have to advise you against having children in the future. You nearly died giving birth. Your womb was damaged as a result. You would be risking your life if you were to give birth again. Ah, here's your baby.'

The nurse entered, holding a tiny bundle wrapped in a white sheet. She leaned over Liz and gently placed the baby in the crook of Liz's left arm.

'We tried to get you to hold her yesterday but you were in too much pain. We've had to feed her with boiled milk and water, but it would be best if you could feed her yourself.'

Liz hardly heard her. She was staring in wonder at her tiny daughter. The only scrap of light in her otherwise dark world. Her baby indeed had a covering of downy black hair. Her little face was screwed up. She looked at Liz with one eye, the other eye still closed. Liz, despite her pain, smiled, her battered eyes filling with tears again. Tears of joy. She had never seen anything as beautiful as her baby. She felt a sudden rush of love despite everything. She kissed the top of her daughter's head.

'My little darlin'. I'm so sorry for everything. But I'll make it up to you. I promise. I'll make sure that nobody ever hurts you,' she whispered softly to her baby. The baby gazed contentedly at her mother. Both eyes open now.

'Will I leave ye for a while? She's just after been fed. She should sleep soon. I'll be outside at my desk. Just call if you need me.'

'Yes, I'd like that, I'm tired myself,' Liz replied. Mother and baby snuggled cosily together, safe in each other's presence. The doctor and nurse left the room, leaving the door ajar. Liz and her baby were asleep within a minute.

*   *   *   *

Nonie and Patsy walked towards the nurse seated behind her desk. She was engrossed in writing reports.

'Excuse me, we're looking for Liz McCarthy,' Nonie said politely.

'Ye called yesterday. She had her baby, a little girl. Both mother and baby are sleeping. I'd rather not disturb them. Mrs McCarthy has been through a terrible time.'

'Could we just see them for a moment? We won't wake them, I promise,' Nonie said.

'I suppose. After all, her own husband couldn't be bothered to call to see her. And 'twas him that caused all the damage,' the nurse said as she rose from her chair, 'follow me.'

She led Nonie and Patsy to the little room near her desk. Silently she pushed in the door and stepped back. Nonie and Patsy looked at the sleeping mother and baby. Nonie walked towards them. She saw Liz's bruised and cut face. Tears sprang to her eyes. Suddenly, Liz's eyes opened and she looked at Nonie.

'Nonie, Patsy, I'm very sorry. I never meant for any of this to happen,' she whispered sadly.

Nonie sat on the chair by her bedside.

'Liz, I know what you did was wrong. Nellie and … John told me. They're very upset. They've gone back to Kildare. Left on the train this morning. But, you didn't deserve this. Nellie told me what Jack did to you. We came in yesterday but we were told that you …. mightn't pull through,' Nonie's voice faltered.

'I've hurt so many people, Nonie, I never meant for anyone to get hurt,' Liz whispered as her tearstained eyes welled up again.

'The nurse said Jack hasn't been in. What will you do now?'

'I honestly don't know,' Liz said crying softly. Nonie stroked her good arm. The baby stirred in Liz's arm and yawned sleepily.

'Who have we here?' Nonie asked softly, smiling through her tears, as she stroked the downy soft hair of the sleeping baby.

'It's a girl. My very own baby girl. I'm going to call her Maria Rose. I don't know what's going to become of us, but I love her and I'm going to mind her,' Liz said proudly.

'She's beautiful Liz. She looks just like you. Doesn't she Patsy?' Nonie turned to Patsy who had been standing silently by the window, hands clasped behind his back, looking out. He turned and walked over to the bed to stand beside his wife.

'Patsy, I don't know what you must think of me. Nellie is your sister. She saved me from Jack. I'm so sorry for everything. I know she'll never forgive me. I don't expect you to understand.'

'She's a lovely lass. Maria Rose,' was all that Patsy said as he stroked the baby's head.

Outside the room, there was a commotion. Somebody was shouting at the nurse. Liz recognized the voice.

'Oh God, it's Jack!' She said, beginning to tremble. Without warning, the door was flung open, and Jack rushed in. He stopped as he took in the scene. Liz, a bruised and battered wreck, cradling a baby, that should have been his baby, and Nonie and Patsy standing beside her, admiring the baby. They stared in horror at Jack's face contorted with rage.

'John Flynn sent ye to check was his bastard born, did he?' He bellowed.

Liz shrank back against her pillow in fear, pulling her baby closer to her. The nurse had followed him in.

'Mr McCarthy I have to ask you to leave. Your conduct will not be tolerated in this hospital. The orderlies are on their way to escort you out.'

'I'll leave when I'm good and ready, now leave me to speak to me wife,' he said menacingly.

'You have five minutes,' the nurse said after a pause and left the room, leaving the door open.

'You,' Jack said, his eyes narrowed, pointing at Liz,

'you're coming home with me tomorrow. But that, that thing there,' he said pointing at the baby, 'is not.'

Liz began to cry.

'Jack, I'll come home if that's what you want, but I can't leave without my baby,' Liz pleaded.

'I will not have that man's bastard under my roof. D'ya hear? Your family don't know that you've had it yet. If you refuse to come home, alone, I'll tell them exactly what you have done. They'll never speak to you again and what will you do then? Where will you go?' he shouted.

Patsy straightened up, and calmly walked towards Jack. He stood in front of the angry man. Jack glared back at him.

'Jack, what's done is done. The baby is innocent in all of this. Can't you find it in your heart to forgive Liz? After all you gave her an awful beatin'. She is sorry for what she has done. If you can't forgive her, at least, let her keep her little baby. Have a heart man,' Patsy said.

'I'll never forgive her. She is my wife and nobody has any right to tell me what to do. I'll be back tomorrow and she is coming home with me. And I'm telling ye, if I see that thing again, I'll kill it!' Jack said, turning and walking out, just as the nurse entered with two orderlies. Jack brushed past them as he stormed out. Everybody was silent for a few moments. The nurse instructed the orderlies to go back to work and she closed the door behind her. Liz was sobbing again. She cradled her sleeping baby to her as she rocked to and fro. Nonie put her arm around Liz's shoulders.

'He'll come round, Liz, once ye go home, he'll come round,' Nonie said soothingly.

'No, Nonie you don't understand, He means it. He'll kill my baby. See what he did to me! What am I going to do?'

'Don't go back to him.'

'I have to go back; I've nowhere to go. I'm very sick still. But I want my baby too. I need her,' Liz replied.

Just then the baby stirred and opened her sleepy eyes. Nonie looked at the baby. She reached out and held her tiny hand.

'She's so beautiful, and so helpless. A little innocent,' Nonie said wistfully.

Liz's crying subsided. She looked as Nonie gazed longingly at the newborn baby.

'You take her. Please, take her and raise her. I'll give ye money. And I know ye'll look after her. Please! I beg ye, look after my baby,' Liz said urgently.

Nonie and Patsy looked at each other.

'Liz, it's John's baby. We couldn't. It's not fair to Nellie. We wouldn't want to hurt her,' Nonie replied.

'Don't tell them. Say ye adopted her. Please!'

'Patsy, what do think? It's up to you,' Nonie asked.

Patsy walked to the window and looked out, deep in thought. Meanwhile, the baby gurgled. The two women cooed in response. Patsy turned and looked at his wife. He knew how much she had longed for a baby all these years.

'Yes. Nonie, if that's what ye both want. Shure, the poor wee baby. She shouldn't be tossed around like that. We'll take good care of her Liz, treat her like our own. Anytime you want to see her, you know where we'll be. We'll tell everybody we adopted her,' Patsy said. Liz smiled through her tears.

'Thank you, both of you. The nurse said she'd have to stay here for a week because she's so small,' Liz said.

'I'll speak to the nurse soon. I don't know what to say yet, but I'll think of something. We better be going now, we'll be in, first thing in the morning. Goodbye Liz, try get some sleep now,' Nonie said, kissing the baby on the top of her head.

She kissed Liz on her bruised cheek. Patsy and Nonie left. Liz heard them speaking to the nurse outside. Shortly afterwards, the nurse came in just as the baby began to wail.

'We'll feed her Mrs McCarthy; you're still very weak. Your sister informed me she is taking the baby home in the morning, because you have to go home with your husband.

This is very irregular, I must tell you. And by rights the baby should remain here for a while longer,' the nurse said to Liz.

'It's what I want. The baby has to go home in the morning with my 'sister',' Liz said, her heart heavy.

The nurse lifted the crying baby from Liz's arms.

* * * *

At seven o clock the next morning, Liz was sitting up in bed cradling her baby. Tears flowed freely down her face as she held her baby close to her chest. The baby snuggled up to her mother unaware of Liz's plight.

'Oh my baby, my baby. I love you so much. You'll never know how much I love you. I'll never forget you. Nonie and Patsy will take good care of you. I'll find a way to see you again, I promise,' Liz whispered softly as she gently kissed the top of her daughter's head. Mother and baby dozed together. Liz woke with a start when she heard the door open. Nonie and Patsy entered, carrying a brown paper parcel, tied with string.

'I made clothes for the baby, remember? So I thought that we'd dress her in them to bring her home in. I called to Father Finnegan last night and she's to be baptised tonight. I was going to call her Maria if that's all right with you.'

'Thanks Nonie, I like the name. I wrote a letter for baby Maria. Will you give it to her when the time is right?' Liz said tearfully, holding a folded sheet of paper. Nonie was changing the baby's clothes at the end of the bed. She paused.

'Why don't you read it out now?' Nonie whispered softly.

Liz took a deep breath. She rubbed her eyes with the back of her good hand. Opening the sheet of paper, her hand shook as she read;

'Eight of May, Nineteen Hundred and Twenty Six.
My darling Daughter,

Today, I hand you over to my dear friends, Nonie and Patsy, who will look after you. My dearest baby, my heart is breaking at the thought of giving you away. I want to keep you, and hold you and feed you. I want to be there for your first tooth, for your first steps, your first words. Due to circumstances, which you cannot understand, I cannot look after you right now. I live in hope that someday I will come and get you and when that happens, nobody will ever come between us again, I promise you. I trust my good friends to mind you. I will always remember you in my prayers, and in my thoughts. I'll never forget you a chroi, and I hope you will never forget me. I make a solemn vow to you, that one day, we will be with each other once again and neither hell nor high water will ever come between us again. I wrote a little poem especially for you, to tell you how much I love you. I hope you like it.

THE ROSE
A single rose, blowing in the wind,
Afraid to tell it's tale,
Many try to touch its heart
But all seem to fail.
And though it's soft warm embrace,
Could warm any soul
Its thorns are always there,
As lost loves take their toll.
But, know this now
Though things may change
And we may someday part
You always belong here
Right here in my heart.

Your loving mother,
Elisabeth McCarthy.'

Liz's words faltered towards the end of reading the

letter. She struggled to regain her composure. Carefully she folded the sheet of paper and handed it to Nonie. Nonie placed it in her coat pocket then picked up the baby, resplendent in her new clothes. Patsy stood beside her. Both of them smiled at the sleeping infant. Liz turned and stared out the open window. Outside, the sun shone in the cloudless blue sky. Birds sang from the trees in the hospital grounds. The sound of ponies' hooves from outside the hospital gates floated in the air. Nonie watched her.

'Liz, that was beautiful, and what a beautiful poem. The Rose; it's so beautiful. Maria Rose that's what we'll call her. It's not too late to change your mind. There must be another way,' Nonie said, cradling the sleeping baby, tears in her eyes.

Liz shook her head sadly.

'No, there's no other way at the moment. Someday, when I'm better, I'll come get her, but I don't know when. Yes, someday my baby and me will be together again. Now, please go. Go now, because Jack will be here soon and…and,' Liz couldn't continue.

She felt like her heart was being ripped out of her. Nonie handed the sleeping infant to Patsy and walked to Liz. Crying, both women threw their arms around each other and hugged each other tightly. A lump formed in Patsy's throat as he witnessed the poignant scene. He gazed in wonder at the infant sleeping peacefully in his arms.

'Thank you Nonie, for doing this for me. You're my best friend. Now go, please. I'll be all right,' Liz said, grief threatening to overwhelm her, as she pushed her friend away gently. Crying, Nonie took the baby from Patsy and cradled her. Together, Patsy and Nonie walked to the door. Turning back, Nonie saw Liz curled up in the bed, her body shaking from the force of her grief.

'Goodbye Liz. I'll take good care of your baby, 'til you come and get her,' Nonie said tearfully.

Chapter Seven

Jack stood in the doorway of the room. In his hand he carried a Hessian bag. Liz was sitting on the bed, facing the window, her back to the door. She had regained her composure. Jack stared at her rigid back.

'I don't want to know anything about…well, you know what. I brought in a clean frock; it's your favourite, the blue one. And some undergarments. I'll wait outside 'til you're dressed,' Jack said as he placed the bag on the bed. He turned abruptly and left the room, closing the door behind him.

Liz didn't move for a full five minutes. Wiping her tearstained eyes one last time with the back of her good hand, she leaned over and picked up the bag. Taking her time, she removed the hospital gown and dressed in her favourite blue dress. Only now, it was stretched slightly over her still swollen abdomen. Glancing down at her abdomen, which until three days ago was home to her precious daughter, she felt the tears well up again. With an effort, she swallowed hard. 'He'll never see me cry again!' thought Liz.

Bending down, she took her bloodstained dress from the bedside table and stuffed it into the bag. She brushed her dishevelled hair. Picking up the bag, she slowly walked to the door. Outside, Jack was pacing the corridor. The nurse looked up from her desk. She smiled at Liz.

'Mrs McCarthy, you must be glad to be going home. Dr O'Connor has already explained to your husband about your weakened condition. And he has also advised him about it being for the best not to have any more children. Go to your doctor in eight weeks time to have your splint removed. Get as much rest as possible, because it will take you a while to recover from … the birth. Look after yourself, Mrs McCarthy,' the nurse said kindly.

'Thank you, for everything. You and Dr O Connor have been very kind. Goodbye,'

Liz said gratefully. Jack reached out to take Liz's bag but she ignored his outstretched hand.

She turned and slowly walked down the dingy corridor, occasionally steadying herself by holding onto the wall. Jack followed behind her. Emerging into the fresh air, Liz suddenly felt dizzy. The pony and trap were tied up outside, just outside the main door. Jack took her bag and put it into the trap. He held out his hand to help Liz up. She ignored his outstretched hand and slowly pulled herself up into the trap. She sat on the edge of the seat, as far away from Jack as she could. When he was seated, he flicked the reins and Penny set off at a trot down the road and out the tall wrought iron gates. They made their way through the city traffic and onto the Ballincollig road. Liz looked out her side of the trap all the way, not once looking in Jack's direction. Jack glanced at her a few times.

'Ignore me if you want. I told your family that you lost the baby. That it died. As far as I'm concerned that's what happened. You better stick to that story if you know what's good for you,' Jack announced, a hard look on his face. Liz didn't reply.

Shortly afterwards they reached the laneway to the farm. Liz quickly glanced at the now empty cottage at the end of the lane.

A minute later, they pulled into the farmyard. The kitchen door opened and Liz's mother followed by her sister in law, Aine and six year old nephew Cormac, came out when they heard the pony's hooves. Liz's heart sank. She didn't want to talk to anybody right now. She carefully stepped down from the trap and Jack led Penny away. Liz's mother ran to her only daughter and throwing her arms around her, embraced her. Stepping back, she held Liz at arms length. Tears were in her eyes.

'Liz, you poor love, losing your little baby like that. Shure, poor Jack is devastated over it an' all. He told us you had a terrible time of it. My, what happened to your poor hand?' Asked Liz's mother, holding up Liz's bandaged wrist.

Jack had joined them by now.

'I fell. When I got the pains. I fell over. And broke my wrist. The doctor said it's a right nasty break,' Liz said glaring at Jack. He flinched.

'Oh, you poor, poor thing. You look awful. Me and Aine have cleaned the house from top to bottom, even the bloodstain from the floor by the stairs, and your quilt. Jack said that's where you lay when you were in labour, before he took you to the hospital. You lost a lot of blood, me poor darlin'. And then to lose your little baby as well...' with that Liz's mother broke down and sobbed loudly. She grabbed the corner of her crisp white apron and dabbed at her eyes. Aine walked over and hugged Liz.

'Liz, I'm so sorry for your troubles. I'll do whatever you want me to, all you have to is ask. We made a stew for ye're dinner. Come on in and we'll serve it,' Aine said, tears in her eyes. Liz stood there, unable to cry. Gently, her mother led her into the kitchen. Jack, Aine and Cormac followed. Liz hesitated as she entered, remembering the last time she was here. Was it only three days ago that her whole life turned upside down? In less than three days, the course of her very life had changed forever. She knew that things would never go back to the way they had been.

They sat around the table, eating a delicious dinner of Irish stew. Only for Cormac chatting happily to his mother there would have been complete silence.

'Liz, Jack didn't know if it was a boy or a girl. Men! What did you have love?' Liz's mother asked gently.

Liz looked at Jack. Of course, Jack never asked what she had. He didn't want to know. Jack looked away from her harsh glare. His face reddened and he lowered his head intent on eating the steaming stew.

'I had a girl. A beautiful baby girl. She was perfect. I named her Maria Rose. She had beautiful skin and a head of soft dark hair,' Liz replied in a cold harsh voice, her gaze still resting on Jack's lowered head.

There was silence.

'Did the hospital take care of the, em, er .... burial?' Liz's mother persisted.

'Yes. Everything was taken care of at the hospital,' Liz replied in the same toneless voice.

'One last question, love. Was she baptised?'

There was a pause. All eyes were on Liz. She stared at Jack again.

'I've no idea. I don't know if my daughter was baptised or not. She could be buried in some killeen somewhere. I don't know.'

'Liz! Remember your manners,' Jack said sharply.

'It's all right Jack. She's not well. She's just had a terrible loss. Liz, maybe you should go for a lie down, after dinner. You don't look at all well. And you lost so much weight,' Liz's mother said worriedly.

They ate the rest of their dinner in silence, all but Liz, who hardly touched her food. She stood up suddenly.

'I'm going to lie down. I'm tired. Excuse me.'

She stopped at the bottom of the stairs, looking for traces of the bloodstain that she herself had seen a few days ago. Her mother had removed every trace. She shivered suddenly. She walked slowly up the stairs and fully clothed lay on the marital bed. She fell into an exhausted sleep. In her dreams, she held her baby in her arms, caressing her and talking baby talk to her. She was in the top field from where she had a wonderful panoramic view of the countryside. The sun was shining, the birds were singing, the cow's mooing in the distance. She swung the infant around and around. The baby gurgled happily and Liz laughed out loud. In the distance, she heard somebody call her name. Turning, she saw John Flynn approaching her, a big smile on his face. She waved happily. As he got nearer, the sun suddenly disappeared and the sky grew dark. A cold wind suddenly blew up. Looking back in the distance, she saw it wasn't John at all, but Jack. His face was like thunder.

'Get rid of that thing or I'll kill it!'

Terrified, Liz clasped her baby tightly to her chest. Jack was approaching fast. She looked into her baby's face. There was nothing in her arms, except an empty blanket.

'No, no, give me back my baby!' She cried.

She sat up in bed suddenly, beads of sweat running down her forehead. Her breath was coming in big gasps. Liz's mother came running into the bedroom. She sat on the bed and held out her arms. Liz clung to her mother as the tears came.

'Mam, Mam, I want my baby, please I want my baby. I can't live without her. I want her so bad,' Liz wailed, rivers of tears flowing down her face. Her mother rocked her only daughter to and fro, gently stroking her hair and her face.

'There, there, I know it's hard, a stor, but the pain will pass in time, just give it a chance. I wish I could take away your pain but I can't. I'm here for you love, to share your awful burden,' her mother said, still rocking Liz.

'You don't understand Mam. My baby is ......' her voice trailed off as Jack's bulk loomed in the doorway. He threw her a warning look.

'I know, I know, love. Your baby is in heaven. It's a terrible tragedy. Try and get some rest now. There, there, now,' Liz's mother said soothingly, as she gently laid her daughter down on the pillow. She kissed Liz on the forehead. Liz drifted off to sleep again as her mother walked out of the bedroom. She paused in the doorway to speak to Jack.

'She's in a bad way, Jack. You must look after her 'til she gets well again. She's really taking it hard. About the baby; and she's very weak,' Liz's mother said in a low voice to Jack. He shrugged his shoulders.

'She'll be all right in a day or two. Don't expect me to mollycoddle her. I have a farm to run. And don't you be mollycoddling her either. She'll be all right,' Jack said, harshly. He turned and marched downstairs. Liz's mother looked at his retreating back as he descended the stairs. What was that about? She wondered.

*   *   *   *

In the weeks that followed, Liz experienced many dark days. After completing her daily chores, Liz would spend the remainder of the day in bed. Gradually, her strength returned. She had moved all her things into the downstairs bedroom. She never slept in the marital bed again. She ignored Jack completely and Jack left her alone. Day after day Jack ate his breakfast and dinner alone at the kitchen table. Jack would leave immediately after dinner to go to the public house in Inniscarra, returning at around midnight. Liz occasionally heard him staggering upstairs.

One evening, four weeks to the day that Liz's baby was born, Jack entered Reilly's pub in Inniscarra. Although still daylight outside, the small low-ceilinged pub was dim inside. He went to the high polished counter and ordered a pint of Murphy's. He looked around and nodded at familiar faces of his neighbours. They nodded in return. He waited patiently at the counter, deep in thought as he waited for his pint to settle. He turned when the door opened. Dan Lucey entered. Pat the bar man eyed the newcomer suspiciously.

'Well Dan, are ya goin' to behave yourself tonight and not drive any more of me customers away?' he said.

Dan looked apologetic as he took off his flat cap and stood there twisting it around and around in his hands. He cleared his throat.

'Sorry for the last night Pat. I suppose I shouldn't have told Joe Walsh that his wife would look better wearing a cloth sack over her head. How was I to know he'd stick up for her? Anyway, well, I think I've learned me lesson this time.'

Pat the barman grunted.

'Hmm. That's what you said after the last fight you caused. This is your last chance, mind.'

Jack couldn't stop chortling. Dan Lucey seemed to attract trouble everywhere he went.

'Another thing Dan, maybe you might stop the lies an' all. Nobody believes a word ya say,' Jack said.

Dan looked indignant.

'When do I tell lies?' he asked.

'Every time you open your mouth!' guffawed Jack as he swallowed a mouthful of creamy Murphy's. Hours later, Jack, Dan and Jackie Murphy were huddled near the fire, downing pints of Guinness. Their words became increasingly slurred and their conversation more animated.

'That was a sad business about your little baby, Jack. Are ye goin to have another one or what?' Jackie slurred as his head swayed. Jack's face suddenly clouded over. He lowered his glass.

'I don't know Jackie. Liz, well, she took it very hard. Don't know if she'll ever let me near her again,' he said with a tinge of sadness.

'But don't they say that the best cure for losing a child is to create another? Your good wife would thank ya if you provided her with another one,' Jackie said.

'Ya Jack. Are ya a man or what? You need to produce a baby sooner rather than later, shure, how old are ya now?' Dan asked, his arms crossed on the table in front of him. Deep in thought, Jack took another swig of stout.

Liz woke just after midnight, to the sound of the kitchen door slamming. She turned over in her bed. Seconds later, her bedroom door was kicked open violently. Startled, she sat up quickly. Jack stood menacingly in the doorway, his large bulk illuminated by the tilly lamp in the kitchen. She looked at him.

'What do you want?' Liz asked, her heart pounding.

'Well, I was down the pub with the lads and they were

sympathising again about 'our terrible loss'. Jackie Murphy an' Dan Lucey said the only way for you to get over losing your 'poor' baby was to have another as quickly as possible,' Jack said, swaying slightly, his words slurred. Even from where she sat in her bed, Liz could smell the whiskey on his breath. She suddenly felt afraid.

'I told them…, I told them they were right. We should have another baby. Only this time I'll make damn sure it's MY baby!' Jack continued.

'Jack, go to bed. You're drunk. You remember what the doctor said, at the hospital. I shouldn't have any more babies because it's too dangerous. I could die or the baby could die,' Liz said, her mouth suddenly dry.

'Oh, I don't care if you die. But it would be nice if I could have a baby of me own. I'm sure I'm man enough to produce a son and not a poxy girl!'

'Jack! Stop this now. Go to bed. Now!' Liz said loudly, her eyes wide with fear.

'Don't you dare tell me what to do in me own house. You're still me wife, whether you like it or not. I have me rights,' Jack said as he slowly advanced towards Liz.

She pulled the colourful patchwork quilt around her as she shrank back against the bolster pillow, in fear.

'Jack, go away, please, you're scaring me.'

Suddenly Jack leapt onto the bed and caught Liz by her good arm. He forced her back against the bolster and straddled her. Without warning, he tugged at the front of her cotton nightdress and ripped it again and again until her breasts were exposed. She started to scream, but he clamped his other hand over her mouth. Terrified, she looked into his eyes. She could hardly breathe because his hand was clamped over her mouth and nose. Panic welled up inside in her. He continued to tear at her nightdress until it was completely shredded. In a frenzy, he started opening his own trousers. Within a minute he entered her.

*   *   *   *

Later, after Jack had fallen asleep on top of her, Liz struggled to push him off. She couldn't shift him. He was too heavy and now that he was asleep he was a dead weight. Eventually, she wriggled out from underneath him, afraid of wakening him. The remains of her nightdress fell onto the floor. Shaking violently she picked up her dressing gown from the chair in the corner and quickly put it on. Taking the washbasin from the stand and a washcloth, she went to the kitchen. Very quietly, she filled the basin with cold water. She removed her gown and for the next five minutes she scrubbed herself all over with carbolic soap, tears mingling with the suds. Finally she dried herself vigorously with a rough towel. She pulled on her dressing gown again and tied the cord tightly. She went to the door of the bedroom. Glancing inside she saw that Jack was lying face down on her bed snoring, his trousers around his ankles. She felt the revulsion rising in her throat. Quietly, she crept into the room and pulled out clean clothes and shoes, from the clothes chest. She crept back out gently closing the door behind her. Hurriedly she dressed, trying to ignore the pain she felt in her abdomen. Suddenly she noticed that she was bleeding heavily again. It was only in the last few days that the bleeding had lessened. Quietly, she went back to her bedroom to get some of her 'rags'.

Afterwards, she sat on the armchair by the dying embers of the fire. She heard the grandfather clock strike two. Clearly in shock, she shook violently as she huddled by the dying fire. Finally the tears came.

'God in heaven! How long more must I pay for my mistake? Haven't I suffered enough? I've lost my precious baby and I don't know if I'll ever see her again. Why didn't you take me when I was ill? Why must I continue to suffer?' She whispered.

The clock struck six. Liz woke with a start. It suddenly

came back to her. What Jack had done. Her trembling had abated she stretched her aching body before easing herself out of the sugan chair. She crept out of the house as the sun lifted itself above the distant hills and inched its way upwards in the golden sky. She stood for a few moments watching the beauty of the new day awakening. She turned and looked at the still, ripple free river below. Despite herself she marvelled at the deep blue stillness of it and the distant roar of the weir. Birds were waking from their night slumber and were chirping sleepily getting ready for the day ahead. For anyone else this would have been the closest thing to paradise on earth, but for Liz, its beauty could not quell the emptiness she felt inside. She tiptoed to the barn and hooked Penny to the trap with her one good hand.

Quietly as she could, she walked Penny down the lane, away from the house. At the end of the lane, she stopped and looked at the little cottage, which until a few days earlier was home to John Flynn and Nellie. She swallowed hard as she leaned her weary head against Penny's silky neck. She recalled the fleeting moments that precipitated the course her life had taken in recent months. The first was falling in love with John Flynn despite her efforts to avoid him. The second was 'that night' when they declared their love for each other and succumbed to their overwhelming passion. And the third, when Jack discovered the truth about her precious unborn baby. Tears pricked her eyes as she climbed into the trap and flicked the reins. She headed Penny in the direction of Ballincollig. At six thirty she pulled into her family's cottage. Her father, sitting at the kitchen table, peered through the small window at the sound of hooves approaching.

'Jesus, Mary and Joseph, 'tis Liz! What's wrong now?' He said to his wife who was cooking breakfast.

He got up and walked out, his wife following behind him.

Liz climbed down from the trap and ran to her mother,

tears flowing down her face. Helplessly she looked at her feet as her body convulsed with shuddering sobs.

'Mam, Mam, I can't stand it any more. I can't go on. Please help me, Oh help me please, I can't stand the pain any more,' Liz cried.

Liz's mother put her arms around Liz and embraced her. Liz clung to her as she sobbed.

'Liz, love, what's happened? Is Jack all right? Come into the house and have a cup of tea.'

Arms around each other, Peggy led her trembling daughter into the kitchen, followed by Michael Moran shaking his head impatiently. Women! Liz's mother steered Liz to a chair at the table and poured a cup of strong tea for her.

Her parents sat beside her and waited till she calmed down a little. With shaking hands she lifted the willow-patterned cup to her dry lips and took a few sips before carefully placing the cup back on the saucer.

'Now tell us what's happened? And how's your poor hand?' Her mother asked gently.

Liz opened her mouth. She looked at them both. How could she tell them? Tell them that her baby was, in fact, alive. That it wasn't her husband's baby but John Flynn's? And that her husband had brutally raped her the night before? She closed her mouth, unsure of where to begin.

'M-My hand is not too bad, it's healing. T-Things got too much for me an-and I feel, I feel terrible and I... I can't go on,' Liz whispered hoarsely.

Her parents looked at her.

'Is that all?' Her father bellowed. 'You come tearing down here at cockcrow just because you feel bad? We thought something was wrong. Liz, you have to grow up and face reality. Your baby is dead! It's hard, I know, but life goes on. Now drink your tea and go back before your husband miss's ya.'

Liz looked to her mother who looked scared. She

always looked scared around her husband. Her mother nodded now, as she looked away.

'Yes, Liz you have to go back, love. Everything will be all right soon. Just give it time. Here's your tea. Would you like a slice of soda bread or bacon?' Her mother got up and moved towards the hearth. Liz moved her chair back, its legs grating on the flagstone floor and stood up. She knew her parents couldn't help her. Nobody could. Her tears had stopped. She glanced around the familiar kitchen, the kitchen where she was witness to many family disagreements. She remembered her father constantly shouting at one or other of them. The almost daily beatings by her father. His wife bearing the brunt of everything. Would life be any better if she moved back in with her parents? She'd never live down the shame of leaving her husband. She'd never get another husband either. In those moments Liz knew she could never come back.

'No, I don't want tea, or anything else. I'm sorry to have troubled ye. I'll go home and get on with the housework. Goodbye,' Liz said with a new calmness as she closed the kitchen door behind her.

She climbed into the trap, flicked the reins and left her parents home. Her parents, still seated at the kitchen table, looked at each other, dumbfounded.

'Jack needs to be firmer with that girl. She was always a dreamer. She doesn't realise when she's well off. Many a girl would love to be in her position,' Michael said.

His wife got up from the table and walked to the tiny window. She looked out at the retreating pony and trap. Tears sprang to her eyes. Her heart ached for her daughter.

Liz entered the farmyard, just as Jack emerged from the house. He stopped suddenly and glared at Liz. She drove past him and climbed down from the trap when she reached the barn. After settling Penny, she walked into the yard. Jack was still watching her through slitted eyes. Defiantly, Liz pushed past him into the kitchen. Jack followed, slamming the door behind him.

'Where were ya?' He shouted.

'None of your business,' Liz replied calmly, picking up the broom with her good hand.

'It is my business. You better tell me now, where were you at this hour of the morning?'

'If you must know, I went to my parents.'

Jack looked suddenly afraid.

'What did you tell them?' He growled.

'Nothing. Nothing at all. How could I tell them they have another grandchild? A child you told them is dead! How could I tell them that you brutalised me last night? I haven't even recovered from the beating you gave me just before I gave birth to my baby. Maria. That's her name. She is alive. She exists! You ever attack me like that again, and I will go to the police,' Liz shouted angrily.

'And what do you think they will do? You are my wife. I can do what I like. I own you! I bought you from your father, remember?' sneered Jack.

Liz knew he was right. Pulling herself up to her full height, she walked up to Jack, her eyes blazing.

'You listen to me, Jack McCarthy. You ever speak to me or look at me or God forbid, touch me in any way, I will drive a pitchfork through you, while you sleep off your drunken stupor. Do you hear me? Don't ever; ever touch me again, because I will kill you. I have nothing on this earth to live for. I am already dead. If I spend the rest of my life in gaol for your murder, t'would be worth it!'

Chapter Eight

'I can't be! Could you have made a mistake?' Liz asked.

Dr White smiled wryly.

'That's what you said on your last confinement Mrs McCarthy! No I'm afraid you are expecting a baby. I estimate your due date is the beginning of March. I'm aware of the circumstances of your last birth. I have your hospital notes here. I see that Dr O'Connor strongly advised you against having any more children. You have put your life in danger by having another baby. Chances are that this baby will die too. I know that losing a baby is very traumatic indeed. After all there is a very high mortality rate in infants born in this country. Thousands of babies die every day. Some women want another baby to replace, well, not replace exactly, the baby they have lost. Hang on. This is strange. According to the notes, your baby was born alive. Sorry to have to ask, but what date did your baby die?' Dr White asked looking down at his notes, pen poised, ready to amend them.

Liz bit her lip. She sat on the chair silently. Dr White looked up.

'Mrs McCarthy, I know it's difficult for you to talk about your deceased infant but I have to amend the notes. How long did your baby live for after birth?' Dr White asked gently.

Liz sighed.

'Doctor, my baby didn't die. It's a long story, but Jack didn't want a girl and he refused to keep her. So I gave her to my best friend and her husband to be looked after. Please don't tell anybody. Especially my family.'

'Mrs McCarthy, are you asking me to lie? I'm sorry, but I have to adhere to a code of ethics. I cannot pretend that your baby died when she is very much alive. I am obliged not to discuss your medical history with anybody, but if I am ever asked, I have to tell the truth. Anyhow, you have far more serious problems ahead of you. Your womb was perforated after giving birth. It hasn't healed at all. Now that you are with child again the situation is extremely grave. I'm afraid to have to tell you that as the baby grows in your womb, you and your baby could die. You will have to be watched closely all through your confinement. It's very important to rest as much as possible. No heavy work. You have to call here every two weeks to be examined. Anyway, lets remove your splint.'

Liz held out her bandaged wrist towards Dr White.

Liz walked out the door of the doctor's surgery, her head down. She turned towards the village and walked. Despite the searing midday heat Liz felt cold. All around her the sounds of people going about their daily business seemed magnified. Horses, and donkeys and carts trudged noisily through Ballincollig. Shawled women stood on the street talking, rush baskets swinging on their arms, passing the time of day. Children scampered happily up and down the main street, squealing in delight. Large horse drawn carts slowly made their way through the village, driven by farmers with leathery brown faces.

Liz stopped on a corner. To her right she saw the nearby church, the church where she had been baptised, where she had received her first Holy Communion, her Confirmation and where she was married three years earlier.

The church where she attended mass every week. Since her marriage she had gone to mass with Jack, but since she returned home after her daughters birth, she went to the later mass alone. Jack continued to go to seven o clock mass as he had done all his life.

Ignoring the sounds of the bustling village, she walked towards it. Approaching it, she saw the tall slim figure of the new parish priest, Father O'Riordan opening the heavy bog oak door. Hesitating for a few moments, she continued. On entering the darkened church interior she couldn't see Father O'Riordan anywhere. She walked up the central aisle where over three years earlier, she married Jack McCarthy. She stopped half way, genuflected and blessed herself. She slid into a pew. For the first time in the last few months she felt calm in this oasis of tranquillity. She looked around at the lofty timber beamed ceiling, the stained glass windows. Fourteen paintings on the walls, depicting the Stations of the Cross. The ornately carved white marble altar. She closed her eyes and breathed in the leafy smell. She felt herself mentally unwind.

'Are you all right Missus?'

Liz jumped as she opened her eyes. Father O'Riordan was standing beside her. He was wearing his long black cassock topped by a white roman collar. Her face reddened.

'I'm sorry, Father, I was just ....' Liz began, 'I don't know what I'm doing here actually.'

'You're Mrs McCarthy, aren't you? I recognize you from mass. I know your parents well. You're married to Jack McCarthy from Inniscarra. May I sit down?' Without waiting for a reply he squeezed in beside Liz.

'Your mother told me about your sad loss. I'm terribly sorry. If there's any way I can help you please let me know. And hopefully God will see fit to bless you and your husband with children in the future. I'll pray for ye,' Father O'Riordan said in his quiet voice.

Liz looked straight ahead.

'Father, if you commit a sin unintentionally and you get punished for it, how many times do you get punished? What if it was a-a mistake, more than a sin? Is it not enough to be heavily punished once?' Liz said wearily.

The priest looked at her, puzzled, a small smile on his lips.

'Well, you know Jesus Christ was severely punished for the sins of every one of his flock. They flogged him, scourged him at the pillar, stoned him, spat at him, crowned him with thorns and finally crucified him. He accepted his fate. What is this 'mistake' you made? Have you been to confession?' He asked.

Liz shook her head. She looked into the gentle face of the priest.

'No Father. I haven't been to confession lately. I'm sorry, I shouldn't have said anything. I wandered in here and for the first time in years, I feel calm. I'd like to sit here for a while by myself if you don't mind.'

'Of course. And remember, if you're truly sorry and ask for God's forgiveness, he will forgive you.'

Liz managed a tiny smile.

'It's not God's forgiveness I have to worry about, Father.'

He smiled back and patted her on the arm.

'Stay as long as you like, my dear. I will be calling on you at your home in the coming weeks. I hope being in God's house will bring you some peace of mind. God bless you.'

With that Father O'Riordan stood up and stepped out of the pew. He genuflected towards the altar before walking in the direction of the sacristy; his shoes click clacking on the stone floor.

*   *   *   *

Later, as Jack sat at the table, Liz served him dinner. She sat opposite him for the first time in months. Jack looked up surprised.

'I see you got your splint off. That's good. You might be more use around the farm now,' he said as he chewed his food.

Liz looked at him for a few minutes in silence. How she hated him.

'I have something to tell you. I'm having a baby. Before you ask, it's yours. Happened the night you raped me. Believe me when I say I don't want this baby. Anyway, Dr White says it's very dangerous for the baby and me. One or both of us might die. I hope I do! Die, I mean. By the way, Dr White knows that Maria didn't die. It's not in the hospital notes.'

Jack stopped, his fork halfway to his mouth. Slowly he lowered his fork and stared at his plate. An uncertain smile slowly spread across his face.

'Well, this changes everything. It's a good omen. A new start. That's great news. Liz, I'm sorry about everythin'. Lets start again.'

'Only if I can go and get Maria!'

'NO!' thundered Jack, 'No, and don't mention her name again, ever.'

'Please, please let me bring my baby home. Please, I need her. I promise, I'll do anything, anything. You're right; it will be a new start. And we'll have a new baby as well and…'

'I said NO! Everybody thinks the baby died. How can we tell them now that it didn't?'

'We'll think of something. I'll….I'll never be complete without my baby, Jack.'

'No, Liz. I'll never have that…. baby here. Ever.'

Liz stared at him, tears glistening in her eyes. She rubbed her eyes and stifled her sobs. Her heart felt like it was breaking, all over again. She looked at Jack.

'Nothing has changed then. There is no new start.'

With that she got up and walked to her bedroom closing the door behind her. Jack stared after her. He shoved his plate away roughly. He put his hands up to his head and rubbed his eyes tiredly. He glanced at Liz's bedroom door sadly. Despite everything, he really loved Liz. He still wasn't over what she had done with John Flynn. More than anything, he had wanted the baby to be his, but she wasn't and he could never accept her.

Chapter Nine
Sunday January 9th 1927

Liz sat up in bed. She glanced out at the moonlit sky. It was a freezing cold night in January. A heavy frost lay thick on the ground outside. The grandfather clock chimed the hour. 1 o'clock. Another pain gripped her and she clutched her abdomen. Surely she couldn't be in labour? She had eight weeks to go. She wondered had Jack come home from the pub yet? Liz struggled out of bed. She pulled her nightgown on. Shivering in the cold night air, she opened her bedroom door and walked to the kitchen door. It was unbolted. Jack wasn't home then. She walked to the hearth, picked up the poker and sat on the armchair. Another pain caused her to double over in agony.

'I hope Jack gets home soon.'

*   *   *   *

The months had passed in a blur. Shortly after she told Jack about her pregnancy, the postman knocked on the kitchen door and handed Liz a letter. Liz recognized Nonie's handwriting. She sat on her bed as she read it, fearful that Jack would come back from the fields. Slowly she opened it.

'Twentieth of June, Nineteen Hundred and Twenty Six.
Dearest Liz,

I hope this letter finds you in good health. Thank you for sending the ten shillings every week. It's not necessary as looking after Maria Rose is pure joy for Patsy and myself. We worry about you all the time, you know. You know where we are if you ever need us. We do hope you will visit us soon although we know things might be awkward between Jack and yourself.

Molly just dotes on little Maria. She got engaged to her young man, Molly that is, not Maria. They hope to get married soon. Molly has already asked can Maria be flower girl. Maria is the happiest little baby in the world. She hardly ever cries. I'm sure she'd much rather be with you, though. We told everybody that we adopted Maria from the Catholic Young Women's Society. We had fierce trouble getting her christened. The day we brought her home, Patsy cycled over to Father Fitzgerald's house in Glounthaune. He told the priest that we had just adopted a little baby, may God forgive us for the lie, and we were anxious to have her christened immediately. Well, the questions he asked Patsy about Maria. He agreed to christen her though, the next day. When we arrived at the Sacred Heart church next day, with Maria looking like a little angel from heaven above, Father Fitzgerald demanded to know the names of her parents so as to proceed with the christening. I had to think fast so I told him Elisabeth Moran; I thought it best to give your maiden name, and John Flynn. Of course he had already met John and Nellie after mass several times, so he was immediately suspicious. He inquired as to the whereabouts of John and Nellie to which I replied they had returned to Kildare ages ago, and why was he asking. He proceeded with the christening eventually. We named her Maria Monica Rose Flynn. Molly and her young man James are the godparents. I hope you will write to me soon and let me know how you are getting on. I bid you goodbye for now.

Your best friend as always,
Nonie.

P.S. Patsy and Molly send their love. And Maria sends all her kisses to you.'

Liz sat there for a long time afterwards, holding the letter tightly to her chest. She cried quietly as she rocked herself to and fro on her bed. She didn't hear Jack as he entered the kitchen and quietly stood in her bedroom doorway. Eventually, she wiped her eyes with her apron, and rose from the bed. She started when she saw Jack standing there. Quickly she shoved the scrunched up letter into her apron pocket.

'What have you got there?' He asked.

'None of your business.'

'I said, what have you got there, and I want an answer NOW!'

Liz stood there glowering at him.

'It is a letter from Nonie. Happy now?'

Liz walked towards the door. Jack stayed in front of the doorway barring her way.

'Might I be right in thinkin' that it's Nonie and Patsy that has your bastard?'

Liz flinched. She turned and looked up at him, her eyes angry.

'You said you didn't want to know. Remember? Well as it happens, yes, Nonie and Patsy are minding Maria for me.'

'I hope you don't have notions that you will get her back, because I'll see to it that you will never have anything to do with her again.'

'Get out of my way,' Liz said between clenched teeth.

Jack stepped back. Liz walked past without a word.

Liz groaned inwardly when she saw her mother, Aine and Cormac arriving in the pony and trap. She knew that Jack had told her parents the previous night. Through the open kitchen door, she watched as her visitors entered the kitchen. Her mother was beaming from ear to ear. She hugged Liz tightly.

'Liz, pet, I'm so happy for ye. Now ye can look to the future. Ye'll have another baby to end your heartache at last. Oh how you suffered, me poor cratoir. Didn't I tell ya that all ya needed was time?'

Liz forced a smile.

'Yes and now we are going to have another baby in the spring. The tea will be wet in a minute. How's Cormac today?' Liz said as she leant down in front of her nephew.

'Mam says, I'm the best boy in the world, Auntie Liz. Mam says you're getting a new baby cos your baby girl's in

'Eaven with Holy God. And that you was very sad 'cos Holy God took your baby. Are ya getting' a girl baby or a boy baby this time? Please get a boy baby so I can play wit 'im,' Cormac said, looking at his Auntie with his big innocent blue eyes.

Aine was horrified. She clamped her hand over her mouth as her face reddened.

'Well, we just have to see what Holy God will bring me Cormac love, and your mammy is right, you are the best boy in the world,' Liz smiled at the cherub like face of her nephew and brushed an unruly black curl from his forehead. He kissed Liz on the cheek before running out to chase the ducks.

'Cormac! I'm so sorry Liz. I hope he hasn't upset you. His mouth runs away with him from time to time. Anyway, we called because we removed all your baby things when you were in hospital, you know, clothes, blankets and the crib. We put them in the attic and we thought you might want to get them out now, so we're here to help!'

Liz stopped smiling suddenly. She turned to Aine.

'Aine, those 'things' were for Maria. Although she's….no longer with me doesn't mean that I'll use her things for this, this ….new baby. I want new things for the new baby.'

Aine's face reddened again and she looked upset. Not knowing what to say, she stared at her feet.

'Liz! That was uncalled for. Aine was only trying to help. What's got into you? You'd think that you'd be happy that God has seen fit to bless you with another child,' Mrs Moran said angrily to her daughter.

'Believe me when I say that God had no involvement with me getting in the family way! And if ye must know, I didn't want another baby, I already have …..' Liz's voice trailed off suddenly, 'I'm sorry, Aine, mam. I just haven't had time to get used to expecting so soon after…. Maria,' Liz said, tears springing to her eyes. Without warning she broke down in tears. Mrs Moran placed her arms around Liz's shoulders and pulled her close. Aine rubbed Liz's arm up and down before putting her arms around Liz's back. The three women embraced until Liz's sobbing eventually subsided.

*   *   *   *

Liz heard the sound of the pony's hooves clip clopping on the frozen ground up the lane towards the farmyard. She knew that Jack would have lain across the seat and while Penny headed back towards the farm from the public house. The pony and trap passed the farmhouse, into the barn. Sometimes, Jack would fall asleep on the journey home and it would be a while before he'd wake up. Ten minutes later, Jack entered the house. Through his drunken haze he saw Liz, sitting by the fire.

'Why're ya still up?' he slurred, swaying unsteadily.

'I need to go to the hospital. I'm in labour. Oh no!'

Jack jumped as Liz let out an ear-piercing scream. She felt another contraction coming. She bent over again, clammy sweat beading on her forehead. Jack unsteady on his feet watched her uncertainly. He scratched his cheek thoughtfully.

'Well, I'm 'fraid you can't go to the hospital. Roads are terrible with the frost, worst frost I've seen in nigh on forty years. Have to wait till mornin'. Anyway, don't ya have a few more weeks to go?' Jack slurred.

'Jack, I already told ya what the doctor said about giving birth, and how dangerous it is. I need to get to the hospital now.'

'And I told you, you have to wait till morning. We'll go, at cockcrow. Surely you can wait for a few more hours. Now, I'm going to bed; I'm tired.'

Liz stared incredulously as Jack calmly staggered up the stairs to his bedroom. Another contraction gripped her and she bent over again. When the pain eased, she knew she only had a few minutes before the next contraction would come. Moving as quickly as she could, Liz went into her bedroom. She plucked her black hooded winter cloak from the clothes chest and her black woollen stockings and black ankle boots. Carefully, she pulled on her stockings and boots. She draped her cloak over her, picked up the patchwork quilt and went out to the barn. As on many nights in the past, Jack was too drunk to unhitch the trap from Penny. Throwing the quilt up on the seat, Liz led Penny and the trap out of the barn and across to the kitchen door. She went into the kitchen to look for a reed taper to light the oil lamps at each side of the trap. As she picked up the reed from the mantelpiece, she felt another contraction coming. She sat down and waited till the pain had passed. Carefully she lit the taper from the dying embers of the fire, and going outside, lit each lamp. She threw the taper on the ground and hauled herself up into the seat. Wrapping her cloak about her, she placed the quilt around her lap. Taking the reins, she made a clicking sound with her tongue and Penny set off down the moonlit lane.

It was eerily silent as Liz steered the pony through the dark lanes towards the Anglers Bridge. The only light emanated from the oil lamps, the half moon and millions of flickering stars. An owl hooted, startling her, as she passed under a frost covered leafless tree. Dark shadowed areas loomed at every turn as Penny's hooves crunched on the hard frosty ground. Liz felt scared and vulnerable. Her breath formed clouds of mist. Beads of sweat rolled down her forehead. She groaned as the next contraction hit her. She let go of the reins as she bent over in pain. Confused, Penny slowed and stopped. She neighed as she tossed her head from side to side.

'God help me. Please let me get to the hospital soon.' Liz cried between clenched teeth.

'Christ Almighty! Is it yerself, Mrs McCarthy? Ya gave me a fright with yer screaming. Whatever is the matter?'

Startled, Penny neighed and she reared slightly. Suddenly scared, Liz gaped at the diminutive figure of Dan Lucey standing unsteadily on the crisp white frosted grass verge. His dingy flat cap was pulled low on his head. His breath formed a misty cloud in the chill night air. As Liz's contraction subsided she stared uncertainly at him. His breath stank of whiskey. She swallowed.

'D-Dan. I –I, well the pains are coming and I have to get to the hospital fast,' she said in a trembling voice, her teeth chattering from the cold.

'Christ,' he muttered raising a hand to his jaw and stroking it thoughtfully.

He looked at her again.

'Where is Jack? Surely he should be with you? Shure, we were at the pub tonight and he said ya had a couple of months to go yet,' he slurred.

'Jack's in no position to accompany anyone anywhere, as well you know. Now if ya don't mind I've got to get to the hospital,' Liz announced haughtily, grasping the reins. Pulling her cloak tightly around her, she clicked her tongue. Penny started off at a gentle trot once again. Dan stared after her for a moment before turning towards his house. He dug his hands deep in the pockets of his shabby grey overcoat and shuffled on. The pony had only gone twenty yards when a loud shriek tore through the still night air once again. Dan turned in time to see Liz doubled over in the trap. He sighed and shook his head. Liz screamed again before dissolving into loud sobs.

'Are ya all right Mrs McCarthy?' he called in a loud slurred voice.

'Dan please, help me!'

With a muttered oath and an exasperated shake of his head, he stumbled back to the trap, his tattered boots crunching on the frost-covered ground. He stared at Liz wondering what best to do.

'Take it aisy Missus. Is the pain gone yet?'

Liz half sat up, her sobs subsiding. Her face was contorted by a mixture of fear, pain and foreboding. She nodded at Dan weakly. She knew it was only moments before the next contraction would strike. She grasped the reins. With another muttered oath, Dan took them from her grasp and climbed into the trap, gently easing Liz to one side. Gently he pulled the patchwork quilt around Liz, tucking it in all round. She looked at him in surprise as he flicked the reins. Penny set off at a brisk trot.

'Dan, I'm sorry, I'm just so scared. The pains are just terrible. You don't know what its like…' Liz whispered.

'Me wife died in childbirth.'

Liz looked at his wrinkled face in the moonlight as the trap swayed from side to side.

'I-I didn't know you were married Dan, how long ago was it? That your wife died I mean?'

'Over thirty year ago it were. I was just nineteen, me wife Julia seventeen. We lived with her family in Queenstown. They had a smallholding, grew the few spuds and a bitta barley. We were so excited about the babby. She had only a week left, God bless her. One Sunday morn, we were alone in the tigeen. Everybody was at early mass. We were goin to go to the next wan. She was screaming like yerself an' I didn't know how to help her. I just …., sat beside her and told her push it out. Every time I tried to leave the room she screamed again, so I stayed. It was pitiful it was. The wailin'. T'was like a banshee. I held her hand, didn't know what else to do. I prayed that her ma would hurry home from mass. Julia said she was goin' to die and I told her hush, she was only havin' a wee babby, not a foal! Next thing she gave an almighty scream and then went all limp. I kept callin' her name and slappin' her cheeks, to rouse her from her weakness. That's when I noticed she wasn't breathin'. I panicked and started screaming her name and shakin' her hard. Nothing. Then her ma and da came in and saw me roarin' like a bull and shakin' their poor little girl like a rag doll. I tried to tell them she just stopped breathin', but they thought I .. attacked her or somethin',' Dan's voice faltered and he hastily wiped his nose as he turned to look at the neat town houses on the Western Road as they rumbled by.

The gas streetlights glinted eerily in the frosty mist.

Liz stared at him. She felt sorry for him. In the moonlight, she saw the tear glistening in the corner of his eye.

'What happened then? Did they believe you in the end? Did .. she have the baby?' Liz whispered.

Dan shook his head as he flicked the reins.

'Julia's baby died inside her.'

'Oh!' Whispered Liz.

'The priest was sent for; this was back in 1896. Lots of women died in childbirth. I didn't know what was happenin'. I was hunted out of the bedroom. Hours later her ma came out of the room crying and the priest went in. The baby was born. Me son; me only child. Dead! Julia's mother was beside herself. She looked straight at me and shouted at me.

'It was him, he beat her, we saw him. He killed his wife and leanbh.'

I couldn't believe it! I just lost me wife and poor child and they thought I did it. I was thrown out, literally thrown out the door, by her da and the parish priest. I'll never forget the door slamming and I lying in the dirt on a rainy Sunday afternoon. I was beside myself with the grief. I walked and walked. Whatever money I had in me pocket, I drank it. I tried to go to the burial, but Julia's da and brothers; all four of them, gave me a hiding I never forgot. Next day I went down to the quay in Queenstown and got on the first boat that would have me.'

Liz had listened in amazement at the longest conversation she ever had with Dan Lucey. A rush of sympathy washed over her for this man. He was hunched over the trap as he led the pony along the dimly lit Grand Parade. She opened her mouth to say something and was immediately seized by another bout of contractions. She doubled over as she emitted an ear-splitting shriek. Dan glanced at her and flicked the reins even harder.

'Hold on Missus. I'll not let you die like my lovely Julia. We're nearly there. Take it aisy now. Gee up, ya mangy pony ya.'

Liz lapsed between consciousness and unconsciousness as the wrought iron gates of the hospital swam into view. She held her swollen abdomen as she lay half slumped across the seat. Dan jumped down from the trap and ran to the gate. He spoke urgently to the gatekeeper who fumbled with a large bunch of keys. Shivering, Dan jumped back into the trap, just as Liz doubled over in pain once again. The gatekeeper watched as the pony and trap lurched forward towards the maternity wing of the old hospital. Dan steered the pony to the door of the maternity hospital. As the next contraction hit Liz screamed again.

The door opened and an orderly peered out.

He started when he saw the woman screaming in pain in a trap and an obviously drunk man jumping down from the trap while the pony stamped impatiently on the hard ground.

'Help the lady please. She has another few weeks to go but her babby decided to catch us all on the hop,' Dan informed the orderly as he walked towards the trap.

'Are ya all right Missus?' the orderly asked.

'Help me! I've been getting pains for over an hour. My baby's not due for another eight weeks.'

'Can you get down? Come on I'll help you,' gently the orderly helped Liz from the trap. He put his arm under her arm and draping it across his shoulder, he helped her in the door to the hospital. As he walked her towards the labour ward he called for assistance from the nurse on duty at her desk. Dan followed at a distance, his flat cap hastily removed from his head, his wispy grey hair flattened against his bony head. He walked behind a sobbing Liz and the orderlies. When she was taken through the double doors at the end of the corridor, he stopped suddenly. Twisting his cap round and round between his grubby wrinkled hands, he swallowed. He barely knew Liz, but she was always kind to him. He was afraid. Afraid she would die in childbirth just like his beloved wife. He had done his best, hadn't he? Standing alone in the empty corridor, he turned abruptly and placing the cap upon his head, he headed for the door.

Minutes later, Liz was in a bed surrounded by doctors and nurses. She was sweating profusely and her breathing was laboured. Dr O Connor was reading her file as the nurses flitted around her. He looked at her eventually, a concerned look on his face. He leaned over and spoke in a calm gentle voice.

'Mrs McCarthy, hello again. I remember you. Last May wasn't it? You had a difficult labour and childbirth. I didn't expect to see you in here again, let alone within the year. There's only a few months between your babies isn't there? We'll be here with you, but I can't lie, you're in for a bad time of it, I'm afraid. Hopefully, everything will be all right. Is your husband with you? I'd like to talk to him.'

'No,' she gasped.

'You didn't come in here, from Inniscarra, by yourself?'

At that moment, Liz screamed again in pain.

'Nurse, get some ether to relax her a bit.'

Throughout the long pain filled night, Liz drifted in and out of consciousness, screaming as her body went into spasms. In her unconscious state, she had a similar dream to the dream when she gave birth to her daughter. Again as she followed the bright light she heard a voice telling her to go back.

'No, not this time. I don't want to go back. Too much pain.'

'Go back now!'

'No, please not this time, please God, let me come to

you.'

Through the mists of pain, Liz was aware of a baby being placed in her arms. In her dreamlike state she tried to hug her tiny baby.

'Maria Rose, my darling baby, I told you we'd be together again. I'll never let you go again,' she slurred as her eyes tried to focus on the infant.

'Mrs McCarthy, you had a baby boy, your second child. You'll be going home soon enough to your daughter.'

'This is not Maria? I have a son? Hello my baby, I'm your mother. I'll never let you go. I let your sister go but I swear nobody, nobody will ever part us,' she whispered weakly, her words slurred.

In her delirious condition, she heard a distant voice. It was Dr O'Connor, a worried look on his face.

'Mrs McCarthy, I'm afraid your baby is very small and weak and I don't expect him to survive. We'll take him away now because you're also very unwell. Try get some sleep.'

Liz was asleep within seconds.

A howling wind was blowing around the walls of the draughty hospital as Liz slowly opened her eyes and blinked. As her eyes adjusted to the light, she heard a movement beside her. Dazed, she looked around and focussing on the figure hunched by her bed, she saw Jack sitting beside there. He looked at her sombrely.

'Liz. How are ya? You've been out cold two days now. I saw the baby. Doctor says he might not…live.'

Liz turned away and looked out at the swirling snow as it spattered against the window.

'Liz, I'm sorry I didn't bring you in here the other night. I was in no condition. I was really drunk. I wasn't expecting… you to… you know have the baby for a few more weeks. When I woke up next mornin' and found you and the pony gone, I vaguely remembered comin' home and you sayin' that you had the pains. I'm so sorry Liz. Well anyway, I ran down the lane heading for your father's place. Jaysus, it was freezin'! The frost was hard on the ground. Dan Lucey pulled up alongside me on me own pony and trap. Well, when he told me how he brought you in here I was mighty grateful to him. Not bad for a man who had drank two bottles of whiskey and at least a bottle of poitin!

He got out of the trap and I drove like the clappers to your Da's place. Michael Og brought me in here yesterday mornin' an' I've been here since. I've done a lot of thinkin'. About all that's happened. I really don't want our little baby to die, but if it's God's will...' his voice cracked with emotion and he took a deep breath, 'anyway, whatever happens, I'd like us to work out our difficulties and start fresh, like. I'll give up the drink and we'll go back to the way things were, 'cos I really miss ya, in all ways. Will you forgive me? What do ya think? Liz?'

Liz lay very still in the bed, thinking. Could things work out after all? While Jack was in the right mood, maybe it was a good time to ask him. She sighed. Without turning around she asked, 'What about Maria?'

Silence. A full five minutes passed before he answered, in an unusually calm voice.

'Liz, I knew you'd ask me about that again. I'm afraid the answer is no. I can't do it. I'm sorry. We couldn't explain where it came from. And who it's father was...'

He stopped as a bloodcurdling scream emanated from Liz. She struggled out of the bed. She held on to the end of the bed as she stood shaking, and screaming. Her long dark matted hair billowed out behind her making her white pinched face appear even whiter. Her black ringed hollow eyes and her white cotton nightgown gave her the appearance of a spectre staggering towards Jack. Jack jumped up and backed towards the open door as he stared at her advancing towards him.

'You bastard, you bastard! You destroyed me. You made me give away my baby. She's not an 'it'! She's a girl!

She has a name. Maria! She is eight months old! You nearly killed my baby and me! You raped me and now our son might die because of the damage you caused me. And you have the nerve to ask me to forgive you! Go to Hell, Jack McCarthy! I hope you'll burn in hell. Burn in hell. I'll never forgive you. I hate you. I hate you...'

Liz slumped to the floor crying and shrieking as nurses and orderlies ran past Jack into the room. Jack, tears in his eyes watched helplessly as two orderlies gently lifted a sobbing Liz onto the narrow hospital bed. One of the nurses looked sharply at Jack while the other nurse tried to calm Liz.

'Jesus, Mary and Joseph, what have you done to your poor wife? Isn't it bad enough that she had to drive herself in here on a freezing cold night? What have you done to her now?'

Before Jack could reply, Dr O'Connor entered the room and walked towards Liz, who had fainted. The doctor held her limp hand and felt her clammy forehead. He turned to Jack.

'I don't know what's going on between you and your wife, but I must ask you to wait outside while we try to settle her. She is seriously ill and you have to stop upsetting her. Now please, wait outside.'

Jack backed out of the ward bumping into the doorway in his haste. He sat down heavily on a nearby bench. Leaning over he held his head in his hands. Tears ran down his face. How did things go so wrong? He thought. God help me. I know I made terrible mistakes. I don't know what to do anymore, he thought, sobbing quietly.

Chapter Ten
April 1934

Liz emerged from the kitchen into the dazzling sunshine, carrying a wicker laundry basket full of dirty laundry. She placed the wooden washtub on a three-legged stool near the water pump. She filled the bucket with crystal clear water and tipped it into the washtub. She refilled the bucket three times, each time emptying it into the washtub. She took the bar of carbolic soap from her apron pocket and started scrubbing the clothes vigourously against the wooden washboard. Later when she was hanging the clothes on the clothesline, she heard a voice calling her. She turned and smiled when she saw her son William, or Will as he was called, running towards her. He was seven years old now. Following close on his heels was his cousin Cormac. They were best friends. Now eleven, he was the image of his father Michael Og, all jet black curls and big blue eyes. She adored her only son. He helped ease the pain of living without Maria.

She still received letters occasionally from Nonie giving her updates on Maria, who was now nearly eight. She had never seen Maria since she handed her to Nonie that day in the hospital. She went to the post office in Ballincollig every week and posted ten shillings to Nonie, with a short letter. On Maria's birthdays and at Christmas she always sent one pound and addressed it to Maria herself. Sometimes she'd send little gifts such as books. Nonie had told her that Maria was an avid reader. She'd write a short note wishing her either 'Happy Birthday' or 'Happy Christmas' and sign it 'from Elisabeth'.

She smiled as Will and Cormac drew nearer. They had spent the morning working with Jack in the top field. Jack also adored his only son. It was his idea to call him William Patrick after his own father. Jack and Liz never spoke to each other since that day in the hospital. She had been very

ill for two months after giving birth to Will. Will himself
was a very sickly child, but with a lot of help from Liz's
mother, he grew stronger. She looked at her young blond
haired son now.

'Mam, Dad and Cormac and me ploughed the top field.
Dad let me hold the reins of the plough. I can't wait to grow
up and be a real farmer like Dad.'

'You'll do no such thing. You'll continue at school and
get an education and make something of yourself. Farming
is not good enough for my son.'

'That's what you always say, but I want to be a farmer.
Dad says when I grow up, the farm will be mine anyway, so
I have to be a farmer. Dad says school is for cissies.'

Liz frowned. She hated when Jack filled Will's head
with notions of becoming a farmer like himself. Over the
years, Jack had acquired more land and had taken on a farm
hand from Inniscarra village. Jack was sixty-three now. He
never touched a drop of alcohol again. He still went to the
local public house at least three nights a week to meet his
friends. Liz was glad, as she couldn't bear to be in the same
room as him.

'Come on darling, its nearly lunch time.'

'Dad said, tell you he'll be down in fifteen minutes.'

Liz grunted. Will looked at his mother.

'Mam, why don't you and Daddy talk to each other?
When I go to Cormac's house or to Seamus's house, their
dad and mam talk. I never ever saw you and dad talk to each
other.'

'We're too busy to talk,' Liz replied abruptly, 'Now go
wash your hands.'

Later Jack, Will and Dan Lucey sat around the table
eating their dinner. Dan was a regular visitor at dinnertime.
Both Jack and Liz were very grateful to him for what he did
to help Liz the night she went into labour. Against
everyone's wishes, Liz insisted that Dan be asked to be
Will's godfather. His eyes filled up with tears when Liz

asked him.

'I would be honoured to be your son's godfather Elisabeth,' he replied unusually subdued.

Will called him 'Uncle Dan' and was very fond of him. Liz smiled as she thought of all the times Dan kept Will and Cormac amused with hair raising tales of his sea faring adventures.

Jack picked up the letter that Liz had placed beside the willow-patterned plate. He opened it and read it. A broad grin spread across his heavyset features.

'Yes!' He shouted punching the air, 'It's a letter from the.., let me see, the E-S-B. Remember I wrote to them last year about that new thing, electra-city when they had the announcement in the Irish Press? Well, they're coming out next month on the sixteenth of June and they'll connect us up!'

Dan and Will looked at Jack. Liz, sitting in the hob of the fire, her dinner on her lap, had been listening.

'Da, what's electra- city?' Will asked.

'It's a new way to run machinery and it gives light. I don't rightly know how to describe it,' Jack replied, scratching his head, 'All I know is, it's the future. And we're one of the first in Cork County to get this electra-city.'

'Electricity is a new form of power. It was brought in in 1927 to power the factories. All the cities and towns have it. It's in Cork city. You can walk into a shop and you have light like you've never seen before. You don't need oil lamps or candles anymore. The E.S.B. lay wires all over your house and they put bulbs in the ceiling…' Liz joined in, then she stopped as she realised this was the closest she came to having a conversation with Jack.

Jack and Will were staring at her open mouthed.

'They have electra-city in the navy boats,' added Dan, slurping his stew.

'Do they now?' asked Jack with interest, winking at Will.

Will rolled his eyes to heaven. Young as he was, he knew Dan was prone to exaggeration.

'Yeah. 'T'was…let me think now, 1919 and I was sailing on the Grace O Malley, to Newfoundland and the navy had just got the ships rigged up with the electro …electra-city….'

'Are ya sure t'was 1919?'

'Of course I'm sure. Well as your good wife says, it lit up the ship like daylight. There was a light in every cabin, on the decks, everywhere, and the cook was cookin' with it an' all.'

'Very peculiar that, Dan. Seeing as how the electra city plant in Co. Clare wasn't built 'til 1927!'

'On me life, I swear …'

Will started giggling followed by Jack. Even Liz managed a smile. Dan Lucey always managed to land himself in it.

'Anyway we'll all find out what it is and how it works next month,' Jack announced and he continued eating his dinner.

Lately, Liz thought more and more about Maria. Nonie had written to her last week to tell Liz that Maria was receiving her First Holy Communion on Thursday May 10th. Liz wrote a letter last night and placed a five- pound note in the envelope towards her Holy Communion dress. She knew Nonie wasn't looking for money towards the Communion but Liz felt it was her duty. She would send a letter to Maria herself on her Communion day.

8th May

Liz entered the busy post office in the middle of the Main Street. In her hand she held an envelope. She looked at it again. On it she had written,

'Miss Maria O'Mahony,
Rose Cottage,
Clash Road,
Little Island,
Co. Cork.'

She stared at the envelope, which contained a short note wishing Maria good luck on her special day. Also enclosed was a five-pound note. Slowly she turned and walked out of the post office without buying a stamp.

'I don't care what Jack or anybody thinks; I'm going to watch my daughter receive her First Holy Communion!' She thought as she walked quickly back to the trap.

*   *   *   *

The sun shone on the little group of children standing outside the Sacred Heart Church, Glounthaune. Little girls in their dazzling white dresses and veils, white ankle socks, and white shoes. Boys in black blazers, short black pants, white shirts and ties, and black shoes, hair slicked back neatly with hair oil. Mothers huddled together chatting. Fathers never attended Communions or Confirmations. Liz stood behind the tall chestnut tree outside the wrought iron church gates. After tying the pony and trap to the tree, she looked among the crowds for Nonie. She edged a little closer. The church bells pealed loudly and the group filtered into the church. Liz stood alone in the empty churchyard. Plucking up the courage, she walked to the church, opened the heavy oak door at the side and quietly entered the dim interior. She slid silently into a pew at the back. She looked at the little group of children listening earnestly to what the priest was saying and strained her eyes to catch a glimpse of Maria. How on earth would she recognise her?

Just then, she spotted a little girl with her back to her. She had long chestnut coloured hair covered by a lace veil. Liz scanned the crowd for Nonie. She spotted her, seated a few seats behind the Communion children, whispering to a young woman who had a little boy of about two seated on her lap. The service continued, the children singing at intervals.

Liz stared at her daughter's slim back. Occasionally Maria turned to whisper to her companion and the two girls giggled discreetly at some private joke, their hands covering their mouths.

Once, Maria turned and looked around the church. Liz stared at the face of her daughter for the first time in eight years. Maria had creamy white skin, the brightest blue eyes Liz had ever seen, full lips and of course, tumbling brown glossy hair, framing her pretty face.

Why, she looks like me! thought Liz.

For a split second, Maria looked at Liz, and then turned to her companion again. Both girls giggled.

Outside the church, Liz waited at the gate as the Holy Communion group and their mothers emerged from the church. The children were impatient now to get home for their favourite part of the day; receiving the tuppence from their neighbours and friends. Mothers clutching their children's hands strolled past Liz until only a few remained. Liz spotted Nonie talking to a young woman and her little boy, and a mother and her young son. Suddenly, Nonie looked up and saw a familiar figure standing by the gate. She shaded her eyes from the glare of the morning sun and her pretty face broke into a happy smile. She whispered something to the young woman and said goodbye to the mother and son. Holding Maria by the hand, Nonie walked quickly towards Liz, a big smile on her face. Liz smiled back.

'Liz! 'Tis great to see ya,' she said beaming as she held out her arms to Liz and the two women embraced warmly.

'Oh Nonie, it's great to see you. How I've missed you,' Liz cried almost overcome with emotion.

Breaking apart, Liz looked at Maria and the young woman. Maria was staring at Liz.

'Liz, this is Molly, my niece, and her little boy Sean, who's two. Molly this is my best friend Liz, from Inniscarra.'

'Hello Liz, Nonie has told me all about you. I'm glad to meet you at last.'

Liz smiled as she shook Molly's hand. She stared at the young woman's swollen abdomen in surprise. Molly smiled.

'Yes I'm expecting again. I have only eight weeks to go. Wish it was over, I feel like a whale,' she announced holding the small of her back as she grimaced.

'Oh that's nice. I hope it goes well for you,' replied Liz.

'I haven't told you everything about Liz. We still have our secrets,' Nonie said looking Liz in the eye and smiling, 'and this is my daughter Maria Rose.'

Surprised, Liz held out her hand to Maria and who gently shook it.

'Hello Maria... Rose, what a pretty name. I'm very pleased to meet you at last. You look so beautiful. Your ...mother told me you were receiving your First Holy Communion today and I had to come. Here, this is for you,' Liz said handing Maria a crisp five- pound note. Maria stared at the note, her eyes shining, and mouth open in surprise. She looked at Liz happily.

'Thank you very much. I've never had a five- pound note! Mammy talks about you all the time. You're really pretty.'

Liz smiled, tears glistening in her eyes. She stroked Maria's shiny hair.

'You're very pretty yourself. Like a rose,' she said softly, staring at Maria.

'That's my name Maria Rose. Everybody calls me Rose,' Maria said shyly as she held Liz's gaze.

Liz glanced at Nonie, tears glistening in her eyes.

'That's a very special name, for a special little girl.'

'Don't fill her head with silly nonsense. She's spoilt enough already,' Molly interjected, a little too sharply, as she rolled her eyes to heaven. Maria's face fell. She looked at her feet.

'Molly, how many times have I told you leave her be? She's only a child,' Nonie snapped, glaring at Molly, 'now take Maria and Sean home in the trap. Liz and me will go in her trap. And, be nice to her. It's her First Holy Communion.'

Molly scowled as she grasped little Sean's hand. She walked quickly towards the trap, tied to the iron railing inside the gate, followed by Maria. Liz watched, concerned. Nonie looked at her.

'Don't worry. Molly is like a cross between a mother and an older sister to Maria. They get on most of the time, but you know families, occasionally they argue and fall out.'

Liz relaxed a little bit. They reached Liz's trap, tied to the chestnut tree. They climbed in, and headed towards Little Island.

'She turned out to be a beautiful little girl, Nonie, thanks to you and Patsy. There was many times I wished I could see her again but things are difficult with Jack,' Liz said as the pony trotted along at a steady pace. A warm breeze blew gently against their faces as they squinted against the late morning sun.

Nonie smiled and looked at Liz.

'It's good to see you again Liz. It's been a long time. Imagine its eight years. How's your son, William isn't it?'

'Will, we call him. Only for him I'd be lost. I kept hoping that some day I'd get Maria back. But Jack was adamant. I begged him many times to let me go and get her. My heart was broken you know. It felt like she was dead. Everybody believes she died. While I was still sick after her birth, Jack raped me one night, after a feed of drink. I couldn't believe it when the doctor said I was expecting a baby again, so soon after Maria. I wanted to die. When Will was born, he gave me a reason to live again. He's in school today of course. My mother is collecting him from school.'

'You've had a rough time haven't you? I was delighted to see you today. I told everybody that we adopted Maria. Nobody knows the truth.'

'Have you any news on…. John and Nellie? I feel really bad about them.'

'They visited just once, that was last year. I think they might have worked out who Maria is. After all she's the head off you. Nellie's not well at all. She's got consumption. She's had it a while now. John really loves her, you know. Anyway, when they visited, John got on very well with Maria, as did Nellie. John has a job in Kildare in a blacksmith. He's very handy you know,' Nonie paused.

She smiled at Liz who smiled back.

'It's so good to see you after all these years. When are we going to meet Will?'

'I don't know. Jack doesn't know I'm here. And I'm not going to tell him. One day I'll tell Maria who I am and we'll be together again. I made a vow to her. In the letter I wrote in the hospital, the day.. , the day I gave her to you and Patsy. I vowed to come get her one day and we'd be together always. Just me, Maria and Will.'

Nonie smile suddenly vanished. She turned away. Liz looked at her.

'Nonie, whatever's the matter?' Asked Liz, concerned.

Nonie hesitated. After a few moments, she looked at Liz with sad eyes.

'It's Rose. I treat her as my own child. After all this time, I never imagined I'd have to hand her back. I don't know if I can. I'm scared of losing her now.'

'Nonie, I'd never do anything to hurt you. But Maria is mine and it was always my intention to get her.'

'I know Liz, I know. I don't want to lose her and I'm

scared.'

Liz patted Nonie on the arm and smiled.

'I know. We'll work something out when the time comes. Don't worry.'

Just then they pulled into Rose Cottage. After climbing down from the trap, Liz and Nonie walked into the dim kitchen. Molly smiled at them as she busied herself putting cups and saucers on the table. The kettle was bubbling on the hearth.

'Sit down there now. I'll just get some rhubarb cake and tea. Maria is gone down the road. She's delighted with her five-pound note. She wants to go to town soon and buy a new dress. A pink dress if you don't mind, and pink shoes. She just loves pink, I suppose it's because she's never had anything pink. I put Sean down in my bed, he's exhausted, poor cratoir,' Molly said as she placed the teapot on the table and sat down. Nonie and Liz sat down too.

Molly, Nonie and Liz passed away an enjoyable hour, chatting and catching up on news. All of a sudden, Liz saw the top of Maria's head as she passed by the garden wall. Nonie was watching Liz watching Maria. She reached out and touched Liz on the hand and nodded. With that, Liz got up and walked out into the glare of the midday sun. Maria smiled shyly when she saw Liz. Liz smiled back.

'Well Maria, have you enjoyed your first Holy Communion day?' enquired Liz.

'Yes, I've had a good day. I got nearly six pounds! I never saw so much money. Molly said she'll take me to town, 'cos I want to buy new clothes and I want to buy presents for mammy and daddy and Molly and Sean and James. I'd like to buy you a present too, Liz, I mean Mrs...'

'You can call me Liz, and please, don't buy me anything. You're a very generous girl, Maria. How do you like school? Your mother tells me you are very clever and you love to read.'

Maria smiled shyly again.

'Ya I love school. My teachers name is Bean Ui Riordain. I love when she reads us stories. And I like English and Irish and Catechism. I don't like arithmetic or Euclid. Daddy reads to me too. He bought me some books; I can't read them yet so he reads them to me. He says one day I'll be reading to him!' Maria said giggling.

'Do you get on with Molly?' Liz asked.

'Oh Ya. She's my cousin but she's like my big sister. And Sean, he's so cute, isn't he?'

'Yes, he's beautiful. Do you look after him,' Liz asked smiling.

'I play with him all the time, and I take him for walks. Sometimes I feed him. He's such a happy baby. When Molly has her new baby, I'll mind him or her too.'

Liz looked at the pretty girl standing before her. Maria had removed her veil and her ringlets were tumbling down her back. Her cheeks were flushed and her eyes were shining brightly.

'You're a very good girl Maria, and your mother is very proud of you. I'm so glad I came today. Well, I must go now, my little boy will be coming home from school soon,' Liz said as her smile began to waver.

She hated parting from Maria. Having seen her now she wanted more than anything in the world to put her into the trap and bring her home.

'Wi-will you call to us again, sometime?'

'Of course. Maybe next time I might bring my son. His name is Will. He's seven. Well I have to be going, enjoy the rest of your day Maria, it was lovely to meet you at last,' Liz kissed Maria lightly on the top of her head. Without warning Maria wrapped her arms around Liz's waist and clung to her. Hesitating at first, Liz put her arms around her daughter and drew her close. She breathed in her freshly washed hair and revelled in the gentle firm embrace of her only daughter. She never wanted to let Maria go. She felt a tear in the outer corner of her eye. She looked up as Nonie and Molly came out and reluctantly released her grip on her daughter. Was that a tear in Maria's eye? Wiping her eye she smiled brightly at Molly as she held out her hand to her.

'Goodbye, Molly it was lovely to meet you. Nonie, I'll see you again, tell Patsy I was asking for him,' Liz said, tears spilling from her eyes, this time happy tears. Nonie threw her arms around Liz and hugged her warmly. Together the little group walked towards the pony and trap, tethered to the twisted sycamore tree. Liz climbed into it and with a final wave at her friend and Maria she flicked the reins and clicked her tongue as the pony moved forward. As the pony trotted down the road, Liz whispered a prayer to God. She smiled through her tears. Had she looked back she would have seen Maria standing in the middle of the road, watching the pony and trap depart; an unexpected sadness welling up inside her.

'Thank you, God for allowing me to see my daughter again.'

As Liz pulled into the farmyard, she saw Jack come out the kitchen door. His face was like thunder as Liz drove past in the pony and trap. He stood at the kitchen door watching her every move as she unharnessed the trap. A shiver of fear ran down her spine as she walked towards the kitchen. Ignoring her angry husband, she walked past him into the kitchen. He followed her inside and kicked the door shut. Liz jumped. Still ignoring him, Liz went about her chores. She fetched potatoes from the vegetable box in the recess above the mantelpiece and placed them in the earthenware sink to scrub them. She felt Jack's eyes boring into her back.

'Where were ya?' he snapped, 'I came in for me lunch and it wasn't there because you were gone. Now, where were ya?'

Liz ignored him and carried on with her work, scrubbing the potatoes clean in the sink. She placed them in the blackened pot and hoisted it onto the swinging crane. In two strides he was next to her, yanking her roughly by the wrist. She twisted out of his grasp and turned on him angrily.

'Oh, so you're talking to me again; after seven bloody years! And trying to break my wrist again as well! How dare you! And since when are you interested in where I go?' she snarled, her eyes furious. Jack was taken aback.

'You went to see her didn't ya?' he yelled angrily.

'Yes! I went to see HER; my daughter! And you know what? She made her first Holy Communion. And another thing, she is a beautiful little girl and….' Liz began to sob, her anger spent, 'she's mine and I love her and I'm proud of her. I'm going to see her again.'

'You will NOT! I forbid you to go anywhere near Little Island again,' Jack shouted as he pushed Liz violently against the wall. She cried in pain. She stood up and suddenly rushed at Jack pushing him hard. He stumbled backwards. Straightening up he reached and caught Liz by the shoulders and shook her roughly, his face a mask of hate. She struggled to free herself from his grasp, her hair coming loose and tumbling over her face.

'Jesus, Mary and Saint Joseph! What are ye doing?'

Both of them stopped struggling and pulled away from each other when they saw Liz's mother and Will standing in the doorway. Will was shocked, his small hand clasped tightly in his grandmothers rough hand. His mouth was open and his eyes wide with fright. Liz quickly regained her composure. She straightened her clothes and tucked stray strands of hair behind her ear. Her face was flushed and she struggled to slow her breathing.

'Nothing Mother, it's.. it's all right now. Thanks for collecting Will from school. Would you like a cup of tea?' asked Liz in a trembling voice. Jack stormed out the door leaving it open. Will ran to his mother and put his arms protectively around her waist. She hugged him tenderly. Liz's mother stared after Jack before turning back to Liz.

'No, I'll be off home Liz. Is everything all right,

between you and .. Jack?' she asked worried.

'Ya. You know how it is Mam. 'Tis life. Nothing I can do about it. I'll be grand, no need to worry about me,' Liz said with a watery smile, 'Will, are you going to help your father in the field?'

Will looked at his mother's sad face. He squeezed her tightly.

'Ya. Are you sure you're all right Mam? Why was Da so cross with you?' he asked worriedly.

She smiled down at her young son and ruffled his fine blonde hair.

'It's just grown up stuff, Love. Never mind about it. You go on up to the field and I'll get on with the dinner.'

Liz's mother reluctantly said goodbye and left the kitchen. Will followed her, glancing back at Liz who was stoking up the fire, the orange and blue flames leaping high. As he closed the door behind him, Liz slumped into a chair at the table. She put her head in her hands and wept.

Chapter Eleven

The sixteenth of June dawned bright and sunny. Jack and Dan Lucey were already out in the fields. Will was helping Liz to milk the cows before he went to school. The E.S.B. were expected at nine thirty to start erecting poles to bring the Electricity supply to the farm.

'Mam, can't I stay at home today. I can help you and Da. I want to see what this electra- electra...' Will began.

Liz smiled as she sat milking a cow, the tin pail between her knees. She expertly pulled the teats and the jets of milk produced a high-pitched tune when it hit the sides of the pail.

'Electricity. No need to worry. The E.S.B. will be here for a few days. We won't be connected to the supply for weeks. Now hurry and I'll walk with you to school.'

An hour later, after walking Will to school, Liz was washing the laundry in the large tin bath in the yard when she heard the rumbling of the motor vehicles approaching the lane from the main road. She looked up, as did Jack who had just returned from the fields. The huge grey motor truck roared into the farmyard followed by a smaller truck. Liz's heart beat faster. She had never been this close to such an enormous vehicle before. She had seen motorcars in the city, driven by the gentry. In the back of the bigger truck were about twenty long bitumen coloured timber poles. Each pole measured about thirty foot long and twelve inches thick. The smaller truck contained huge rolls of black cable and tools.

Two men jumped down from the bigger truck as another two emerged from the smaller one. They walked towards Jack. Liz watched as the men spoke to Jack amid much gesturing towards the fields and the farmhouse and looking at plans. The men returned to the bigger truck and switching on the ignition, slowly drove towards the fields. Later, Will returned from school and Liz was amazed to see about twenty local children were following him. Walking straight past the house, the group of children headed for the fields. Having completed her chores, Liz followed the children. As she neared the fields, she noticed the tall bitumen dipped poles, dotted across the fields in a straight line. She spotted the trucks in the top field. She could see the team of four men digging an enormous hole. She was surprised to see, not only the group of children, but also a lot of local farmers and even some of their wives. They were after all, the first people to get electricity in the Inniscarra area. As she entered the top field she saw one of the workmen tie a long rope to one end of the poles. The other end of the rope was attached to the big truck. Seconds later, the truck slowly drove forward until one end of the pole was hovering over the four foot deep hole. The truck continued to drive forward until the pole slowly rose in the air until it was standing upright. The crowd cheered! The remaining workmen quickly filled in the hole with a mixture of mortar and earth. Liz smiled.

After a few days all the poles were erected. Liz came out of the kitchen one morning to the astonishing sight of a workman seemingly 'walking' up the only pole erected in the farmyard. On closer inspection she saw that the man had clamps attached to his boots and a thick belt around both his waist and the pole. Ten days after the first pole being erected it was time for the electricity to be switched on. Liz's family arrived at nine o clock to inspect the newly installed light fixtures in the ceilings and the one wall socket in the kitchen. Jack proudly showed his father-in-law around his newly modernised house and cowshed. Michael Moran shook his head.

'Can't understand what all the fuss is about,' he grumbled, 'there's nothing wrong with the way we've done things for hundreds of years.'

'That's the problem. It's time to move with the times. Electra-city is the way forward. Any minute now the E.S.B. will connect us up and you will see.'

Shortly after two o clock, the man from the E.S.B.

arrived. By that time most of the Moran and McCarthy families were present. Fifteen minutes later, the E.S.B. man flicked the switch on the wall near the kitchen door. The kitchen instantly flooded with light. Everybody gasped in amazement.

'Look at the light thing on the ceiling, it's like a glowing egg!'

'God in heaven! Would ya look at that! It's a hundred times brighter than an oil lamp!'

'Of course its bright, ya eejit, it's the middle of a sunny summers day!'

'Don't it show every little bit of.... well you know. The walls look very dingy or somethin'. Don't they Liz? And I never noticed the cobwebs above the mantelpiece before!'

'Peggy Moran! I can't take you anywhere anymore, because you open your big mouth and immediately stick your even bigger foot in it.'

'Now we've seen it what else does this electra, electra-city do Jack?'

Jack smiled. He was delighted with all the interest in the new electric lights. He looked at Liz. She was staring wistfully in the direction of the door.

Later that evening after Liz had gone to bed, Jack and Will sat at the kitchen table. Jack puffed away contentedly on his pipe. Will was reading Robinson Crusoe. Occasionally they'd glance at the ceiling light in awe. After a while Jack put his pipe back in the pipe bowl and yawned.

'Time to go to bed, Son.'

'Can I read in bed, Dad, with the new light in my room?'

'Twenty minutes, no more! I'm going up now,' Jack said as he got up and stood under the light bulb. Will stared in surprise as his father stood beneath the bulb and blew at it like you would blow out a candle.

'Da-ad,' Will called as he walked over to the light switch, finger at the ready.

Jack turned and smiled sheepishly as it dawned on him. He shook his head.

Jack watched from the end of the stairs as Will flicked the switch off and the kitchen was once more plunged into darkness.

*   *   *   *

Two years passed. Liz continued to write and send money to Nonie. Occasionally she enclosed a short note for Maria. In it she would politely ask how she was getting on in school. Liz would write about her son, herself and the farm. She continued to buy books for Maria because Nonie had told her that she loved to read. She'd post the books separately, wrapped in brown paper and addressed to Maria herself. Sometimes when Liz received a letter from Nonie, there would be a short note enclosed from Maria. In her childish scrawl, she would thank Liz for the latest book and tell her about school, her friends, Molly and her 'parents'. Liz looked forward to these little notes from Maria and looked forward to the day when they could live together as mother and daughter.

Her relationship with Jack disintegrated further and they now lived separate lives. Only for Will, life would be unbearable. He was nearly nine now, tall and fair-haired. His brown eyes were like Jack's, but in most other ways, he was like Liz. He was a very bright pupil at school. When he came home from school, he'd get changed and go out to the fields with his father. In the evening Liz would look out for father and son as they returned from the fields. She was very proud of her handsome son. She would have liked to have had more children, but circumstances being what they were, she knew she was lucky to have given birth to Will. Much as she had abhorred being raped, she could see the good that came from it in the shape of Will. Christmas was fast approaching. It was a fairly mild winter so far. Liz walked to the post office in Ballincollig with her letter to Nonie. Also enclosed was a note and a pound note to Maria for Christmas. Liz was worried about Nonie lately. She was suffering from tuberculosis for a few months now. She didn't complain much. In her last letter she announced that she felt much better. After purchasing a stamp, Liz slid the letter into the slot of the post box and set off for home.

Days later, as Liz prepared dinner; she looked out her kitchen window on hearing the sound of pony's hooves approaching. She stared in surprise as her father and mother got out of the trap. Her parents only visited two or three times a year. She walked to the kitchen door and opened it.

'Well, this is a surprise. Are ye staying for dinner? We're having...' Liz stopped when she noticed the solemn expressions on her parents' faces.

'Liz, I hate to be the bearer of bad news. I was in the city this mornin' and I bumped into Miss Crowley, you know, that you used to work for. She asked me if I heard the news an' I asked her what news? She said your good friend Noreen died, Sunday night. T'was T.B. Anyway she's being buried tomorrow in Caherlag graveyard at twelve o'clock. I told Miss Crowley I'd tell ya,' her father said sadly as he rested a hand on her shoulder.

Liz felt as if she had been kicked in the stomach. She couldn't take it in. Nonie! Dead? Dead at the age of thirty-seven. Her mothers voice came to her like sunshine cutting through a fog.

'Liz, Liz come in out of the cold. I'll make you a cup of tea. It's a terrible shock for you. I know how close ye were.'

Liz's mother led her gently into the warm kitchen and helped her to the chair beside the fire. Her mother filled the kettle and placed it on the swinging crane above the flames of the fire. Liz's father searched through the cupboards of the pine kitchen dresser. He cursed under his breath.

'What kind of home is this? There isn't a drop of whiskey or poitin or anythin'.'

'Would ya calm down? Can't ya see Liz is in shock?' His wife scolded him.

'I was lookin' for somethin' to give her for the shock,' he replied through gritted teeth.

At that moment Jack entered the kitchen with Will. It was nearly dark outside now. He closed the door behind him.

'Michael. Missus Moran. How are ye?' He asked as he sat at the table. He looked at Liz and the frozen expression on her face.

'Is there somethin' wrong?' he asked.

Will went to his mother.

'Are you all right, Mam?' He asked taking her hand in his. It was icy.

'Jack, we came to tell our Liz here, that her friend, Noreen or Nonie as she was called, died the night before last. She had T.B. And as you know, herself and Liz were very close. She's being buried tomorrow at Caherlag at twelve. I'm afraid Liz got a bit of a shock and I was looking for some whiskey, to take the edge off, but ye don't have any,' Michael Moran said.

Jack looked at Liz, sitting very still, staring into space. He'd seen that look before, after he attacked her the first time. He knew that Liz and Nonie had been corresponding all the time.

''Tis all the same to us. We can't go to the funeral. And it's not like she was family or anythin',' he said matter of factly.

Liz turned and looked at him. She stood up suddenly still holding Will's hand.

'I am going to the funeral tomorrow and neither God nor man will stop me,' she said defiantly.

'Ah sure, you have to take her to the funeral of her best friend, Jack,' Michael said.

'I'll go on my own. I'm quite capable of looking after myself. Now if ye don't mind I have to get the dinner.'

Liz turned away from the group and placed the pot of spuds on the swinging crane. Everybody stared at her. Her parents walked to the kitchen door, Jack followed. When they went outside, Michael turned to Jack.

'Jack, let her go to the funeral. It's the right thing to do. She's got to pay her respects,' he said.

'Would you let your wife go to a funeral on her own?' Jack asked.

Liz's mother looked indignant. Michael shook his head.

'I see your point, but Liz is a different kettle of fish to Peg here. She's more headstrong. More independent. Let her go to the funeral Jack.'

'I seem to remember you tellin' me before we wed, that Liz had notions about herself. You advised me to sort her out quick,' Jack said. Michael eyes narrowed.

'Now Jack, it's seldom I interfere between man and wife, but Liz has been a good and faithful wife and its only fair she goes to her friends funeral. I trust you to do the right thing by Liz.'

Jack helped Liz's mother into the trap, her husband climbed in the other side and with the oil lamps lit on either side, they set off in the dark. Jack stayed outside looking up at the stars, as the night air grew chillier with the frost that was already hardening the ground. He knew he could stop Liz from going to the funeral if he wanted to. He was afraid she might meet John Flynn and they might rekindle whatever they had had. Where would that leave him? And Will? What if she wanted to take the child, her daughter? No, he had to stop her. He went back into the warmth of the kitchen. Will was sitting at the table and Liz was serving the dinner onto the two plates. She never sat with Jack and Will for meals. Jack sat at the table. He looked at Liz.

'Sit down for a minute,' he asked.

Will looked at him astonished. He had never seen his parents sit down together at the table. Liz sat on a chair. She didn't look at him. Jack ate his dinner with great big gulps.

Eventually he stopped chewing.

'I forbid you to go the funeral,' he said without looking at her. Will watched his mother. She showed no emotion.

'All right,' she replied calmly.

She got up again and left the kitchen.

Jack was surprised. He could hardly believe it was so easy. He continued eating. Worried, Will ate his dinner too. Liz went to her bedroom and lay down on the bed, suddenly exhausted. Her tears ran onto the pillow as she buried her face in it. Oh Nonie, why did you die? A week before Christmas. Today is the twentieth, which means you died on the eighteenth. And what's going to become of Maria? My poor little girl must be devastated. I don't care what Jack says; I'm going to the funeral.

*   *   *   *

The ground was white with a sparkling coating of frost as she made her way down the driveway next morning in the pony and trap. She shivered involuntarily. She wore her heavy black cloak with the hood and the travelling blanket was wrapped around her lower body. Will had left at his usual time this morning to go to school. Jack was already out in the fields. As soon as Will had left, Liz hurriedly got dressed and harnessed the pony and trap. She went straight to the Sacred Heart Church in Glounthaune. She knew she was early for the mass. Tying the pony to the bare chestnut tree outside the church, Liz slowly made her way in through the gates and up to the church door. She rubbed her hands together in an effort to warm them. She opened the heavy door and then the inner door. As her eyes grew accustomed to the dimness of the church, she saw the pine coffin lying on a table, just below the altar. She let out a gasp. Slowly she walked up the aisle towards it, tears already running down her face. She bit her lip to stop herself from crying out loud. When she reached the coffin, she stopped. For a few moments, she stood very still in the near darkness as she tried to comprehend that Nonie was gone from this earth. She reached out her ice-cold hands, placed them on the lid of the coffin and laid her head on top of them. The sobs she had been choking back burst from her like an avalanche. Minutes later she heard a sound behind her.

Straightening up, she saw Patsy standing at the back of the church. He looked dazed. He seemed older than his years. He shuffled up the aisle till he stood silently beside Liz. Liz and Patsy looked at the coffin in silence for a few minutes. Liz touched his arm.

'I'm so sorry, Patsy. Nonie was truly the most wonderful person, I have ever known. She was my only friend in the whole world. And you. I owe ye both a debt that I can never repay. How's Maria taking it?' Liz asked softly.

'Nonie loved you too Liz. As for Maria Rose, that child brought more joy to us than you'll ever know. 'Tis we owe you the debt,' Patsy said as a solitary tear rolled slowly down his cheek, 'I..loved my Nonie more than anything on this earth. I don't know what I'm going to do without her. How will I live without her?' He asked, turning his pain filled eyes towards Liz. She put her arms around his shoulders and hugged him for a few moments.

Behind them, they could hear the sounds of mourners entering the church. Liz quietly slipped to the back of the church as more people entered. She looked around for Maria. She spotted her as she entered the church walking between Molly and her husband James. James, an extremely tall thin young man was holding a little girl aged about two in his arms. Little Sean who was five, held onto his other hand. Maria clutched Molly's hand tightly. Bewildered, the child looked around her, her tearstained face showing her anguish at the loss of the person that was central to her world.

Suddenly Liz started. Entering the church was John

Flynn and Nellie. Memories flooded back. Was it ten years since John Flynn had worked for her husband? He looked the same, his greying temples the only sign of ageing. Seeing Nellie was a bigger shock. Gone was the curvaceous body and in its place was an almost skeletal frame. She looked gaunt and grey and feeble as her husband assisted her to a pew.

Mercifully, they didn't see Liz. She pulled the hood of her cloak up around her ears. After everybody was seated, the priest began the mass. Liz struggled to concentrate on what the priest was saying as the memories refused to go away. Her one night with John Flynn flashed through her mind, followed by the horrific attack by her husband and the subsequent birth of Maria. Her cheeks were aflame at the memories. She looked at Maria. She longed to go to her, to comfort her, tell her the truth about who she really was. Maria sat between Patsy and Molly, crying quietly, yet with a dignified air. The irony wasn't lost on Liz. Maria, mourning the death of her 'mother', was unaware that she was in the presence of both of her real parents.

After the service, the mourners filed out of the church in silence. Liz remained where she was. She didn't want to risk bumping into John and Nellie. She waited until she was sure the horse drawn carriage containing Nonie's coffin was on its way up the steep hill to Caherlag graveyard. After a suitable length of time she emerged from the church. The frost was thawing under the watery sun. She untied the pony and climbed into the trap and headed up the hill a mile or so until she came to the graveyard. She pulled up and tied the pony to a nearby tree. She carefully made her way towards the small group of black clad mourners inside the wall of the graveyard. Up here at the top of the hill, a mist still hung over the graveyard adding an eerie atmosphere to the burial. With her hood pulled up over her lowered head, Liz discreetly made her way to the edge of the crowd. Desperately trying to peer over the shoulders in front she could make out where Molly and James were standing. Although she couldn't see her, she knew Maria was standing between Patsy and Molly. Shortly afterwards, the burial service was over and people began to make their way out of the graveyard. Liz hid behind a tree until she thought everyone had left the graveyard. When she looked at the newly filled in grave she saw that Patsy and Maria were still standing at the graveside. Looking around, Liz walked to the grave. At the sound of footsteps crunching towards them, a tearful Maria turned and stared in wonder at Liz. With a loud sob, Maria fell into Liz's arms. She buried her face in Liz's heavy cloak as she cried her heart out. Liz hugged her daughter close for the first time in nearly ten years. They clung to each other as if they'd never let go.

Outside the graveyard, John Flynn was helping his sick wife into their trap when he happened to glance back at the grave. In the grey fog, he noticed the dark hooded figure hugging Nonie's little girl Maria. With a start he realised it was Liz. And she was hugging the little girl who was born around the time that Jack attacked him and Liz.

'John, what's the matter, love?' Nellie asked him.

'Nothing, my dear. Come on let's get back to the house,' he replied as he tucked the travelling rug around Nellie. He glanced once more at the two figures, embracing in the fog.

*   *   *   *

Christmas Day arrived. Since the funeral and the subsequent row afterwards Liz was on autopilot. She hardly ate at all and sleep didn't come until the early hours of the morning. On top of grieving for Nonie, she worried terribly about Maria. The poor child was devastated at the loss of her 'mother'. Liz longed to comfort her. She knew it was futile to ask Jack could she come live with them. Especially after the fight that ensued on her return the day of the funeral.

Only for Dan Lucey and Will being present in the kitchen when she walked in, it would have been far worse. Dan instinctively knew that trouble was brewing and stayed until the early hours of the morning, giving Liz the chance to escape to bed early.

*   *   *   *

Liz shivered as she swung her legs onto the floor. Weary and cold she dragged herself to the kitchen and proceeded to light the fire. She walked to the parlour and gazed at the tall Christmas tree in front of the window. She had always loved the fresh pine smell Christmas trees and the earthy smell of holly but today it failed to delight her. The tree almost reached the ceiling. Will and Cormac aided by Dan Lucey laughed a lot when attaching the festive decorations to it. Normally Liz lent a hand but this year couldn't face it. After Jack and Dan planted the tree in an old tin bucket and dragged it into the parlour, the boys hung the homemade ornaments from its branches. Old cigarette and matchboxes were transformed into gaily coloured boxes dangling from the tree. Paper chains made from crepe paper and tin foil, criss crossed the tree and cotton wool dotted it to resemble snow. A shiny foil star made by Will topped the tree. After Will went to bed the previous night Jack brought in the new bicycle and carefully leaned it against it the tree. A tall red candle surrounded by sprigs of red-berried holly and tory tops nestled in the window. On the high mantelpiece was an equally tasteful arrangement of holly and tory tops. Holly sprigs were placed above every available picture and photo on the walls. On the highly polished sideboard next to the nativity crib, was a generous supply of alcohol for their friends from the neighbouring farms who turned up on Christmas evenings after six for a bit of a chat and a sing song. Two dozen bottles of Murphy's, two big bottles of Jameson whiskey and a four bottles of Jennings red lemonade were neatly stacked at one end. Liz returned to the kitchen as the fire crackled into life. A trussed plucked goose hung upside down from the ceiling near the stairs ready, to be cooked for dinner. The iced Christmas cake and Christmas pudding sat side by side on the dresser. Noises came from overhead signalling that Jack was up. Liz sighed. She wished this day was over.

All Christmas day meant to her was a lot of extra cooking and cleaning. Normally she looked forward to Cait, Pat and their children calling in the evening, but not today. Jack came downstairs. Without so much as a glance at Liz he pulled on his old overcoat, Wellingtons and flat cap and marched out into the drizzly day to milk the cows. He'd come in in an hour and change his clothes to go to eight o clock mass. Only after mass would he eat his breakfast, put before him on the table just before Liz and Will left for nine o clock mass.

Liz took down the goose, rinsed it in the sink before placing it in the special earthenware roasting dish. She stuffed it with a parsley and thyme bread stuffing. She hung the pot of porridge on the crane ready to cook for Jack and Will's breakfast. Next she peeled enough spuds, turnips and cabbage for the dinner. A thud upstairs brought a little smile to Liz s lips. Will was up and in a second would run downstairs to see what he got from Santy Claus. Right on cue, he raced down, smiled at Liz before dashing past into the parlour. Liz smiled again at the boyish whoops of joy coming from the parlour. He flew back into Liz and hugged her tightly just as Jack came into the kitchen and removed his Wellingtons.

'Dad, guess what Santy brought me? A new bike! I can cycle to school and up the village and over to Cormac's house and Danny's house and ….,' Will gushed his eyes shining brightly.

'All right, all right, I get the picture,' Jack smiled, holding up his hands. He glanced at Liz who quickly turned away. She had been in a funny mood since her friend's funeral. She'd better snap out of it fast, Jack thought.

*   *   *   *

The merriment was well underway by six o clock. Earlier, Dan Lucey had arrived for Christmas dinner bringing a bottle of Jameson for Jack, a pair of delicately embroidered handkerchiefs for Liz and a paper bag of bullseyes for Will. Liz was touched by his kind gesture.

'Thank you, Dan, they're beautiful,' she'd said, a tear threatening to roll out of her eye.

'You're doing all right, girleen. I know you're upset about .. your friend dying so close to Christmas, but time is a great healer,' he'd said softly, patting her gently on the arm.

He seemed to instinctively know how she felt. She dabbed her eyes with one of the handkerchiefs and smiled gratefully at him.

Liz was sitting beside the turf fire in the parlour with Cait, Mary Hogan and Mary McDonagh. Jack, Dan, Pat, Ned Hogan and Sean McDonagh were sitting near the Christmas tree, each with a bottle of Murphy's in their hands. Will, and four of Cait and Pat's eight children were coming and going between the kitchen and the parlour. Liz struggled to stay focussed on the conversation going on around her, smiling every so often. Another two hours and the women would be brought home by one of the men and thankfully Liz could finally go to bed while the men would continue to drink and talk into the early hours. Suddenly the lights went out. Another power cut. Power cuts were more frequent during wintertime. Seconds later and Jack had lit a couple of candles, kept for such emergencies. He walked into the kitchen returning with the tilly lamp kept in the cupboard of the pine dresser. Having lit it, the conversation resumed as if there had been no interruption whatsoever. In despair, she watched the clock until Cait announced she wanted to go home. Pat, her husband, offered to drive the three women and three of his own brood home. Danny, his twelve-year-old son, wanted to stay with Will. After waving goodbye to the women as they set off, Liz trudged wearily to her room and sank gratefully on to her bed. For the first time in days she slept. Not even Dan Lucey's off key singing woke her.

Chapter Twelve

'Rose Cottage,
Clash Road,
Little Island,
Co. Cork.
25 of January 1937.

Dear Elisabeth,

I hope this letter finds you well. Just a few lines to thank you for your lovely letter. And the ten shilling note you send every week. Its very thoughtful of you to think of Patsy and Rose at this time and the money comes in handy too. Patsy is taking Aunt Nonie's death a lot harder than expected. He hasn't gone back to work yet. He hardly eats anything and doesn't talk to anybody. Nearly every day he takes the pony and trap and goes up to the graveyard alone and does not return until after dark. Then he sits near the fire until bedtime. I am hoping that with time, his grieving will ease. He takes no interest in Rose at the moment. She is back in school, thank God. She was very close to her mother, being an only child. She does not cry or fret as much now but at the start the poor child was very upset. I'm writing to inform you so you won't worry too much about Rose or Patsy.

I find it particularly difficult at times to deal with their grief. What with my own children Sean and Katie. My husband James is a sergeant in the army and is away a lot. I myself, miss Nonie terribly. She was so good to me always. Anyway, if you're ever near Little Island, do call in.

Yours,
Molly Fitzpatrick.'

Sitting inside the hob by the crackling log fire, Liz read Molly's elegant handwritten letter. How she longed to bring Maria here and look after her. Liz had sent ten shillings to Molly just like she had every week since Maria was born.

I'll have to stop sending money or Molly will start to wonder why I'm sending it, thought Liz. There was no point in revealing who Maria's real mother was now. Liz carefully folded the letter and put it back in its envelope. She stood on the chair and reached up behind the flour bags above the mantelpiece. She removed the loose stone at the back and placed the letter with all the other letters from Nonie. She pushed the stone back into place and stepped down from the chair. Just then, the kitchen door burst open and Will ran in, followed by Jack and Dan Lucey.

'Mam, Mam, guess what Dad bought in Cork? He bought a wireless. Look!' Will said excitedly.

Liz looked up to see a smiling Jack carrying a wireless. He put it up on the kitchen dresser and they all gathered around to look at it. It was two foot tall made of a highly polished dark wood. On the top was a large round knob with two smaller knobs either side of it. In the front was a circular beige coloured cloth grille. PYE was etched in capital letters below the grille. Jack took a length of black cable from his pocket.

'Dad says when the wireless is on you can hear people talking and singing on it!' Will announced excitedly.

'First, I have to put this aerial thing out the window and hang it up high to get a signal,' Jack said. '

'I'll go get the ladder,' Dan offered.

Will followed him. Minutes later, Liz saw Jack at the top of the ladder which was propped against the bare sycamore tree in the front garden. He was fastening the aerial to a branch near the top of the tree. Will came back into the kitchen, and standing on the table, opened the window as Jack fed the aerial in through it. Liz closed the window against the biting wind. Jack came in from the yard stamping his feet and blowing his hands against the biting wind. He pushed the aerial into the socket at the back of the wireless set. Jack removed the bulb from the kitchen light and after inserting the lead and the bulb into an adaptor, placed the adaptor into the light. Will switched on the kitchen light and the kitchen flooded with light.

Jack immediately started fiddling with the knobs on the wireless and loud noises unlike they had ever heard before emanated from the strange wooden contraption. Liz and Will drew back frightened. Jack continued turning the knobs this way and that and suddenly,

amid the crackling and hissing, they heard the sound of a man talking. He seemed to be talking about the weather!

'And the outlook for the next few days is for storms to continue, with gale force winds increasing in velocity. Heavy rain may cause severe flooding. Temperatures will remain at minus 1. This is Radio Eireann. Good afternoon,' a male voice eloquently crackled.

'And that was the one o clock news bulletin followed by the weather report. A discussion on the forthcoming constitution being drawn up by the leader of Fianna Fail, Eamonn De Valera follows these messages,' announced another male voice as a lively tune jingled from the wireless. Liz, Jack, Dan and Will, their mouths open, stared mesmerised at the wireless box on the kitchen dresser.

*   *   *   *

1938

Liz carefully folded the clean clothes as she unpegged them from the clothesline. Behind her the sun was low in the sky as it was about to dip below the horizon. The sky was a conflagration of crimson and gold, the sun a shining sphere. Liz turned as she heard the sound of horse's hooves trotting up the lane. She was surprised to see her brother Michael Og. She smiled as he pulled up alongside her and dismounted.

'We weren't expecting you till tomorrow. The hurling match doesn't start 'til three o clock. Don't you think you're a bit early to hear it on the wireless?' She said playfully.

He didn't smile. He was holding a rolled up newspaper in his hand.

'Liz, I have to talk to you. Is Jack inside?' He asked.

'Ya, he's listening to the wireless with Will,' she replied as she picked up the wicker laundry basket, 'what's wrong?'

'I'll tell ya inside.'

They both walked into the kitchen. Jack and Will were sitting on chairs close to the wireless listening to the news bulletin. Jack sat, ear cocked, listening intently, his pipe dangling from the corner of his mouth. Will looked up. His eyes lit up when he saw his uncle.

'Hello Uncle Michael, are you coming tomorrow to listen to the match?' he asked.

Jack looked up. Michael stood near the hearth looking uncomfortable.

''Tis mam who sent me. She was reading The Cork Examiner today and she saw something… I think you better read it yourself Liz,' he said sombrely as he handed the newspaper to Liz. It was folded open at the death notices. He pointed at a recent death. Slowly Liz took the newspaper and walked to the window.

'Patrick O Mahony, beloved husband of the late Noreen O Mahony (nee O Sullivan) and father of Maria Rose, died at his residence Rose Cottage, Clash Road, Little Island, yesterday Wednesday, 24th of August 1938. Requiem Mass is at Sacred Heart Church, Glounthaune, at 7.00 pm today and burial is on Saturday 27[th to] Caherlag graveyard at 10 o clock.'

Liz's hands began to tremble before she got to the end of the death notice. Tears sprang to her eyes and she put her hand to her mouth to stop crying. Jack rose and walked over to Liz. Carefully, he took the paper from her shaking hands and read the notice. A loud sob escaped from Liz's mouth. Will didn't say a word.

'I suppose you will want to go to the burial or maybe the mass tonight?' Michael Og asked gently. She nodded, tears streaming down her cheeks. Jack opened his mouth to speak. Michael Og caught his eye and shook his head. Jack fell silent. Michael Og helped his sister to a chair at the table.

'Make your mother a cup of tea,' he instructed Will who immediately went to the blackened kettle simmering on the hearth. Jack cleared his throat.

'I'll drive you to the church for the burial if you like,' he offered. Liz nodded her head. Apart from the shock of reading of Patsy's death, Liz was worried for Maria. What would become of her now?

Later that night Liz tossed and turned in her bed. Suddenly she sat up in bed. Something had woken her. Somewhere outside, she heard an unusual sound. It sounded like a cat yowling. It must belong to one of the neighbours. She lay down again and turned away from the window. However, the yowling didn't stop, if anything it grew more eerie. It was a low-pitched steady sound that didn't let up. After another hour, Liz got out of bed and walked to the little window. She peered out into the moonlit garden, trying to determine what part of the garden the bloodcurdling noise was coming from. She didn't see any cat. Sighing with frustration, she sat on the edge of the bed while she pulled on her shoes. Dressed in her white nightgown she opened her bedroom door, walked through the kitchen to the parlour, and quietly opened the top half of the door. She leaned out; her ear cocked first one side then the other as she looked all around the garden. A full moon glowed like a glowing white orb in the sky lighting up the countryside. Finally her eyes came to rest on one of the trees at the end of the garden. With a shock, she saw, not a cat, but a human form standing with their back to her beside the gnarled trunk of the oak tree. She narrowed her eyes, leaning further out to get a better look. She saw that the person was about four foot tall, had long white grey hair and was dressed in grey. It was from here that the spine-chilling noise was emanating. There was something very unearthly about the small person and the hairs stood up on the back of Liz's neck. She drew back from the door suddenly and closed the top half of the door.

Calm down, you're dreaming, that's all. There's nothing out there. It's just your imagination, Liz thought. After taking a few deep breaths to calm herself, Liz carefully opened the top half of the door. She immediately looked towards the tree. Nothing. She sighed. She could still hear the yowling noise. She leaned out over the half door and peered out again. She let out a piercing scream. Just outside the door to her left, not six feet away was the little person she had seen earlier.

Liz looked into the grotesque grinning face, from whose misshapen mouth the unearthly yowling was coming from. It could only be the Banshee! Liz had never been so terrified. Frantically, she slammed the door shut and bolted it. Trembling she backed away from the door, afraid that, somehow, the banshee might break down the door. She was too afraid to go back to her bedroom, so she ran upstairs.

Taking deep breaths in an effort to stop her trembling, she stood on the dark landing. Then she quietly went into Will's bedroom and got into beside him. He grunted and turned away from her. She lay in the bed, turned away from the window. She could still hear the yowling outside. She pulled the quilt up over her head. All of a sudden she heard another sound. It couldn't be. It sounded like the cock crowing! Only thing is, cocks never crow at night. She covered her ears and closed her eyes tightly trying to erase the memory of the horrible face.

Next morning, Liz woke with a start when the cock crowed from his pigsty perch. Will turned and yawned.

'Mam, what are you doing in my bed?' He asked in surprise. Embarrassed, she got up.

'I-I was a bit upset about my friend Patsy. That's all,' she replied as she walked out of his bedroom. Jack was just coming out his bedroom door when he bumped into Liz. She walked quickly past him and down the stairs.

Later, as the family ate their breakfast, Liz cleared her throat.

'Did anyone hear that .. that noise last night? It sounded like a cat. Went on all night. I could hardly sleep,' she said.

'No,' chorused Jack and Will.

'Maybe it was the Banshee. Grandmother told me about the Banshee. How they turn up three days before a death and they make a horrible wailing noise,' Will said.

'Well, in that case the Banshee is too late, Patsy died two days ago!'

'Jack! Have respect for the dead,' Liz said angrily.

'Grandmother says the Banshee only appears if there is a death in the family. So your friend Patsy doesn't count,' Will announced as he ate his bread and jam.

'I'll have no more talk about Banshee's or deaths. I heard the cock crow as well. Did ye hear him?' Liz said.

Will sighed dramatically.

'Ah mam, did you hear the pigs squeal and the sheep baa and the…'

'Be quiet boy. Liz, are you sure you heard the cock crow?' Jack asked in a strange voice.

'Yes, I'm telling the truth. Did you hear it too?'

Jack went very quiet. He suddenly looked fearful.

'Jack, whatever is the matter?' Liz asked, scared.

After a few moments, Jack stood up and walked to the window and looked out.

'People say if you hear a cock crow at night there will be a death in the family. Hearing the banshee can be dismissed as an old wives tale, but not a cock crowing at night.'

Liz and Will stared at Jack's back.

'Right, that is definitely enough of this talk of … ghostly sounds in the night. Just forget I ever mentioned it. I might have dreamt it. Now, Jack I think you should milk the cows and Will, you help him.'

*   *   *   *

Next day Jack and Liz travelled to the Sacred Heart Church in Glounthaune. Both of them hadn't uttered a word on the journey. It was a beautiful sunny day. They had left Will at her parents' house. On reaching their destination, Jack jumped down from the trap and tied the reins to the chestnut tree as Liz alighted from the trap. They were early. Without waiting for Jack, Liz quickly walked towards the church. She hesitated before she pulled the heavy door open. Inside the dark church Liz could see the simple pine coffin on the table in front of the altar. She walked towards it. Tears in her eyes, she rested her hand on the lid.

'Oh Patsy, why did you have to die? You just turned forty. At least you're with Nonie again. So wherever ye are ye're together again.'

'Liz!' A familiar voice called from the door of the church. She froze momentarily then turned to see John Flynn framed in the light. Slowly he walked towards her. He smiled.

'Liz. It's good to see you although I wish it were under happier circumstances. How have you been?' He asked.

He looked older and tired.

'JJ-ohn! I'm fine. How have you been? Look, Jack is outside and I don't want any trouble. Not today. Not here. How did poor Patsy die?'

'I think from a broken heart. He never really recovered from Nonie's death. Molly said he just faded before her eyes. Died in his sleep.'

'I see. Well at least they're together again. Is Nellie here too? She must be very …'

'Liz, Nellie is dead. She died three months after Nonie, God rest her soul. Consumption. I miss her terribly. I felt so bad about…well you know, what happened between us. She was very hurt. I promised her that I would never betray her

172

again. She forgave me.'

'Oh John, I had no idea. I'm so sorry for your loss. I felt bad also about… it. I never meant to hurt her the way we did. She was a lady.'

'She was indeed. I….'

'Liz! What in God's name is going on? Is this the real reason why you wanted to come to the burial? To see him again? Is it?' Liz looked past John to see Jack standing in the doorway, his eyebrows knitted together in fury. John looked at his feet. Liz turned and hurried towards Jack.

Jack's eyes were blazing. He continued to stare at John's back.

'Jack, will you calm down. We're at a funeral. Have some respect. Nothing is going on,' Liz said between clenched teeth.

People were beginning to file into the church now. Liz went and sat at the back of the church, leaving John standing there dejected. After a few moments, an angry Jack followed her. John sat in a pew near the top of the church. Liz watched the door waiting to see Maria enter. Maria was now twelve. Liz hadn't seen her since Nonie died nearly two years earlier.

She saw Molly enter the church with her husband, a young woman and two children. They walked slowly towards the top of the church. With a shock Liz realised that the young woman was Maria. How she had grown! She was almost as tall as Liz now. She looked far more mature than her years. Her long chestnut hair reached her waist. She had grown even prettier if that was possible. Today, her sad eyes were tearstained. Shortly afterwards the priest began the ceremony. Afterwards, the pallbearers carried the pine coffin out of the church, followed by Molly, her family and Maria. Liz watched as Maria walked down the aisle behind Patsy's coffin. As the little group passed Liz and Jack, Maria saw Liz. With a start, Jack realised that Maria was Liz's daughter. His anger resurfaced when he saw John Flynn a few paces behind Maria. Liz touched Maria on the arm as she passed. Through red-rimmed eyes, Maria managed a little smile.

Jack and Liz followed the mourners out of the darkened church into the brilliant sunshine. Jack grabbed Liz roughly by the arm. People turned and stared in surprise, John included.

'You're coming home with me now,' Jack whispered in her ear as he pulled her by her shawl, away from the crowd. Liz struggled out of his grasp, the shawl falling on the ground. She bent down to pick it up, and then she turned on him.

'I told you before, don't ever touch me again,' she hissed angrily through bared teeth.

'You better get in the trap now if you know what's good for you. See these people here; I don't know them and I don't give a tuppeny toss about them. You wait till I get you home,' he said in a low voice, his nose nearly touching hers as he looked down at her. She looked helplessly towards the crowd as they stood around the church grounds. Maria was watching them, along with John, Molly and her family.

Embarrassed, Liz threw her shawl across her shoulders as she quickly climbed into the trap. Jack untied the reins and climbed in beside her. As Jack flicked the reins, Liz looked towards the dispersing crowd again and saw John standing near the gate, watching her.

John had been on the point of marching over to the couple Jack grabbed Liz roughly. He stopped himself in time. He knew it would only make things worse for Liz. He watched helpless, as they scuffled with each other and the threatening manner in which Jack spoke to Liz. When they got into the trap, he caught her eye, could sense the fear and the hopelessness she felt. How he longed to go after her. He never stopped loving her and he knew now, he never would.

After picking Will up at her parents', Liz, Jack and Will continued on to the farm in Inniscarra. Will detected the frosty atmosphere between his parents. Although they didn't speak much to each other, he hardly ever saw any hostility between them. Liz actually jumped from the trap as soon as it had stopped in the middle of the yard and ran into the house. Will stared after her then looked at his father who looked furious. Will was surprised to see his father march into the kitchen without unharnessing the pony. Will slowly got down from the trap and walked towards the kitchen where he could hear his father shouting angrily at his mother. Carefully opening the kitchen door he sidled in.

'You'd better admit the truth now. The real reason why you wanted to go to that bloody funeral!' He yelled at her back.

Liz was standing, looking out the kitchen window, trembling. She wasn't in the mood for Jack. She was utterly distressed. From Patsy's death, from seeing her estranged daughter and also from seeing John Flynn again. She realised she still loved him. She had a terrible sense of foreboding. She shook her head.

'Jack, not now please. I did nothing wrong.'

'You did nothing wrong! You meet up with the …man you had a relationship with, whose bastard you gave birth to…'

Liz spun around, her temper rising. Then she caught sight of Will's frightened face.

'Jack can't you see you're scaring Will? Won't you stop this now? It's not going to do any good dragging up the past now.'

'It's about time he knew exactly what his mother is,' he replied in a menacing voice. He turned and looked at the frightened boy cowering near the kitchen dresser.

'Will, I hate to be the one to tell you, but it's about time you heard the truth.'

'No, leave him alone. You're frightening him!' Liz cried as she made to cross the room. Jack grabbed her by the arm; his face contorted with rage, his eyes wild with hate, and pushed her hard. With a scream, she fell in a heap beside the table.

'Mam!' cried Will as he rushed to help her, 'Da, what did you do that for? Leave her alone.'

'You wouldn't say that if you knew the truth,' he replied callously. Will helped Liz to her feet. A trickle of blood stained the corner of her mouth. She wiped her mouth with the palm of her hand. Crying, Will put his arm around his mother's shoulders. She looked at Jack. Suddenly, she was no longer afraid. She raised her head defiantly.

'Before you were born, son, your mother had another baby. I told everybody she died at birth. The reason I did that....' Jack didn't get any further because with a scream, Liz lunged at Jack. She pulled his hair as hard as she could while he struggled to catch her by the arms. With one hand dragging his head downwards by the hair, she rained blow after blow on his back while kicking him on the shins over and over again. Jack eventually managed to grab her free hand and catching her fingers bent them backwards until screaming in pain, she let go of his hair. Still bending her fingers backwards, he continued to squeeze as she slumped to the floor, howling in pain. With a sickening crunch the fingers on Liz's left hand, snapped.

Will who was rooted to the spot with fear, suddenly sprang at his father and tried in vain to pull him off Liz.

'Dad, dad, leave her alone you broke her hand, stop! Please,' he sobbed.

With a swipe of his hand Jack slapped him away. Will fell against the table knocking over a chair. He sat on the cold flagstone floor, gasping for breath, tears pricking his eyes. Unsure of what to do and trembling in fear, he watched his father, breathing hard, suddenly let go of Liz and stepping over her. He staggered towards the open door, still breathing hard. Will immediately crawled to his mother's side where she lay crumpled in a faint. Carefully he raised her clammy head and brushed her hair from her forehead. He gently lifted her left hand, its twisted fingers already beginning to swell. Her eyes opened suddenly, wide with fear, and unable to talk, she opened and closed her mouth several times, the only sound coming out was a strange gurgling noise.

'You bastard! What's gotten into you? Why did you hurt her?' Will shouted at his father who was clutching his chest, his face red and puffy, his hair wild, his breath coming in deep gasps.

'The baby, that your mother had, was not fathered by me. Do you understand? You're mother had another man! She tried to pretend that the baby was mine. I only found out the day before it was born. The man, he worked for me, lived with his wife, yes, he was married! They lived in the cottage at the end of the lane. I gave him a job; a home and he took me wife as well! When the baby was born, it was a girl, I told your mother she could come home, but not the baby. Next day she came home without a word. Left her baby with her friends Nonie and Patsy. Oh, she had it all worked out, of course! The man, who she was with, was related to Patsy. So your mother had it all planned that she could see the baby any time she liked. And him as well! I told everybody that 'our' baby had died at birth, to protect HER! It was the happiest day of me life when you were born, Will. At least, I knew for sure that you were me own,' Jack gasped, tears running down his cheeks, still breathing hard.

Half sitting up, supported by Will, a crying Liz whispered,

'Why don't you tell him the rest? Well? I committed a sin. I know I made a mistake. A terrible, terrible mistake. A lot of people got hurt but, tell me, how long more will I be punished? For the last twelve years I have been paying a terrible price, over and over again. The only good thing, the only thing that keeps me going is my son. Without you, Will, I have nothing to live for...'

'So, my father is telling the truth?' Will asked, hurt and disbelief clearly showing on his tearstained face. Liz, holding her injured hand clasped to her chest, sat up straighter. Tears in her eyes, she reached out her good hand to stroke Will's face. He pulled away from her and looked at the floor.

'Will,' she whispered crying, 'they are other things too. I wanted to protect you. I didn't want this to happen. I....'

Jack's sudden moan interrupted her. Will and Liz looked at Jack, just as he bent over, eyes squeezed tight in pain, clutching his chest. He slowly slumped to his knees and keeled over on the hard stone floor.

'Will, help me. I can't ...breathe. Go ... and get... your uncle Pat.... Quick!' he gasped, his breath coming in deep gulps. Hesitating for just a second, Will sprang to his feet and ran out to the barn. Saddling the horse quickly, he jumped on the Clydesdale's back and galloped out of the yard.

Liz looked at Jack warily. He looked back at her.

'Why did you do that, Jack? You have destroyed everything and hurt people. What will become of us all now?' Liz asked sadly, as she crawled over to where Jack lay, her injured hand hampering her. She sat beside him and gazed at his face scrunched in pain. His face was a strange grey pallor, his eyes dilated, lips tinged with blue. A solitary tear rolled out of the corner of his eye, down his cheek.

'I loved ya, Liz. More than you'll ever know. I couldn't believe that I was married to the most beautiful woman in Ireland. I wanted to kill John Flynn, because not only did he father your baby, he was much younger and better looking than me. I- I couldn't compete with him. I knew he loved you. He still does. I saw your daughter today. Maria. She's the head off you, Liz. I wish...I wish, now, that...' he broke off as he squeezed his eyes tight and started to sob quietly, his breath getting shallower. Liz reached out her good hand and gently lifted his clammy head onto her lap. Tears ran down her face, mingling with blood from her swollen lip, as she looked into his eyes.

'Jack, I made one mistake, which I was never going to do again. I hurt you, I hurt Nellie, and I lost my only daughter. John Flynn respected you, Jack. I.. I cared about you too and I know how much I hurt you. But, we can move on now. I don't want to fight with you any more. We have a son. Things will get better, we'll get the doctor for you and, and...,' she stopped as great gulps engulfed her. Jack was looking at her, his expression soft. In the distance they could hear the sound of horse's hooves approaching.

'No, Liz, this is the end. I...I'm not going to make it. There is one thing you can do for me.... before...I...go.'

'What?' She asked, stroking his forehead.

'Forgive me. For.... everything I did to... you. I really.... hurt you,... made your life hell. I'm sorry for...hurting you. I love...' he gasped, 'you.'

Horses hooves sounded outside the kitchen and footsteps hurried towards the door. Will, his uncle Pat and his two cousins Patrick and Danny, both in their late teens, burst into the kitchen and stopped. Liz was huddled on the floor, her hand twisted and swollen. Lying on the floor, his head cradled in her lap, lay Jack. His glassy eyes stared heavenwards; his breathing had stopped, forever. Liz was weeping openly over his dead body.

'I... forgive you. Goodbye...Jack,' she sobbed, stroking his forehead lovingly.

Pat walked to Liz and carefully lifted her up off the floor. Will walked over and knelt beside his father. He leaned over and picked up Jack's lifeless hand, already growing cold. He suddenly bent down and embraced his father as great choking sobs ripped through his body. Pat gently placed a weeping Liz on the sugan chair by the hearth.

'Dad, Dad, wake up. Wake up! Please, please,' Will howled. Pat knelt beside his nephew and his brother in law.

He closed Jacks eyes and put his arm around his grief stricken nephew. Just then Dr White entered through the open door with a farmhand, sent by Pat to fetch him. He knelt beside Jack and taking his limp hand, felt for a pulse. He turned to Pat and shook his head grimly.

'I'm sorry Will. He's gone,' the doctor said patting the grief stricken sobbing boy on the head. He turned to look for Liz and caught sight of her slumped in the chair by the hearth. Looking closer he noticed the injured hand, the bloody mouth and the listless appearance. He walked over to her and was shocked at the condition she was in. He carefully lifted up her hand and examined her fingers. Four fingers were clearly broken, a jagged piece of bone sticking out an awkward angle from her middle finger. More people entered the kitchen, among them Liz's parents.

*   *   *   *

Liz woke up to the sound of keening. How long had she slept? Pain shot through her left hand. She held it up and examined the splint, fashioned from pieces of wood and wrapped around each of her broken fingers with strips of white muslin. Her hand rested on a flat piece of wood also bound firmly with muslin. It all came flooding back to her in the darkened room. Dressed in her nightgown, she struggled out of bed. She felt faint and weak and her legs felt shaky. She ached all over and she had a pounding headache. Gingerly she walked to the closed bedroom door. A feeling of nausea washed over her. She opened the door and stopped as she took in the scene. In the dim candlelit kitchen Jack was laid out in his best suit, in a plain pine coffin, on the kitchen table, in the centre of the floor. The chairs were pushed back against the walls. Lighted candles were placed all around the coffin. A peat fire burned in the grate. Jack's sister Cait who was weeping, her husband Pat and their eight children and two grandchildren, were seated around the kitchen along with Will, Liz's parents and her brothers and other mourners. Local women, wearing black shawls, were keening in unison, in steady high-pitched voices. The kitchen door was open and the crowd had spilled outside. Everybody turned to stare at Liz. Liz's mother walked towards her. She held out her arms to Liz who didn't move.

'Liz love, how are you? How's your poor hand? Whatever happened? We asked Will but he hasn't said a word since yesterday, when his poor father died,' Liz's mother said softly, stroking Liz's arm, 'Poor Jack. He had a heart attack, Dr White said. You were out cold yesterday when we came. The doctor put the splint on your broken fingers. Jack will be removed to Ballincollig church tomorrow and buried in the graveyard next to the church the day after.'

Liz was watching Will. He looked up once and then looked away. Liz wanted to go to him. She opened her mouth to call him but no words came out. She tried to go to him but her mother held her back.

'There, there, a stor. Would you like a cup of tea? Aine, come over and help me with Liz,' Mrs Moran called to her daughter in law. Aine came over and gently steered Liz in the direction of the bedroom while Mrs Moran went to pour a cup of tea. With a last glance at Will, Liz allowed Aine to lead her back to her bed.

Chapter Thirteen

A cool breeze blew across the graveyard as the mourners gathered near the open grave. Liz felt a bit stronger today. Dressed in black from her boots to her caipin lasa, she stood at the side of the grave. Will stood at the foot of the grave between his uncle Pat and cousin Danny. Liz glanced at him. Will hadn't come near her or spoken to her since his father died three days ago. Liz herself had barely uttered two words since Jack died. It was hard to believe that only three days ago, she had been at Patsy's funeral. Little did she know her husband would die the same day.

An image of the strange creature she had seen last week came back to her now. It must have been the banshee after all, warning of an imminent death. And the cock crowing in the middle of the night; Jack had been right. He knew a death would occur in the family.

'Liz, Liz can you hear me? It's over love, come, your father and me will take you home. Pat is taking Will,' Mrs Moran gently led Liz by the arm away from the graveside as the two gravediggers began to shovel earth on top of the coffin in the grave. She glanced back at the grave. Will was standing in the same place staring at his father's grave.

*　　　*　　　*　　　*

Liz sat at the kitchen table while her mother hung the kettle on the swinging crane. Her father was standing at the open door waiting for Will and Pat to come. Liz could hear the pony's hooves trotting up the lane. Mr Moran stepped out in the yard talking to Pat. Will opened the door and walked in. Liz stood up shakily.

'Will love, I- I've hardly seen you. Come here darling, I…' she began.

'NO! I never want to talk to you again. You killed him. You killed my father. I hate you.'

Mr Moran and Pat rushed into the kitchen when they heard Will shouting.

'What the devil is going on here?' demanded Mr Moran.

'She killed him. It's all her fault! They had a fight, the day me da died. He told me, he told me what SHE did,' Will was hysterical now, glaring and pointing at his mother.

Liz was speechless. She shook her head. It was like being stuck in the middle of a nightmare.

'Ya, MOTHER, why don't you tell them the truth,' Will continued trembling with anger.

'Will, have you taken leave of your senses? Your father is hardly cold in the grave. Have some respect and for you're mother an' all,' Mrs Moran said.

'My father told me that she...she had another man. Before I was born. And she had a baby. And she was trying to pretend the baby was me Da's but it wasn't. It was a man who worked for him, who lived in the old cottage. The baby was born and Da told everybody that the baby died. But it didn't die. SHE, gave the baby to her friends Nonie and Patsy in Little Island, 'cos the man was related to them,' Will gushed angrily glaring at his shocked mother.

His eyes were wet with tears.

'Will, please you don't know what really happened...' Liz began, her knees beginning to give way. She sat down heavily.

Her father strode across to her and leaned over her.

'Is this true?' he asked her in a low growl. She looked at the floor, unable to speak.

'Answer me, is it true?' he shouted as he lifted up her chin roughly. She stared at him with a dazed expression as she began to cry.

'Dad, please....'

He raised his hand to strike her but Pat caught his outstretched hand in time, and pulled him back.

'Don't hit her Michael. Can't ya see the state she's in?' Pat said.

Liz's mother slowly crossed the floor and sat down heavily in the chair beside her daughter. Her eyes were wet with tears.

'Liz, Love, your baby, your little girl Maria, you said she died. How could you? How could you tell us that your baby, our little granddaughter, was dead? Where is she now? Please a cailín, you have to tell us,' her mother begged taking Liz's good hand in hers.

Struggling to control herself, Liz took a few deep breaths and looked around as every pair of eyes were on her.

'Ya, it's true,' she whimpered in a defeated voice, 'I had a..an affair with John Flynn. It was only the one time it happened. I got a fright when the doctor said I was going to have a baby. John Flynn guessed it was his baby and the day before I had her there...there was a big fight between Jack and John and me. Jack nearly killed me. He broke my wrist too, remember? Anyway, he told John and Nellie to leave. When Maria was born, he came into the hospital and said he was bringing me home but I...I couldn't bring my...my baby home,' Liz broke down as great choking sobs tore through her body. Nobody spoke. After a few minutes she wiped her face with her sleeve and continued.

'Jack had already told ye all that my baby died. I had no choice but to come home 'cos I was very sick after the beating I got, an' the birth. He forbade me to ever see my baby again. I didn't want to live anymore. I begged Jack many times over the years to let me bring her home, but he wouldn't. The doctor warned me not to have any more babies because my womb was badly damaged. One night, not long after the birth, Jack came home drunk from the pub and ....he...raped me. I couldn't believe it. As ye know, Will was born early. Will,' she said, turning to her son, 'you gave me the strength to live. You are my reason for living and I am truly sorry for everything. Jack forgave me just before he died and asked me to forgive him. We made our peace at last, after twelve years. Now I beg you, to forgive

185

me also. I love you so much.'

Will had sat crying quietly, his face like stone, as he listened to his mother. His whole world had been turned upside down in just three days. He lost his father and as he turned to look at his mother, tears streaming down his face, he knew he had lost his mother too. He knew he could never forgive her. He jumped up, ran out of the open door and headed towards the fields.

'Will, don't go!' Liz cried, struggling to her feet. Her mother helped her to sit down again as she sobbed hysterically. For a few minutes, the only sound that could be heard was Liz crying.

'You deserved everything you got, you whore!' Michael hissed, 'Come on Peggy, we're going home. Pat. Will you go find the lad? I will never set foot inside this house again. And you, you're no daughter of mine. Come on Peggy.'

Liz's mother looked at her daughter sadly. Liz nodded at her mother. Her mother suddenly threw her arms around her daughter and clasped her to her as she cried into her hair. Liz broke away.

'Go on mam, I'll be all right. Look after yourself. I love you and I always will,' Liz said crying. Her mother was also crying as she squeezed Liz's hand one last time.

'I love you too, a stor, may God be with you,' Mrs Moran straightened up and walked out to where her husband was waiting impatiently in the pony and trap. The sound of the pony's hooves faded into the distance.

'Liz,' Pat said kindly, 'I'll go and get Will and bring him to my place for tonight. All right? I'll call up sometime tomorrow. I'm very sorry for everything's that's happened. Look after yourself. Get some rest eh?'

He walked out the door and pulled it out behind him. Seconds later the sound of hooves disappeared down the lane. Wearily, Liz put her arm on the table and rested her head on it as finally, the dam inside her broke, and a torrent of grief unleashed itself.

It was a sunny day as Liz walked out of the kitchen door. Nonie and Nellie waved to her from the garden. Beside them Will and Maria were laughing as they chased each other. She smiled at them.

'Liz, come and say hello to our guests,' called Jack jovially from behind her. She turned and smiled at him. Patsy and John were standing beside him; all three were drinking bottles of Murphy's. John was looking at her, love shining in his eyes. She stared at him. Suddenly, the sky turned dark grey. Out of the corner of her eye she saw Patsy begin to fade slowly before her eyes. She blinked and looked again. He was nearly gone. She backed away and walked back to the garden. Nonie was beginning to fade also and Nellie. Maria and Will vanished in an instant.

'Will! Maria! Come back!' she called, frightened.

She turned and walked back to the men. Patsy was gone. Jack was beginning to fade now.

'John, what's happening? Why is everybody leaving?'

He smiled at her, lovingly.

'They're dead. Remember? And Will and Maria don't belong to you any more. It's just me and you now, my love.'

'No. No. I want everybody back. I won't hurt them again. Please come back, Jack and Nonie. Patsy, Nellie, please!'

Liz woke with a start when the cock crowed. She was still at the kitchen table. She moved stiffly, blinking in the early morning light. It was all a dream. She sat up and rubbed her face. It felt sticky and grubby. Her eyes were swollen and crusty. She felt cold and sweaty. In the last few days she'd lost not only her husband, but also her son and her entire family. What was she to do now? She didn't know how to run a farm.

'Pat said he'd call today with Will, so I'll wait till he

comes, ya, that's what I'll do. It's too early now so, I'll make myself a cup of tea and wait,' she thought.

At twelve o clock, Liz heard the sound of hooves approaching.

At last, Will was coming back. She'd have to sit down with him and talk about what they were going to do. She tried to straighten her crumpled clothes and flicked her mane of hair off her face, patting it gently. She smiled, as she looked anxiously at the kitchen door opening, eager to see Will. The door opened and Pat walked in, a solemn expression on his face. He closed the door behind him.

'Where's Will?' asked Liz her smile vanishing. Taking off his cap, he sat opposite her.

'Liz, Will doesn't want to come back here. I tried to reason with him, make him see sense.'

'But, he must come home. He's all I have left. I'll go with you and talk to him,' Liz said.

Pat shook his head sadly.

'Will refuses to speak to you, Liz, I'm sorry. Now, about the farm, you know it has passed on to Will now that poor Jack, may he rest in peace, is gone. Will has asked me to take it on and work it until he is older. But Liz, I don't know how to say this, but you see, Will wants you to leave…'

'Leave?' Liz said, unable to believe what she was hearing.

'Yes. As I said, I tried to reason with him but he said…that he never wants to see you again.'

Liz left out a sob as tears sprang to her eyes. Was there no end to this nightmare?

'But, where doe's he expect me to go? What doe's he expect me to do?'

'He has instructed me to give you a sum of money to help you out.'

Liz couldn't believe her ears. She shook her head defiantly.

'No, no, this is not right! I am his mother; He is the child! He can't order me around like that! I'm going up to talk to him now,' Liz said getting up from the table. Pat got up too.

'Liz, it's no good. He won't talk to you under any circumstances. I tried talking to him; he blames you for his father dying. And he has rights. He is the only son. Now that his father is dead, all this belongs to Will.'

'What about my rights? This is my home, and my son is telling me, I have to get out. Where am I supposed to go? And I have broken fingers. I can hardly stand from the weakness. Tell me, where am I supposed to go?' Liz cried hysterically.

Pat shifted uncomfortably.

'I'm real sorry Liz, but that's the way things are. You know that. I have two hundred pounds here for you,' Pat said, taking out a bundle of rolled up notes from his trouser pocket, 'That will help you to… well to get some place to live 'till you get on your feet. Here, take it.'

Liz looked from his face to the bundle of notes, tears running down her cheeks. She would not beg again. Standing up straight, she held out her hand for the notes. Pat put them into her outstretched hand. She looked him in the eye defiantly.

'Thank you, Pat. Will you tell my son, I will pack today and I will leave here first thing tomorrow morning? Tell him, tell…him, I'll wait here till then in the hope that he will call to see me. And will you tell him… I love him with all my heart and I always will,' Liz said crying again.

Pat looked at her sadly.

'I'll tell him. And Liz, I'm really, really sorry about all this business. Cait and myself always had great time for ya. You could …. Stay with us 'til….,' he began.

'It's all right Pat. You have a house full already. I – I couldn't live there and not here, but thanks for offering,' Liz said.

'We'll miss ya, Liz. God bless you, and be with you. Will you write and let us know where you are?' Pat asked his eyes glistening with tears. Liz nodded, unable to speak. She stood on tiptoe and kissed him lightly on the cheek.

'I'll be off now, goodbye,' with that, Pat put back on his cap and with one last look at Liz, he nodded at her, then turned and walked out the door. For a long time, Liz stood and stared at the kitchen door, the rolled up pound notes clasped in her hand.

Next morning in the early morning sunshine, Liz brought out the last of her bags and heaved it up onto the trap. She had risen at cockcrow this morning and after boiling a big pot of water, had a leisurely wash in the tin bath. She chose her red skirt, and her new fitted white high-necked blouse. She brushed her long black hair carefully and let it hang loose, unable to tie it up with one hand.

After thoroughly cleaning the house, she went to the loose brick at the back of the mantelpiece. Carefully, she pulled out a brown paper package and placed it on the kitchen table. She pulled out the black leather drawstring purse and counted the collection of shillings and pence; her wages from her time working in Crowley's. Over a hundred pounds. Next, she opened her collection of letters. Most of them were from Nonie. One or two were from Molly, and a few from Maria. Maria. Liz smiled as she read the simple notes written by her daughter. Liz contemplated visiting her daughter in Little Island and telling her who she really was. That she, Liz was her mother. At last she could be with her daughter. But, what if Maria rejected her? Like her son did, and her husband, and her parents? She closed her eyes. She shook her head. No, I can't take any more hurt. Maria is with the people she grew up with. She has friends. She wouldn't want to go away with a stranger, even if it was her real mother.

She sighed. She gathered up the letters and her wedding ring, wrapped them in the brown paper and placed it back in the opening. She pushed the brick firmly back into place. Taking a blank sheet of paper she composed a short note to Will. Long afterwards, she couldn't remember what she wrote. She placed the folded solitary sheet of paper on the kitchen table. She picked up her shawl and wrapped it around her shoulders, suddenly cold.

Now strangely calm, she strolled into the garden and sat on the wooden seat. She had no idea where she was going to go, although she had already decided to head for the city. There was nothing for her here anymore. She gave a sardonic laugh. How unlucky can one woman get? To lose two children in a lifetime, only, her children didn't die, they were alive. She swallowed back a sob as another wave of crying beckoned. There was no point in crying any more. There was nobody to hear her. Nobody to comfort her. Will hadn't come back at all, despite her prayers. She got up and walked slowly around the garden, savouring every smell, every sound, every flower and tree, committing them to memory. The garden was always spectacular this time of the year. Overlooking the River Lee, today it was a shimmering blue as it roared onwards towards the city. She wandered around the cobblestone yard and the sheds, stood beneath the old oak tree, and looked down the deep well. She smiled as she looked at the ESB pole, remembering the day when it was put there.

Dan Lucey on his way up the lane, stopped when he saw Liz heading towards the fields. He had heard tales in the public house. Terrible stories about Liz and some other fella. He didn't know if they were true or not. All he cared about was his good friend Jack McCarthy had died. A heart attack, some said; others implied something more sinister. Dan had seen Liz at the funeral. She looked terrible. And her hand was in a splint. That's why he had waited until the funeral was over before calling on Liz. She'd need help now to run the farm. Dan's eyes widened as he noticed the pony and trap harnessed and ready to set off. Stranger still, there were several bags stacked neatly on the seat and floor of the trap. Looks like someone is going on a journey, he thought. He looked at Liz again in the distance. 'Tis herself is going away, he thought sadly. Unsure of what to do for a few seconds and consumed with a strange sadness, he turned and walked back down the lane without a backward glance.

Liz strolled to the nearest field and closing her eyes, she took slow deep energising breaths, drinking in the clean air. She felt a new tranquillity, a new determination. She was free, for the first time in her life; she was free.

*   *   *   *

Rose had sat and listened in stunned silence, hardly believing her ears at times. At times she put her hand to her mouth to stop crying.

'I remember John Flynn. I met him a few times with his wife Nellie. They were at Nonie's funeral, and again at Patsy's funeral. He was my father? Molly used say... well; Molly said some nasty things about you, called you horrible names. She could be very vindictive. When I asked her who my father was she said she didn't know.'

'Nonie didn't tell anybody about you, except that she adopted you. Nobody ever asked where she got you,' Liz paused, ' you are married? Have a family?'

Rose smiled.

'Yes. Tim and me have been married twenty-five years. We have ten children.'

Liz's eyes widened in surprise.

'Goodness! Ten?' she exclaimed.

Rose smiled.

'My eldest is nearly twenty five- my youngest is four months. It's not easy. I'm a grandmother...'

'A grandmother? Oh this is a most surprising day. How

many grandchildren, dear?'

*'Five. Four boys and one little girl,' Rose announced
proudly.*

*'That makes me a great grandmother. Oh dear, I must
be older than I thought! My, what a family. Was that one of
your children with you today?'*

*'Yes that's Adrienne. She's eleven, tripped and broke
her finger. She probably is my quietest child. Doesn't speak
much. We call her 'the bookworm'. She's always reading.'*

*Both women paused. Rose looked around the ward. Liz
looked forlornly at her long lost daughter.*

'Are you happy, Maria?'

*Rose turned away while she pondered the question.
Mentally, she journeyed back over her life. Was she happy?
She turned to her mother, a woman who she had thought
about, for nearly forty years.*

*'Happy? I don't know what happy is, to be honest. I
seem to have had a hard life for one reason or another all
my life. Things... that's how they turned out. I'm not meant
to be happy. Life is hard, rearing the children. Tim is a good
man I suppose. Very easy going. Maybe I do love him,' she
whispered, 'Did you ever meet John Flynn again?'*

*Liz folded her hands together and sighed wistfully. She
looked out the window at the drab grey sky. The sound of the
traffic came to her, contrasting with the tranquillity of the
ward. Rose waited patiently for her newly found mother to
reply. She glanced at the elderly woman as she lay
motionless, her eyes closed.*

'Yes,' she whispered.

Chapter Fourteen
April 16 1941
Belfast

Sirens wailing, the ambulances and fire brigades headed northward as they raced along the streets of Belfast. It was six o clock Easter Tuesday morning. Shrieking men, women and children, most of them in their nightclothes were running for cover, fearing more bombs. In the distance, thick black plumes of smoke billowed upwards. Liz, in her starched white nurses uniform, black cape and tin hat over her now shoulder length hair, clutched the dashboard as the driver swerved around another corner.

She stared incredulously at the sight before her. The ambulance screeched to a halt behind a row of ambulances and fire brigades. Up ahead orange flames climbed upwards amid a cloud of dense black smoke. The early morning air was punctuated with the sounds of people screaming in terror. The entire street had been reduced to a heap of burning rubble. Belfast had been bombed from the air only hours earlier. Liz spotted a dented blackened street name plaque jutting out of the rubble. Greencastle. She looked at the driver and the other ambulance man. They were equally shocked. They had driven up from Dublin along with other ambulances and fire engines. The request had come from the Taoiseach, Eamonn De Valera, himself, within an hour of the bombing, which began at two a.m.

For a few moments, it reminded Liz of the burning of Cork, all those years ago. She forced herself back to the present. She jumped down from the khaki coloured ambulance and took in the devastating scene. Screams of pain, terror and anguish filled the early morning air. Her colleagues Paddy the driver, and John stood silently next to her, gaping in horror at the people fleeing from the bombed street. Seeing the occupants of the other emergency service vehicles moving forward to assist the injured, Liz sprang into action.

'Come on, the fire engines are trying to get nearer to put out the fires. Let's help the injured.'

Liz, Paddy and John scrambled over mounds of smoking rubble and debris towards the victims. People littered the streets, clothes blackened by the force of the bombs. The dead were easy to spot, their vacant eyes staring glassily, covered in blood. Injured people were screaming in pain and shock and calling for loved ones. Paddy stopped to help a woman, covered in blood; her eyes open wide with shock. He grasped her by the arm and led her back to the ambulance. Looking around at the scene of carnage, Liz spotted a blood-covered hand sticking out from a pile of debris. She ran towards it.

'John, help me. There's somebody under here,' she shouted as she started to pull stones and rubble away from the victim uncovering more of the bloodied limb. John ran to help her and together they pulled away heavy pieces of masonry. Carefully, Liz grasped the blackened limb and gently pulled. Suddenly she staggered backwards still clutching the arm. To her horror she saw that it wasn't attached to a body. She screamed. John stopped digging with his bare hands and stared in shock at Liz standing still holding the bodyless limb. Appalled, she dropped it on the road. She looked at John. John continued to dig for a few more minutes, and then slowly he stepped backwards.

'We can't do anything more for that one. I found another body part under the stones. Lets walk on for now.'

For the next few hours the emergency services from both Dublin and Belfast worked side-by-side, locating people buried under what were once houses. Ambulances ferried the injured to the local hospitals. The dead were put to one side temporarily, the rows of bodies increasing alarmingly. The walking wounded waited patiently, sitting on boulders as the nurses and ambulance personnel attended seriously injured patients. As the day dawned sunny and warm, the heavy pall of grey smoke temporarily obliterated the sun. The helpers struggled on weary, tiredness and shock beginning to set in. The unmistakable stomach-churning stench of death was everywhere. People still searched for loved ones, but now it was in silence. Most of the fires had been extinguished now, the cloud of smoke slightly lifting.

At five thirty, Liz and Paddy carried a timber-framed stretcher bearing a badly injured young woman to the ambulance. Gently, they slid the patient into the ambulance, which contained another three patients sitting on one side, leaning against each other. John was still helping the injured, venturing farther away. Liz closed the back door and Paddy put the ambulance into gear and slowly pulled away to make another trip to the nearby hospital. Liz wiped her arm across her sweaty brow. Her crisp white uniform was now a blackened bloody mess and her face was streaked with soot and sweat. They hadn't had time to eat all day and water was in short supply. Her throat was dry.

'Liz!'

She whirled around in surprise. A tall black streaked man, in a fireman's black trousers held up by braces, over what was once a white shirt, black boots and tin hat, strode purposely towards her. Squinting against the sun and smoke, she peered at the blackened figure. Her eyes widened in surprise. She gasped.

'John! John Flynn! What are you doing here?' she asked, as he stood in front of her. He too looked weary, his face equally streaked with black. He smiled grimly.

'Same as you, by the looks of it. What a disaster! Hundreds of people dead. Hundreds more injured. I came up in the middle of the night with the Dublin fire brigade. How many more bloody bombs are those Nazis going to drop on us? So much for Ireland stayin' neutral! There have been bombs dropped practically all over the country now. Sure, only a few weeks ago three people were killed in Carlow when a Nazi bomb fell on their house, and now this. When will it end? When will this damn 'Emergency' end? Well,

I'm glad to see a friendly face in the middle of this hell on earth. And a beautiful face at that. I heard about Jack. I'm sorry Liz. I actually felt sorry… for him. About what happened.'

Liz looked downwards at her feet.

'Well, that's all in the past now. Anyway, we got orders to go back. To Dublin, I mean. You see I live in Dublin now. It's a long story. I really must go look for our man. We'll be leaving soon.'

'We're going back soon too. You look exhausted. Me too,' he shifted awkwardly from one foot to the other as he glanced around, 'Liz, could we …meet, maybe when we get back to Dublin? To catch up, you know?'

Liz looked up into his blackened face. She still felt that thrill she felt all those years ago. A smile slowly made its way to her full lips as her tired face began to redden.

'Ya, I'd like that. I don't know what shifts I'll be working this week. This bombing has thrown us all up in a heap, but I work in St. Kevin's Hospital, on James St. I'm a nurse. Oh, by the way I changed my name back to my maiden name, Moran.'

'I'll find you, rest assured. I suppose we'd better help more of these poor people before we leave. Are you coming?'

Together, they walked towards the debris littered streets, milling with hundreds of Emergency personnel, volunteers and locals.

Chapter 15

John hesitated on the street outside St Kevin's Hospital. He wore his good grey serge suit, white shirt and navy tie. His oiled hair was neatly combed back. He looked up at the tall grey building. It was two days after the bombing of Belfast. He had read in the Irish Press that over seven hundred people died in the bombing and over fifteen hundred were injured. He was still haunted by the images of the dying and the injured. Taking a deep breath, he bounded up the steps and in the main door of the hospital. Just inside the door on the left was the reception desk. A slim uniformed nurse in her early thirties, sat behind the desk, head down, writing. John approached the desk. He cleared his throat.

'Excuse me, I'm looking for a nurse.'

The nurse looked up and smiled.

'Well you've come to the right place. Hospital! Lots of nurses here!'

'Right. Her name is Liz? Or maybe Elisabeth, McCart.... Moran?' John asked hopefully.

'Liz Moran? From Cork? Ya I know her. A good nurse. I'll just check the roster to see if she's here,' she pulled a hard covered book towards her and flicked through the pages.

'I'm afraid she's not here at the moment. She's due in tonight at eight and will work until eight in the morning. Sorry,' she said regretfully. Deflated, John ran his hand through his hair as he tried to think. He turned to the nurse again.

'Look, I'm sorry for bothering you, but I don't suppose you could tell me where she lives?' he pleaded. The nurse smiled coyly.

'Depends on who's asking,' she replied, nonchalantly.

'Well, my name is John Flynn, and Liz and me, we're old friends and....'

'I know who you are from Liz's description. She asked me to keep an eye out for ya, and if you came by to tell you she lives in Crane Street. Just around the corner. No 9. And if you were to go there now I'm sure you'll get a big welcome. Hi John, my name is Sinead. Liz and myself are good friends. Good luck!'

John's eyes shone with gratitude. He grasped her hand gratefully and shook it.

'Hello Sinead and thanks, I've got to run.'

John turned and ran out the door and down the steps. He knew Crane Street. He turned left and strode purposefully up the street, turned the corner and looked at the numbers on the doors. He walked along the row of three storey Georgian houses until he came to no 9. He looked up at the neat grey building with the bright red front door. In the distance he heard church bells chime. Twelve o clock. Slowly he walked up the steps to the front door. He grasped the lion shaped brass knocker and rapped it loudly three times. He waited. He turned and watched the horses and traps trotting up and down the busy street in the midday sunshine. He heard the door creak open behind him. He turned around ready to ask for Liz and found himself looking into those familiar blue eyes. She looked at him in surprise.

'John! How did you find me?' she smiled at him happily.

He smiled back.

'You have a very nice friend at the hospital. Sinead?'

Liz opened her mouth wide then clamped her hand over it. Her face reddened in embarrassment.

'I never thought you'd…. come in, come in,' she stood back and held the door open for him. Gratefully he entered, his large frame almost brushing against her. Closing the door, she turned and led him up two flights of stairs to the first floor. Her flat door was open, she ushered him inside and closed the door. He looked around at the small, airy and neat living room. He could see a tiny kitchen area just off it.

There was one other door in the room, which obviously was the bedroom.

'Would you like a cup of tea, John?' Liz asked as she made her way to the kitchen.

John followed her.

'Ya, I'd like one please. This is a nice flat. I live on Bay View Avenue, just off the North Strand and unfortunately my flat is not half as nice as this,' John said still looking around. Liz put the kettle on the single gas ring and lit it with a match. The fluorescent blue flame flickered weakly.

'This might take a while. The tea, you know with the gas rationing. The Glimmer an' all that. I have some biscuits that I baked last week. How did you end up in Dublin, John? And in the fire brigade an' all!' Liz said as she got two cups and saucers from the shelf.

'Well, living in Kildare, it seemed natural to move to Dublin. At the start of the war, fire brigade personnel were needed. I was too old to join the army. So here I am. I don't know about you but I'm sick of this bloody war. Did you hear that that was the second bombing in Belfast? Only a week earlier the Dockside Road was bombed. There's the shipbuilding yard, engineering works, airplane factories, all contributing to the war effort. Northern Ireland wasn't expecting to be bombed; after all, Ireland is neutral. But we forgot Northern Ireland belongs to the English. I'm sick of the shortages, the rationing. That Hitler fella is a madman. If only the Yanks would join in, the war would be over sooner. But they're neutral too. Anyway, more importantly, how did you end up here in Dublin? Is your son Will with you? How old is he now?'

Liz's eyes suddenly looked sad. She said nothing as she carried the tray into the table in the centre of the living room. John sensed her sadness and her pain. She placed the teapot in the centre of the small circular table, covered in a white lace tablecloth. She pulled out a chair and sat down. John sat opposite her and watched as she poured the tea into the two

201

china cups.

'Will is fourteen now but regretfully he's not with me. It's a long story. I'm ....I'm not sure if I can talk about it. It still hurts so much,' she said without looking at him. Tears formed in her eyes.

John reached across the table and clasped her hand gently. She looked at him and saw the concern in his eyes.

'Tell me Liz. I can't take away your pain, but I'm here for you now. We're both free. We can't hurt anybody anymore. And I won't let anybody hurt you ever again. This time nothing will part us again, my love. I'll always be with you,' he said as tears appeared in his eyes. Clasping her hand tighter, he reached across the little table with his other hand and gently wiped her tear filled eyes. She closed her eyes as he gently rubbed the tears from her cheeks. The unexpected tenderness was too much for her. A sob escaped from her lips. Shakily, she took a sip of her tea. Taking a deep breath, she began to talk.

'The day of Patsy's funeral, Jack convinced himself that I had arranged to meet you there....'

For the next two hours John listened, sometimes in disbelief at Liz's misfortune.

'That day when I left the farm, for the last time, I still prayed Will would call to see me and tell me it was all a bad dream. I write to him every few months. Send him birthday presents, Christmas presents. I never get a reply. I still send money to Maria too, for her birthdays and Christmas, and sent her my address. I asked her to write. But she never did. I don't even know if she knows who I really am. Maybe that's why she doesn't reply. After I left the farm, I stayed in Cork city for a week in a lodging house. I knew I had to get out of Cork. I couldn't take the chance of bumping into my family or Will and they ignoring me. It would hurt too much. I decided to come to Dublin and train as a nurse. I used my maiden name, because I knew they wouldn't accept me if they knew I had been married and if I have children. I'm qualified now, passed my exams last year. The nuns at the hospital are very nice to me. I am even thinking of becoming a nun,' Liz half smiled through her tears. John was looking at her.

'Well, you can forget about becoming a nun,' he announced solemnly.

'What? Why?' Liz asked puzzled.

'Because, now that I've found you, I'm going to marry you and you can't become a nun if you're a married woman!'

Liz looked at him in astonishment. He pushed back his chair, got up and walked to Liz, pulling her out of her chair. He put his arms around her and embraced her gently. He kissed her hair softly.

'Marry me Liz!'

She hugged him.

'Yes,' she whispered in his ear. He squeezed her tight.

Chapter Sixteen

In the weeks that followed Liz and John were inseparable. They went to St Catherine's church and applied to be married. Liz had to present her Marriage Certificate and Jacks Death Certificate. John had to show his Marriage Certificate and Nellie's Death Certificate. The wedding was arranged for the 5th of August 1941. It was to be a low-key affair. Just Liz and John of course, and Liz's friend, Sinead, from the hospital, and John's friend Thomas from the Fire Brigade. Liz was staying on at her job at the hospital. Matron had told her she was too good a nurse to lose. John would move into Liz's flat after they got married. They spent many hours happily strolling hand in hand in Phoenix Park in the long hot evenings, or along O'Connell Street. Their affection and love for each other was clearly evident to their friends and colleagues. John often jokingly suggested he move into Liz's flat immediately, to which she'd playfully slap him. They were very excited about their forthcoming wedding and talked of little else.

'Do you think we should go to Cork, talk to Maria? Tell her the truth, because I don't even know if she knows who we are, that we are her real parents. She might come live with us,' Liz asked as she sipped her tea one afternoon in Bewleys. John drank his tea thoughtfully. He put down his cup and held her hand.

'Liz, Maria is fifteen, nearly sixteen. She's almost an adult. She must know the truth by now. I remember meeting her as a child. For ages I didn't realise who she was. I suppose I blanked it out of my mind. I had hurt Nellie so much and I swore I would make it up to her. I loved her very much you know,' he said softly looking at her directly. Liz nodded.

'I know John, I loved Nellie too. She was a beautiful person; kind and gentle. She loved you more than life itself. I was ashamed of how much we hurt her; she didn't deserve it. And yet she helped me when I needed her most. Don't ever be afraid to admit your feelings for your dear wife. I understand.'

'I know. It's just that I love you in a different way to the way I loved Nellie. Anyway, what I'm trying to say is, about Maria. I was totally charmed by her, she is a lovely young lady, and she has a lot of your ways. Your softness, your beauty, your strength. The day of Nonie's funeral, I saw you and Maria in the graveyard. I so wanted to talk to you, but Nellie was very sick by then. The journey on the train was tough on her. And I didn't want to upset her any more than she was. Anyway, you said yourself, you wrote to Maria and she didn't reply. The only life she knows is in Cork. She has Molly and her cousins and her own friends. Do you really think she would give everything up to come live with strangers? Because although we're her birth parents, that's what we are to her; strangers.'

Liz thought for a moment. She sipped her tea.

'Yes, I suppose you're right. But I'm going to write to her anyway and invite her up for the wedding, tell her the truth if she comes,' Liz said, she continued sipping her tea while the late afternoon sun streamed in the tall windows. Later, as they strolled hand in hand back to Liz's flat, they heard a strange sound from far off. It grew louder. A teenage couple in front of them suddenly looked upwards. Liz and John followed their gaze and stared in horror at the sight of about twenty airplanes, as they appeared high above Dublin city. John grabbed Liz by the arm and hurried her to a nearby tree. Cautiously they peered out from the cover of the oak tree at the planes as they flew overhead. People were running for cover in all directions. Everyone in Ireland was in a state of panic after the recent blitz on Belfast. After about an hour and no noisy explosions, Liz and John anxiously scanned the sky for the Luftwaffe planes but they had disappeared as quickly as they appeared.

On the evening of the thirtieth of May, John arrived at

Liz's flat, breathless. She opened the flat door to him, dressed in her new russet coloured skirt and a short sleeved beige blouse. The skirt was shorter than she was used to, falling just below the knee. John left a long low whistle as she twirled around to show it off.

'Liz love, you look beautiful. What a short skirt! I hope you don't get us arrested tonight.'

Liz pushed him on the arm laughing.

'This is the latest fashion, due to the rationing. I'm wearing my new pair of silk stockings. Well, my only pair!'

'I can see,' John said staring at Liz's shapely legs. She slapped him again laughing. He put his arms around her waist, lifted her up in his arms and swung her around as she squealed in delight. He smiled lovingly at her. She bent down and kissed him passionately on the lips. Gently he lowered her as he continued to kiss her. Eventually, they pulled away, their eyes locked, their arms still around each other.

'I love you so much Liz. I can't wait for you to be my wife. Please let me stay here tonight. I just want to lie beside you and wake up with you in my arms,' John whispered naked desire in his eyes. She continued to stare into his cornflower blue eyes, smiling.

'I love you too Mister John Flynn and in only nine more weeks I'll be Mrs John Flynn, so you'll have to be patient. The wait will be worth it! Now come on, let's go to the pictures!'

Hand in hand they skipped down the steps and strolled up James Street, heading towards the picture house, in the balmy evening sun. Later, they kissed passionately on the steps of Liz's flat.

'That was a good film wasn't it? Clark Gable is handsome isn't he?' Liz said dreamily, arms around John's neck. He pretended to scowl.

'Oh I see! 'Tis Clark you fancy is it? Well Vivien Leigh is a bit of all right. You be careful I don't run off to America

207

and marry her instead!' he said smiling. He looked into Liz's eyes again,

'Are you sure I can't come up for a cup of tea before I walk the three miles back to my poky little flat?'

'Don't try and make me feel guilty! Besides, I'm on the early shift tomorrow. Have to be in for eight. I need my beauty sleep. Goodnight love, I'll see you tomorrow after work,' Liz said kissing him again.

'Goodnight, sweetheart, sweet dreams,' John kissed her again, and reluctantly let her go. He walked down the steps, watched by Liz. He turned and smiled.

'I love you,' he said tenderly. Liz smiled and blew him a kiss.

'Love you too.'

She watched, smiling, as he walked swiftly up the street, then turned and walked up to her flat. She walked to the window and looked out at the evening sky, a conflagration of reds and golds. She smiled dreamily as she hugged herself, before closing the timber shutters.

*   *   *   *

A loud noise woke her from her sleep. She half sat up and listened. 'Must be dreaming,' she thought, and then lay down again. Ten minutes later as she was beginning to doze off, a loud bang shook the whole building. She jumped from her bed and ran to the window. She opened the timber shutters and pulled back the lace curtain. In the distance, she could see orange flames coming from two areas, black smoke billowing upwards. Another bang shook the building turning the sky red for a few moments as another bomb struck its target. She cowered as she heard the loud drone of an airplane flying low over the house.

'Oh God! No! We're being bombed. Dublin's being bombed!'

She dressed hurriedly and rushed from her flat. The

other occupants, Mr and Mrs Mullins, the elderly couple from upstairs, shuffled down as fast as they could. They looked terrified.

'We're being bombed Liz,' Mr Mullins announced unnecessarily.

'I know, lets go downstairs to Mrs Kelly the landlady. We'll have to get out of here, just in case,' Liz said as she tried to usher them downstairs. Mrs Kelly was just coming out of her flat on the ground floor, clad in her nightgown and slippers, curlers in her hair, held in place by a fine hairnet. The short round old woman looked frightened.

'What are we going to do? Where are we going to go?' she asked panic stricken, as the air raid sirens cut through the night air. Everyone looked to Liz for answers.

'I think we should stay here, in the hall, near the front door. We could be in more danger if we go out on the street,' she said. Just then the night was shattered by another loud bang. Mrs Mullins, in her late sixties, clung to her equally frightened husband. Mrs Kelly huddled beside them. Liz opened the front door a crack. People were running past in their nightclothes, screaming in terror, not knowing where they were going. She closed the door quietly. There seemed to be no explosions nearby, they seemed to be more towards the north side of the city. The sound of fire brigade and ambulance sirens could be heard above the wail of the air raid siren. John! The thought of John flashed through Liz's head. He wasn't due to work tonight but it being an emergency, he might have gone in.

Hours passed. One more loud bang was heard, though not as near as the previous ones. The little group huddled together on the stairs. Suddenly, the air raid siren stopped. Fire brigade and ambulance sirens continued to cut through the night air. The group waited for another half an hour. Liz stood up and stretched.

'I think it's safe to go back to bed now. I have to go to work in a few hours time. By rights I think I should go there now. Only thing is, the nurses on duty will need to be relieved at their usual time so I think I'll try get a few hours sleep. Ye should go back to bed, too,' Liz said suddenly tired. She yawned.

'Oh no, we couldn't go to sleep now, could we dear? We wouldn't make it down the stairs in time if the bombing started again,' Mrs Mullins announced in a shaky voice, holding tightly to her husbands arm.

'Well I can't sleep either. Why don't ye come into my flat? I'll make a nice cup of tea. I have a drop of meths for the primus. Come on. See ya in the mornin' Liz. You better get some sleep. You'll be busy by the looks of things. Goodnight,' Mrs Kelly said as she led the way to her flat.

'Goodnight,' Liz said as she went back to her own flat. She looked at the clock on the mantelpiece, five forty five. She lay on her bed and tried to sleep. It was difficult, with the sound of the sirens. Suddenly, the alarm went off at seven. She could only have been asleep for an hour. Still tired, she got out of bed and went to the window, opening the shutters. In the distance she saw great plumes of black smoke rising from the still smouldering buildings. She dressed quickly in her uniform. She ate a slice of bread and had a cup of milk then left to walk the short distance to the hospital. Two ambulances were parked outside the entrance to the hospital as she rounded the corner. Two stretchers were carried into the hospital, along with another two walking wounded. She quickened her step and ran into the hospital to be met by utter mayhem. Doctors, nurses, orderlies and ambulance men were running here and there. Injured patients were either lying down or sitting down while waiting on beds. Liz jumped right into the fray and tried to organise patients as more and more were brought in. Sinead, her friend who had been on the night shift, updated her. She was exhausted. Liz looked at her friend with concern.

'You go home now Sinead. You've done enough. I'll

take over now.'

'I'll stay another hour, that's about all I'll last anyway,' Sinead replied in a tired voice, as she turned to go back to work. Liz and Sinead worked frantically with the other hospital personnel. Sinead looked up as another patient was brought in on a stretcher. A grey hospital blanket covered the patient from head to toe. Sinead sighed. Another dead one. The dead ones were put in a little room down the corridor. She looked at her clipboard. Twenty-two dead bodies were brought in already. She pulled back the blanket to reveal whether it was male or female. The difficult task of identifying them would happen later. Some of the bodies unfortunately were blown to pieces. She looked at the bloodied male face. She began to write on her clipboard then stopped. She looked closely at the face of the dead man again. She swallowed hard as she looked around. Liz was tending an injured child. Sinead looked at the man again.

'Could you bring this one into Matrons office please? It's just over there. And shut the door behind you,' she instructed the puzzled orderlies.

Slowly, Sinead pushed through the throng towards Liz.

'Liz?' she called quietly.

Liz turned around.

'Yes, Sinead? Are you going away? I'll be with you in a minute,' Liz called as she dabbed at the open wound on the distressed little girl's forehead. She applied a dressing to it then put strips of sticking plaster on it to keep it in place.

'Liz, you must come with me now,' Sinead implored.

Liz quietly followed her through the throng, towards Matrons office. Sinead stopped outside the door. Liz stopped too. At that moment, Matron approached.

'Matron, please wait. Don't go in your office for a while,' Sinead said quickly.

Matron and Liz looked at her mystified. Sinead looked sadly at Liz.

'Liz, there was a body just brought in. It's in Matron's

office…' Sinead began.

'What the devil is a corpse doing in my office?' Matron demanded.

Sinead looked at Liz. A shiver went down Liz's spine.

'Liz, I don't know how to say this, but it's … John! I'm so sorry.'

Liz's heart pounded in her chest. All the noise and chaos in the background seemed to stop as she struggled to take it in. She swallowed hard as she looked at Sinead.

'John? But, how? Are you sure?' Liz babbled.

Matron opened the door to her office and pushed it in. Liz looked at the stretcher on the floor inside, covered by a grey blanket. Sinead bit her quivering lip as Liz slowly advanced towards the body. She stooped down. Catching the corner of the blanket, she slowly pulled it back to reveal John's bloody and swollen face, his open eyes glassy. Her hand flew to her mouth as she suppressed a scream. With a start she noticed he was in his pyjamas, once brown, now torn, blackened and bloody. She stared for a minute. Matron and Sinead had entered the room behind her and closed the door.

'John, John! Wake up. You can't be dead. We're getting married, remember, darling? We were going to be together forever. We love each other, so much, you can't be….' And then the tears came. She leaned over him and gathered his bloody blackened body to her as her body shook with anguished sobs. She rocked to and fro, John clasped tightly to her. Matron and Sinead looked on helplessly, Sinead with tears in her eyes. As her crying got louder, Matron went to her and gently tried to prise Liz away from her dead Fiancé, but she refused to let him go, her tears falling onto his injured blackened face. Matron looked at Sinead and nodded. Sinead knelt beside the grief stricken Liz. She put her arms around her friend and gently with Matron's help, managed to extricate the sobbing woman from the dead man. Weak from shock and grief, Liz allowed herself to be helped to the nearby chair. Matron carefully pulled the blanket over John's face. Crying, Sinead squeezed beside Liz, and put her arms around her. Liz clung to her friend as her whole life; all her dreams came crashing around her.

'I'll come home with you Liz, you need to go home now, there's nothing more you can do here,' Sinead whispered as she helped her friend stand up.

Supporting her friend, Sinead led Liz out of the office, through the milling people, out the door and down the noisy bustling street, in the early morning sunshine.

*   *   *   *

Liz sat in the front pew of the St Catherine's Church, the church where they were to be married. She glanced at the pine coffin a few feet away from her. She had placed a single red rose on top. The coffin contained all her dashed dreams. John was forty-four. Father O'Sullivan conducted the service. Sinead, Matron and a few of her colleagues, along with some of John's friends from the fire brigade sat in the seats behind. John had no living relations except for his secret daughter, Maria. Liz had thought about having him buried in Dublin so she could be near his grave. After giving it a lot of thought, she decided the only place he should be buried was in Kildare, next to his dear wife Nellie. She discovered that one of the bombs dropped by the Luftwaffe a week ago, had dropped directly on top of the North Strand next to John's street. John had been in bed asleep. Hadn't felt a thing. His chest had been ripped apart in a second. Other bombs had fallen on North Circular Road. Another bomb fell in Phoenix Park causing extensive damage to Aras an Uachtarain and the American Embassy. Twenty-eight people were killed in the bombing raid, and forty-five injured. De Valera was outraged and called upon the German Government for an explanation. Ireland was neutral and for almost a year now German bombs had 'accidentally' been dropped all along the east coast and midlands, as well as Northern Ireland.

Liz felt a tremendous amount of guilt. The night of the bombing, John had pleaded with her to let him stay at her flat and she turned him down. If only... He would still be alive today. The service over, Father O'Sullivan walked from the altar and shook Liz's hand. She sat there, numb, a solitary tear trickling slowly down her cheek. The pallbearers lifted the coffin onto their shoulders and slowly made their way down the aisle of the church. Sinead held out her hand to Liz and led her outside. As the coffin was slid into the back of the motor hearse, a sudden gust of wind blew the lone red rose from the coffin. Liz watched as it swirled in the summer breeze before floating gently to the ground. She remembered the poem she had written fifteen years earlier for her baby when she had to give her away and the words floated to her now.

But know this now,
   Though things may change,
And we may someday part,
   You always belong here,
   Right here in my heart.

Chapter Seventeen

Liz lay back against the pillow as the memories of John came flooding back. Her wrinkled face scrunched up in pain. Rose rubbed her teary eyes. She reached for her mother's hand and gently squeezed it.

'I had no idea. If you had come for me at any time, I would happily have gone away with you. When I found out about you, Molly convinced me that you never wanted me in the first place. Did you ever see Will again? Where is he now?'

Liz closed her eyes tightly. When she opened them she had tears in them.

'After John died, I fell apart. I continued nursing at the hospital for a while but my heart wasn't in it. Sister Agnes at the hospital took me under her wing. She was a Sister of Mercy. She worked mainly in the children's ward in the role of social worker. I worked with her. I saw first hand the suffering, the poverty and the abuses of little children. I found my calling. I told Sister Agnes I wanted to become a Sister of Mercy and I wanted to work with children. She was one of the few people who knew my life story. She didn't judge me like others would.

Eventually she found me a position, back in Cork. At Mount St Josephs Residential Home in Passage West. I needed to get out of Dublin. Every day working in the hospital reminded me of John. I knew by going back to Cork, I would run the risk of bumping into my family. I found a great sense of peace at St Josephs. It was a simple life, a peaceful existence, although hard work. I loved working with the children. I've been there since 1941.

At the end of the war, I wrote to Will. I promised myself it was the last time. Needless to say, I didn't get a reply. Six months later, I was called in to the Mother Superiors office.'

*   *   *   *

'Come in,' Mother Superior called from her office. The door opened and Sister Elisabeth poked her head in.

'You sent for me, Mother?' she asked.

'Come in Sister Elisabeth, you have visitors.'

A puzzled Sister Elisabeth quietly entered the wooden panelled office. Dressed in a nuns long black habit, she was hardly recognisable. Two men stood up, caps in their hands. She turned to look at them and cried out in surprise.

'Pat! Wi-Will!' she gasped.

Nobody spoke. Mother Superior glanced from one face to the other.

'I have to go about my duties now. Ye can stay here as long as ye need. Goodbye,' she said in her authoritive voice, before leaving the office.

'How are ya Liz, I mean Sister Elisabeth? You're a nun now. Isn't that grand?' Pat, Jack's brother in law said, holding out his hand.

Liz smiled as she shook it warmly with her two hands. She smiled at her son, her eyes misting over. Shyly he looked at her. He had changed so much. He had grown tall and his hair was still blonde and neatly combed. His skin was lightly tanned. He was wearing a black serge suit with a starched white shirt. She noticed how much he resembled his late father, although he had her eyes. He didn't smile, just kept staring at her, then he'd glance back at his uncle. Pat nodded at him reassuringly.

'It's so good to see you again, Pat. And Will,' Liz smiled, glancing at Will, 'how's Cait and the children. And the grandchildren?'

'Cait is fine. She sends her good wishes and shure, all the children are grown up now. The youngest is twenty-two. We've a few extra grandchildren too. Nine altogether,' Pat announced proudly, he stopped smiling,

'Liz, I- we came to see ya because we thought it only right you should know about your poor mother. She died two months ago. Will here asked me to come with him to tell you. He said you always wrote him, since…, well these past few years. And you told him you were here.'

Liz sat down heavily on the nearby sofa, her mind in a whirl. She stared out the window at the sea.

'Poor Mam, I missed her so much and now…' she gulped hard to stem the tears.

Pat motioned to Will to sit in a chair before sitting on the chair opposite.

'Poor Mam. What about, what about my father? How's he holding up?' Liz asked.

'Your father passed away two years ago Liz. By the way, he was never the same after…, after you left. On his deathbed, he was begging you to forgive him. He blamed himself you know. He used say, if only he hadn't forced you to marry Jack, things wouldn't have turned out the way they did.'

'Things happen Pat, and we can't turn back the clock and do it all over again. We only get one chance at life, that's all. One chance. I just wish… I wish I could have been there at the end,' Liz said crying softly. Will was watching her, unsure of what to say. What do you say to the mother you've shunned for years? How could he? He had grieved over the death of his father, but after banishing his mother from her rightful place, her home, he grieved like he never imagined. Pride stopped him from replying to her loving letters. She never gave up on him. Pat saw the way he looked at her. He stood up suddenly.

'I'll wait outside. The gardens look beautiful and this view! Take your time,' he said opening the door and walking out.

Liz looked at Will. Her son. Her flesh and blood.

'How are you, Will? How's the farm going?' she asked gently, dabbing at her eyes. He shifted uncomfortably in his seat.

'The farm is going well. Pat was great all these years.

I'm eighteen now…'

'I know. Last January,' Liz interrupted, smiling.

Will smiled back.

'Anyway, Uncle Pat thinks I'm capable enough now to run it on my own. Cormac, you know Michael Og's son? He's twenty-five now. He's married and has a child, a little boy, Seamus. He bought Dan Lucey's farm a few years back after he died. So Cormac's farm is next to mine and we help each other with the work.'

'Dan Lucey, dead too? Oh, he was a rascal he was, I never forgot his kindness to me the night you were born. Behind it all, he was a true gentleman. And little Cormac, all grown up with his own little son. How things change,' Liz said wistfully.

'Mam, I'm sorry, for everything. I was hurt and angry. Out of my mind with grief. My father died and I found out I had a sister. I couldn't handle it. And when you wrote to me all those years, I often wrote letters in reply but I didn't send them, I'd tear them up in a rage. I don't know why. A part of me died with Dad but worse, a bigger part of me died when you left. I know it was me who drove you away. When I see Cormac and his wife with their son, it brings it all back to me. I needed to see you, to tell you. I love you, Mam, an' I've missed ya,' he was on his feet now, tears running down his face, 'can you forgive me, for all I've done to you?'

Liz rose to her feet. She held out her arms and Will fell into them. They cried together for all they had lost. For Jack, her father and her mother.

'There's nothing to forgive, my son. I am your mother.'

$*$ $*$ $*$ $*$

Rose was smiling as she held her mother's hand.

'I'm glad ye made up. Imagine, I have a brother. I know I grew up with Sean and Katie but they weren't my real brother and sister, we fought like cats and dogs all the time.

As they got older they'd throw it in my face that I was not even related to them. And I have my very own brother!'

Liz suddenly turned away and tears trickled down her face again.

'What's wrong mother?' Rose asked concerned. Liz patted Rose's hand before turning around again.

'Mother, I'm sorry. This is too much for you. You're not well. Why don't you rest for a while?'

'You don't understand Maria, Will and me talked for ages. He told me he had a young lady! He wanted me to meet her. We healed a lot of our emotional wounds that day. He promised he'd call again. He never did. That was the last time I saw him. Three weeks later, Mother Superior called me into the office. I was smiling from ear to ear. I thought it was Will come to see me, but the only one there was Pat. And he looked dreadful.'

*   *   *   *

It was late afternoon on a dismal cold October day as Cormac, Will and Danny trudged wearily into the farmyard. Leaves swirled around their feet.

'Well Will, are you meeting the gorgeous Fionnoula later?' Cormac asked laughing, slapping his cousin playfully on the back. Cormac was the head off his own father, well built with dark hair that curled around his shoulders.

'I'll bet there'll be a weddin' before next summer. Isn't that right Will boy? Old man Sullivan reckons you're a great catch for his daughter, or so he keeps tellin' me Da,' Danny chuckled dodging the playful dig aimed at him by his cousin Will. Danny was Pat's third son. He was the shorter of the three young men and stockier. He was twenty-three and married to a girl from Ballincollig village. He had two young children, a boy and a girl.

'I won't be going anywhere if we don't get them cows milked,' Will grinned, 'and as for getting' married, I'm never getting' married. There must be more to life than getting wed and having children. No that's not for me at all, at all.'

'Ah, sure you have to give us a day out. Why should Cormac and meself be the only ones to suffer? And that Fionnula, well there's a girl and a half. If I was free you'd have a contender for her affections,' Danny winked at Cormac.

'She wouldn't even look at ya, now come on, let's get them cows milked!' Will called as he flicked the switch in the cow byre. The byre flooded with light instantly, and Cormac went to the corner to drag over the heavy milk churns. Will and Danny fetched a bucket each and proceeded to milk the herd. Cormac got another bucket and started milking a cow. Light-hearted banter filled the cowshed as the young men milked the cows. None of them saw or heard the sparks that flared from the single strand cable running from the switch up along the high ceiling. They didn't see the pile of hay smouldering at the back of the byre. Twenty minutes later, the milking complete, they left the byre, switching off the light and closing the door behind them. Sparks danced through the air onto the mounds of hay.

Will called goodnight to the other two before walking into the kitchen. Cormac and Danny mounted their horses and rode down the laneway. At the bottom of the lane Danny turned right, while Cormac turned left; both living on the next farm either side of Will.

Will stoked up the dying fire in the grate and pulled the swinging crane over the flickering flames, with yesterdays stew heating slowly in the old blackened pot.

Things hadn't changed much in the farmhouse since his father died and his mother left. He switched on the wireless and smiled as he heard a traditional hornpipe on it. He sat in the sugan chair by the hearth. For two years after his mother's departure he hadn't come into the house. The memories were too painful. Gradually, accompanied by Pat and Danny he'd come in. Last year he told Pat he wanted to live there again. Although he thought the world of Pat and Cait and his cousins, it could get very noisy in their house!

He smiled happily as he relaxed in the chair. He was glad he went to see his mother. She even agreed to come out for a visit sometime in the future. And his cousins were right; Fionnula was a fine girl, slim with blonde hair and very pretty. He indeed would marry her. Contented, he dozed.

He woke suddenly. The cows were mooing. Strange. He grabbed a tea cloth and carefully lifted the pot of stew from the crane. He hoisted it onto the table. What was wrong with those cows, they were still mooing. As he turned towards the kitchen window he could see a bright light glowing in the yard. He ran to the door and pulled it open. Bright flames leapt from the roof of the cow byre into the night sky.

'Oh no,' he cried. He looked about him in desperation. He wouldn't have time to go get help. He ran to open the door of the byre to let the cows out, then sprinted to the well. Frantically he lowered the bucket and pulled it up, full of water. He ran to the byre where the cows were bellowing in fear. They hadn't made any attempt to get out. The byre was well alight now. Will ran to the door and screamed at the cows to move. He ran in and started to push the nearest one out. She wouldn't budge, just mooed pitifully.

'Come on, move ya stupid heifer, come on get out, ya amadan,' he screamed.

Over at Danny's farmhouse, Danny was sitting at the table bouncing his baby daughter on his knee. His wife Mary smiled from she was standing, at the hearth, stirring the dinner. Danny's son, five year old son, Padraig was at the kitchen window. He pulled back the red gingham curtain and gazed out. The sky was red and orange tonight. He watched mesmerised.

'Come on Padraig, your dinner's ready, sit down will ya,' his mother called.

'Can I watch the sky a little longer, it's really pretty tonight, look Da,' Padraig called.

'Will ya do as your mother says. Now come away from the window,' Danny said firmly.

Padraig sighed and just as he released the curtain from his grasp, Danny saw a red glow from outside. He leaned across the table and pulling the curtain back, peered outside. He stared at the orange and red glow for a few seconds.

'Jaysus, Mary and Joseph!' he screamed, jumping up and setting the baby on the floor, 'Will's place is on fire! Mary, run next door to Da's place and tell him. I'm going to help Will.'

Danny was already putting on his Wellingtons and jacket. In seconds he was out the door and running towards Will's farm. He didn't have time to saddle the horse. He ran as fast as he could down the lane, a quarter of a mile up the hill and up the lane into Wills yard which was now an out of control inferno.

At that moment the cows stampeded from the byre towards the fields.

'Will! Where are you?' Danny shouted over the noise of the roaring inferno and thundering hooves. He ran to the open door of the house and looked in. Empty. He ran back and looked all around. He could still hear mooing sounds from the burning byre. He ran as close as he could, his hands held to his face, but the heat and flames kept him back.

'Will! Where are ya?' he yelled frantically.

He turned at the sound of horse's hooves racing up the lane. His father and a few farmers jumped down and calling to each other started filling anything they laid their hands on with water. Danny ran back to help.

'Where's Will?' Pat asked filling a bucket with water from the well.

'I don't know Da, I've called him an' he doesn't

answer,' Danny replied, tears running down his face.

'Well keep looking for him. Go on,' Pat shouted, worried.

Just then Cormac ran up the lane into the yard his mouth opened wide with horror.

The group of men frantically tried to put out the blaze without success. They wrinkled their noses against the overpowering stench of scorched hay and burning flesh.

'Oh God, look!' shouted Cormac. Everybody turned and watched sparks from the byre leap onto the thatched roof of the farmhouse. Everybody stared in disbelief. More neighbours arrived to help. Within minutes the roof of the farmhouse was well ablaze.

'He must be in the byre,' shouted Danny, returning to the yard after searching the entire house.

'No! He can't be,' Cormac said crying, he ran towards the byre, followed by Danny and Pat. They were beaten back by the flames and the heat once again. They looked on in horror as the byre roof crashed inwards and red flames shot higher into the sky. Shocked, the three men stood still, at the realisation that Will must somehow have been in the cow byre when the fire started. Around them men continued their frantic quest to put out the inferno. Minutes later the blazing roof of the farmhouse collapsed with a resounding crash. Cormac and Danny closed their eyes and wept helplessly. Tears ran down Pat's face. In the distance the peal of fire brigade bells cut through the sounds of the out of control fire.

*   *   *   *

The ruins of the farmhouse and outbuildings still smouldered as a new day dawned. Dark grey clouds drifted upwards as the sun rose higher in the sky, casting an eerie red glow on the burnt out remains of the farmyard. Around them hung the smell of smoke and burnt flesh; the stench of death. Cormac and Danny sat on the grass verge near the gate. White tear tracks streaked their blackened faces. Cormac held his head as if in pain. Danny watched as his father and another farmer edged their way into the pile of rubble, which had once been the cow byre. Some of the men had gone home already. Others stood around murmuring quietly. The fire brigade truck was still parked among the debris. Danny got up suddenly and walked slowly towards the byre. His father and his neighbour were staring into one corner, talking quietly amongst themselves. Pat glanced up when Danny approached. His blackened face, and the sadness in his eyes told Danny they had found Will's charred body.

*   *   *   *

Liz's body shook with her sobs. Rose bit her lip hard as she dabbed at her mother's eyes.

'I'm sorry about that Maria,' Liz sniffed loudly, 'anyway, he called to tell me that Will had had an accident on the farm. The cow byre had caught fire. A faulty wire, or something like that. Will ran in to get the cows out and in the ensuing panic got trampled by the cows. The cow byre was well alight by the time Pat reached it. At first he didn't know where Will was. Sparks from the fire landed on the thatch of the farmhouse and within seconds it was alight. The whole lot went up in flames. It wasn't until hours later when the fire was put out that....that his body was found. Pat didn't go into details. I couldn't have handled it. I went to his funeral in Ballincollig. He was buried with his Dad. Nobody recognised me because I was in my nun's habit. I thought my heart would finally break. I had nobody anymore. Everybody in my life had died, except you. I saw myself as a jinx. I couldn't bring myself to go back to the house in Inniscarra, what was left of it. I don't know what became of it. Anyway, only for the Sisters of Mercy, I would have given up. My

work kept me going.'

Liz looked up as footsteps approached. A nun dressed in a black habit smiled down at Liz.

'How are you feeling Sister Elisabeth?' she asked softly. Liz smiled weakly.

'I'm not too bad now Sister Catherine. This is my daughter, Maria.'

Sister Catherine tried to conceal her surprise. She held out her hand to Rose and shook it warmly.

'Pleased to meet you, Maria.'

Rose got up suddenly.

'I've got to go now. M-mother, I'll call tomorrow. Get some rest,' she leaned over, kissed Liz on her lined cheek and whispered, 'goodnight Mother.'

Liz gazed into her daughter's face and smiled, a tear filled smile. Rose smiled back then turned and walked out the door.

Rose walked through the tall door, past the reception desk. She glanced at the date on the calendar as she walked in. 12th June 1972. She climbed the stairs, and walked along the corridor to St Bridget's ward. She stopped in surprise. The bed was empty and made up ready for the next patient. She turned around and walked out again. Looking around frantically, she saw a nurse coming out of the next ward. She rushed up to her.

'Excuse me Nurse, could you tell me where...Sister Elisabeth is? Has she gone back to the Home?'

'Are you a relative?'

'Yes, she's my mother.'

'I'm afraid your mother took a turn for the worse. She's in a private room. Come with me.'

Rose followed the young nurse down to the end of the dark corridor. The nurse opened the door and peered in first. She turned to Rose.

'Before you go in, I have to inform you, your mother is

extremely ill. She's not expected to pull through, I'm afraid. I'm sorry,' she whispered.

Rose walked quietly into the modest darkened room. A priest dressed in a black cassock with a white dog collar, was bending over Liz, hands clasped, praying. Rosary beads were entwined in Liz's clasped hands. Her eyes were closed. Sister Catherine sat on a chair near the end of the bed, praying quietly. A white candle burned on the bedside table. The priest motioned to Rose to come nearer. She tiptoed quietly to the narrow bed and knelt over the old woman who seemed smaller and frailer since yesterday. The skin on her white face was paper-thin. With tears in her eyes, Rose bent over her mother and rubbed her ice-cold hands. Liz half opened her eyes and looked at her daughter.

'Maria, my dear, all my pain will be gone soon; my purgatory will end at last. I hope I have atoned for my sin; I'm going to be with John. God has been good to me and brought you to me one last time. I am so happy to have met you, my darling girl,' she rasped, her voice barely audible. She closed her eyes again. Rose opened her mouth but no words came out, she continued rubbing Liz's hands. She sat on the edge of the bed and gazed into her mother's face. Liz's breathing became slower and shallower. Ten minutes passed before Liz finally took her last breath. Rose's tears brimmed over as she huddled over her dead mother, stroking her lifeless hand, her lifeless face. Rose cried a lifetime of tears. The priest, the nurse and Sister Catherine stood back respectfully until Rose finally straightened up. She kissed her mother one last time.

'Goodbye mother, I won't judge you. I knew you just a short time, but I know now that you always loved me, and I love you with all my heart. I've lost you all over again,' she whispered in the dead woman's ear. She got up from the bed. With one last look at Liz from the doorway, she turned and walked away, almost blinded by her tears. She wiped them away with the palms of her hands.

*   *   *   *

Thick bushes and briars all but covered the ruined walls of the tumbledown old farmyard. Grass was almost waist high. The ancient well was still visible, under a covering of brambles. Alongside it the blackened stump of a tree. Rose was standing in the centre of the burnt out ruins of the outbuildings, which were almost razed to the ground.

Earlier, she had attended the burial of her mother, Sister Elisabeth, in Ballincollig graveyard. Her final instructions were to be buried with her son, Will, and husband Jack. Rose looked around at the small crowd clustered at the grave. It was a hot sunny day. Most of the people were Sisters of Mercy from the convent in Passage West. Several men and women in their fifties stood solemnly near the graveside, heads bowed reverently, hands clasped together. Rose surmised they probably were Jack and Liz's nephews and nieces.

Rose turned and walked towards the overgrown farmhouse. The front wall was almost intact, completely covered inside and out with ivy. The remaining walls were almost obliterated. She walked through the doorless opening. The burnt out hearth was still visible, complete with swinging crane. She peered through the tiny window opening, at what was once the front garden and now only a wilderness of overgrown bushes. She shivered in the cold, and turned to leave. Something above the blackened mantelpiece caught her eye. She walked towards it and saw a brick sticking out at an odd angle. She reached up and tugged at it. It came away easily, disturbing the crumbling mantelpiece. She peered into the darkness. What did she think would be hidden behind the brick? Didn't her mother tell her she removed everything from behind the brick the day she left the house thirty-four years ago? She scrabbled around in her black handbag until she found a box of matches. Striking a match she held it up near the opening between the bricks. Peering in she saw something glint in the match light. She reached in, scrabbled around and felt .. paper! She gazed in astonishment at the tattered brown package, aged from years in the dark. Carefully she pulled it out and unfolded it.

She blinked in the warm June sunshine as she walked outside. She blew at it to remove the layer of dust. Her eyes widened in surprise when she recognized her own childish writing on the bundle of the letters it contained. She also recognised Nonie's writing. She felt a lump in her throat as everything, her entire past, fell into place. She felt a slight bump and delved into the package again. She gazed at the wedding ring her mother had placed there years earlier.

Her husband Tim had parked the grey Morris Minor at the end of the overgrown lane, next to the little cottage. At first neither of them spotted the cottage, it was so overgrown. Only on getting out the passenger door did Rose see it.

Tim was leaning against the car smoking a cigarette. He looked up when Rose walked towards him.

'Well, love, are you glad you came? Did you find what you were looking for?' Tim asked, smiling at his wife and draping his free arm across her slim shoulders.

She looked at the ring clasped in her hand before smiling up at him.

'Yes. Yes, I've found the missing pieces of my life at last. Come on, let's go home and I'll tell you everything.'

THE END